CHAPTER ONE

Panic clawed at Megan's chest as a forceful knock at the door promised an end to her quiet life. Though she didn't know who had come, she was certain of the reason.

Megan hurriedly crammed the last of her belongings into a suitcase and zipped it shut. As she wheeled it into the foyer, she cast a final, loving look around her home. She would miss the abundance of pillows on her bed, the weekends spent tending to her rose garden, and Twinkles, her dog—the closest thing she had to a child. Most of all, she would miss teaching at the university, where she delighted in opening young minds to the wonders of the universe. Unfortunately, her universe was about to shrink to the size of a prison cell.

The pounding escalated to hammering, and a raised voice called out her name.

Megan had expected the Special Security Force to track her down, just not so soon, which didn't bode well for Dolores's attempt to destroy the alien machine. Regardless of whether her friend succeeded or failed, Megan had provided aid and comfort to what the authorities would surely call a conspiracy to commit treason.

"Coming!" she shouted, hoping to prevent the agents from forcing their way inside. Bracing herself for the worst, she flung open the front door.

Before her stood a figure, cloaked in shadows and as inscrutable as a sphinx. Megan masked her surprise with a frown, straightening to her full height of four feet eight and a half inches. It was Obadiah Wallner, once a member of the Council that had deciphered the extraterrestrial transmission and built the machine Dolores sought to destroy.

His gaze fell on the suitcase. "Going somewhere, Doctor McCullough?"

Megan popped her head out the door, her eyes sweeping the vicinity. Surely, Obadiah hadn't come alone. But there was nobody else there—no agents, no cops, no soldiers. Just a driver waiting at the curb from the ride-hailing service Obadiah must have used.

"I have to admit," she said, "I didn't expect to be arrested by the Director of National Intelligence himself. Should I be honored? I think not. I'm not telling you anything, if that's what you hoped by coming here." Her voice rose an octave. "What did you do to Dolores? For that matter, what happened to Stephen and his family? Did you already cart them off to prison? How dare you do that to a child! And yes, I helped them. That's what decent human beings do when faced with injustice. It's about integrity and compassion, not that you would know. So, take me away. I'm ready."

Obadiah ran a hand down his face. "May I speak?"

Megan took a deep breath, trying to still the pounding of her heart. "I suppose."

"Stephen Fisher activated the machine," he said. "He calls it a Beacon."

As Megan digested the unexpected news, her eyes swept over Obadiah. His eyelids drooped and lines were carved into his normally smooth face. He also wasn't wearing a tie, which was as unusual as the stain on his dress shirt. She reached out and moved aside the lapel, revealing a bloodstained handprint. Her chest tightened. "Where's Dolores?"

A pause. "I'm afraid she's dead. The witnesses claim she took her own life. I'm sorry."

Megan's body went rigid, a bone-deep chill seizing her core. Despite her friend's terminal diagnosis, she never would have done that, not in a million years. "You killed her."

Obadiah's shoulders fell. "She was my friend too, Megan."

She bit off a retort, recalling that Dolores had considered Obadiah an ally inside the Administration they both served. But friendship often clashed with ambition. Megan had the scars to prove it. "Then whose blood is that?"

He looked down at his shirt, as if seeing the stain for the first time.

PROPHET

THE SEQUEL TO MELODY

David Hoffer

ISBN 978-1-7357548-3-3

eBook ISBN 978-1-7357548-2-6

First Edition / January 2025

Cover design by Damonza.com

PART I – A CHILD IS BORN

And the dragon stood before the woman who was about to give birth, so that when she bore her child, he might devour it.

— Revelation 12:4

"General Beckman killed Stephen Fisher, believing him to be a threat. I tried to intervene, but—" his voice trailed off.

Numbness spread through Megan's chest, her worst fears realized. Her best friend was dead, and the self-declared emissary from another civilization, murdered. "That's what you do, isn't it? Pick up the pieces as the world burns. At least Dolores tried to rectify her mistake before the end. Doing the right thing isn't easy, a lesson you obviously haven't learned."

Obadiah dropped his eyes.

Fearing the answer, she forced herself to ask, "What about the wife and daughter—Fran and Melody?"

"I've put them in protective custody."

Megan exhaled, not realizing she had been holding her breath. She loved that kid more than her dog. "I bet Franny takes great comfort in being protected by the same people who murdered her husband. Are you about to make them disappear, like you tried to do with the father?"

Obadiah's lips compressed into a thin line. "That wasn't my doing. Keep in mind, Mrs. Fisher could face serious charges. Her husband had an arrest warrant for two counts of willfully communicating classified intelligence, and she's an accomplice. Then there's aiding and abetting an attack on a federal facility—that's domestic terrorism. I have no intention of pursuing those charges, but that decision is not mine to make."

"What did you do with them?"

"I placed them in a secure location. Secrecy is a shield, and their safety relies on that. Nothing will happen to that family under my watch. Believe me."

"I'm not sure what to believe," Megan said. With nothing left to lose, she asked, "Are you going to arrest me? I harbored a fugitive and knew about Dolores' plan. In your world, that makes me a terrorist."

"That's not my intention, though I strongly advise you not to say those types of things in front of a law enforcement officer." He glanced at the suitcase. "Besides, you can't take personal belongings into prison."

"I wouldn't know."

Obadiah leaned against the wall and rubbed his eyes, his hands shaking. Obadiah, shaking. The most emotionally uptight human being she had ever encountered.

"I need to talk with you," he said. "And not about that."

Against her better judgment, Megan gestured for him to come inside. "You might as well sit down."

Obadiah stepped over the threshold and sank into the couch. After staring at him for a moment, Megan fetched a glass of water and pulled her largest sweater from a dresser. She placed the drink on the living room table, which he downed immediately, and tossed the sweater onto his lap. She then pointed to the restroom. "You're a mess and you smell. Go get yourself cleaned up, then we can talk."

Obadiah nodded gratefully and followed her directions. While he washed and changed, Megan went to the kitchen and poured herself a generous glass of wine. Tears welled in her eyes as she mourned the end of her long relationship with Dolores. They had been friends for years, weathering life's storms while Dolores climbed the ranks at NASA's Jet Propulsion Laboratory. Megan raised her glass, silently toasting the memories of her best friend—now all that remained.

After finishing one drink and pouring another, she returned to the living room. Obadiah emerged from the bathroom wearing the sweater, which fit his tall frame like a crop top. She sat on the opposite side of the coffee table, uncertain what to expect. "All right, tell me what happened."

Obadiah only stared at his hands, his grief apparent.

Megan hadn't spoken to him in a long while, not since her involvement with the Council. His team had helped decipher the transmission that produced the blueprint for the machine. Of all the government officials she had dealt with back in the day, Obadiah had been the best. He had also protected the civilian scientists, like her, from bureaucrats who constantly second-guessed the project. In truth, she had liked him.

Her anger fading, Megan pressed the wine glass into his hand. Never had she seen Obadiah so flustered. It shook her. "Relax," she said. "Start with Melody. Was she hurt?"

Obadiah took a long sip of wine. "Both the daughter and the mother are fine. I know where Melody came from, Megan. I expect you do too."

Not quite ready to trust him, Megan said, "I have no idea what you're talking about."

"Uh-huh. Anyway, after the General was killed—"

"What? Another person dead?"

"Stephen Fisher killed him where he stood. I don't know how."

Megan had an inkling, recalling how Stephen had once rendered her unconscious with a mere touch of his hand. She had endured a brutal headache for weeks afterward. "Sounds like he got what he deserved, the bastard."

"Paranoia finally pushed the General over the edge. This may come as no surprise, but I believe Stephen's not of this world."

Megan snorted. "He announced to the world he's a messenger from the civilization that sent the transmission during that interview with Max Mystery. You're behind the times, Obadiah. Odd for someone who heads up national intelligence."

"I follow facts, not unfounded claims."

"It's not so unfounded now, is it?"

"Then how did he get here?"

Megan shrugged, admitting the same question remained foremost in her mind as well. Stephen was undeniably human—Obadiah had tested his DNA. So, how could he be from somewhere else?

"Then there's his daughter, Melody," Obadiah continued. "When she took my hand, I saw patterns, textures, and colors inside not only her head but everybody's. I also saw these—I'm not sure how to describe it—threads moving through her flesh. It felt like she—"

"Reached inside of you," Megan finished for him, having experienced that herself when Stephen touched her. "I understand."

The creases in Obadiah's forehead eased. "That was my hope. I've concluded the daughter is like the father."

Megan had already deduced that for herself. "And?"

"You're not surprised?"

"I'm smarter than you."

He sighed, rubbing the stubble on his beard. "Did you and Dolores ever speculate what would happen if Stephen entered the Beacon?"

Megan thought back to her time on the project. "Measurement precipitates what physicists call a wave function collapse," she said. "Light, for example, can be a wave or particle depending on whether it's being observed. Dolores theorized that Stephen, strictly by being there, could trigger this collapse, enabling particles to interact instantaneously at a distance. Aside from scale, that's not fundamentally different from creating a wormhole in space. In theory, the perfect mechanism to enable superluminal interstellar communication."

"Are you telling me the thing's a phone?"

Megan absently swirled the wine in her glass. "If it is, we never got it to work. One reason, and this is just me, mind you: there are two humanoid figures in that blueprint we used to build the machine. Pretty sure Stephen is one and Melody the other." She was about to ask why he cared when the answer came to her. "You let them inside the chamber!"

Obadiah nodded. "When I followed shortly afterward, I found Stephen dead and his wife and daughter in tears. Dolores had—"

"Killed herself. I still find that hard to believe."

"More shocking is what's happening inside that chamber right now."

Megan's heart skipped a beat. She leaned forward, clasping her hands together. "Tell me."

"That's the reason I came here. I think you're the only person who can understand what's going on." He drained the glass and wiped his mouth with his sleeve. "But it's not something I can explain. I need to show you."

CHAPTER TWO

The roar of the helicopter's rotors diminished to a moderate chuffing as the craft bounced onto the helipad within the Nevada National Security Site. Megan, a nervous flier to begin with, vowed never to set foot in one of these deathtraps again. Too loud, too bumpy, and not even a glass of wine to calm her nerves. Out the window, a constellation of lights burned against the reddish hue of a sun not yet ready to broach the horizon. Strange to think that Dolores and Stephen were still alive when it had set.

Since her last visit years ago, the town of Mercury had grown into a small city. Judging by the number of troops patrolling the airfield, the armed presence had grown even more—a stark reminder that the government's focus had devolved from understanding the Beacon to exploiting its technology for military use.

A soldier hefted the aircraft door aside. Obadiah leaped out, gesturing for her to follow. Ducking her head, Megan gladly fled the claustrophobic confines, her breath easing as her feet hit the tarmac. Obadiah hurried her toward a waiting Humvee, where she climbed in through the passenger door. He took the driver's seat.

Leaving the airport behind, they traveled along a narrow road through the desert plain toward a distant black hummock on the horizon. Mounds of debris flanked them on either side—piles of rebar, discarded vehicles, and pyramids of aggregate—remnants of the hurried construction from a time that seemed an age ago. As the odometer turned, the hummock slowly grew into a massive black dome that loomed over the desolate landscape like a pagan monument to an ancient god. But to Megan, it had become a gravestone, marking the death of her best friend and the father of a young child.

Megan had been part of the original team that built the device using a blueprint deciphered from the alien transmission. They dubbed it the Gravitational Wave Amplification Device—G-WAD for short, a name only a government committee could love. Stephen referred to it as the Beacon, a term she much preferred. Despite the differing names, not a single scientist had a clue how the thing worked.

The dome revealed only the upper third of the outer sphere, peeking over a crater gouged from the earth by a hundred-kiloton nuclear weapons test. A cylindrical stem extended like a stick on a lollipop from the sphere's base to the injection chamber deep underground—the beating heart of the device. Now, it had become a crime scene.

"What am I going to find in there?" she asked.

Obadiah kept his eyes fixed on the massive dome ahead. "There's a blue haze covering the ceiling and floor of the chamber. Sensors detect activity, but you'll have to tell me what they're measuring and what it means."

"A blue haze," she repeated. Never had she seen anything like that. To her eyes, the chamber had been filled with impenetrable darkness, nothing more. "What else?"

"Beyond that, I'd rather your judgment not be influenced by what I've observed."

Megan glanced out the window at the birds circling the Beacon, another familiar yet inexplicable phenomenon. "You're being awfully mysterious about this, Obadiah."

"It's not something I can properly describe. Like I said, you need to experience it for yourself."

The Humvee ascended the earthen embankment that cradled the dome of the Beacon, decelerating as it neared the checkpoint—the only access through a twelve-foot-high security fence crowned with razor wire. A familiar face emerged from the sentry shack.

Obadiah flashed a badge. "Has anybody been allowed inside since I left?"

"No sir," said the sentry. "Just as you ordered."

"That order remains in effect."

"Yes, sir." Placing a calloused hand on the door frame, the sentry peered inside. A hint of a smile creased his weathered face. "Doctor

McCullough."

"Hey Buzz," she said, glad to see his welcoming face. "How've you been?"

"My hip is sore and my knees creak, but otherwise, I'm just fine. It's sure nice to see you again, though I regret the reason for your visit."

Overcome by grief, Megan could only dip her chin. The gate rumbled open.

Obadiah activated the headlights as the vehicle traversed an earthen tunnel. They emerged beneath a forest of metal lattice struts supporting heavy panels made of *draconium*, an alien alloy with the curious property of absorbing electromagnetic radiation while, in theory, amplifying gravitational energy. The material teetered on the edge of instability, threatening to decompose into radioactive sludge if not for the uninterrupted flow of electrical power.

Following a sharp right turn, Obadiah navigated the narrow winding road down the sides of the crater. Power lines hummed, and the air grew chilly as the road leveled off at a clearing. In the center stood a cinderblock building holding an elevator that transported passengers to a control room that monitored activity inside the chamber. He brought the vehicle to a halt, and they stepped out into the cold. Megan, shivering, rubbed her bare arms to generate some warmth. Noticing her discomfort, Obadiah removed his suit jacket and draped it over her shoulders, engulfing her in wool. They entered the elevator and were soon standing before a reinforced steel door. Obadiah tapped in the security code, and with a metallic clack, the door to the control room swung open.

Lights flickered to life, and a musty odor assaulted Megan's nose. Obadiah led the way inside. She followed, and the moment she crossed the threshold, stopped dead in her tracks. A trail of blood stretched from a crimson pool to a glass lift on the opposite side of the crescent-shaped room.

Beads of sweat formed on Megan's forehead as the haunting image from her worst nightmare flashed through her mind. Once again, she was a child looking at her mother's lifeless form draped in a purple shroud. Like Dolores, her mother had committed suicide. But unlike Dolores, her mother had done it out of misplaced faith in a leader of an apocalyptic cult.

That same sense of helplessness gripped her now, for she had failed her best friend. Megan drew a shaky breath to quell the pounding in her chest. Stumbling back into the corridor, moisture welled in her eyes. "I shouldn't have come here."

A pained expression softened Obadiah's features. "I'm sorry. I should have warned you."

"Is that where—" she began but couldn't finish.

"Where Stephen was shot, yes. His family dragged him to the lift, which took them inside the chamber. The bodies have been recovered, but I ordered nothing else be touched. I didn't want to risk disrupting the phenomenon."

As if that mattered. Her best friend was dead, a father murdered, and his wife widowed. A sudden suspicion percolated into speech. "Am I here to provide cover for the President? You're part of the Cabinet, as were the General and Dolores. When word gets out about what happened here, a shitstorm is going to descend on the Administration. I can just imagine the press conference, where the President will say, 'Let me introduce Doctor McCullough, professor of astrobiology and a founding member of the Council that deciphered the transmission. She'll explain why murdering an emissary from another world isn't a total and complete screw-up.'"

Obadiah held out his hands. "That's not fair."

Megan turned on her heel and retreated toward the elevator. He raised his voice. "Inside that chamber, I can see and hear what others can't. I'm concerned, Megan, not only for my sanity, but what might be happening in there. Please, we go in and come right out. After that, I'll take you back home. I swear."

Megan's pace slowed, her curiosity boring through the anger she knew had little to do with Obadiah. Since the machine was built, speculation had raged as to its purpose. Solving that mystery had been the driving force of Dolores' life, and for a time, her own. But that wasn't the only reason she turned around. Trying to get it together, she took a halting breath. "Fine, but afterward, you take me to see Fran and Melody. I need to know they're safe."

"Agreed," he said at once.

With leaden steps and a resigned sigh, Megan reentered the control room. She bee-lined to the main console, averting her eyes from both

Obadiah and the blood on the floor. Computer equipment, oscilloscopes, and screens from an array of sensors crowded the tabletop. Notepads were open, pens laid aside, and mugs sat unattended, as if left in a hurry. Animals cowered in cages stacked next to the console, subjects for the always fatal experiments—another reason Megan loathed this place. "Did Stephen say anything before going into the chamber?"

Obadiah handed her a handkerchief, which she used to wipe her eyes. "He was in no condition to say much of anything."

"Might have been wise to ask."

"There was a lot going on."

"Still."

Megan studied the various controls, dials, and screens on the console. The shield was down, allowing gravitational energy into the injection chamber. Her gaze shifted to a live screen fed from cameras set at different angles within the chamber. A light blue haze enveloped both the floor and the ceiling—just as Obadiah had reported. More intriguing were the multispectral sensors displaying activity across light bands from ultraviolet to infrared. But what really caught her eye was the output from the laser interferometer. What was usually a flat line now showed gravitational waves oscillating wildly off the chart. Those waves distorted space-time, stretching and squeezing everything inside. On any other day, this would have filled her with wonder, but amidst the death and despair, it seemed an ill omen.

"You went in there, yes?" she asked.

"For a brief time," Obadiah said.

Megan looked him over. "Do you feel alright?"

"Why wouldn't I?"

"You never saw the rabbits."

His eyebrows drew together. "Do the sensors detect elevated levels of radiation or any other dangers?"

"Not that I can tell. But everything that goes in there dies…horribly. At least, that used to be the case. Out of curiosity, why didn't you contact Tara? She knows more about the machine than I do and still works at NASA."

"I thought you'd have a better handle on the big picture. Besides, Tara's married to Stephen's brother, Eric. Even if she'd agree to talk to me, they're both abroad. Can you turn off the cameras before we go in there?"

"I suppose. Why?"

"I'd prefer no prying eyes or ears."

Megan disabled the live feed. "You're being awfully weird about this."

"Being cautious is all. Please follow me."

Trying not to picture Stephen being dragged along the ground, Megan gingerly stepped over bloodied footprints to enter the glass lift. An aperture irised open overhead, its blades overlapping like those of a camera's diaphragm. The lift ascended through the ceiling into a vertical tunnel, then emerged through the floor of the injection chamber. It came to a stop, depositing them on a raised platform in the middle of the cavernous room. As the cabin door slid open, Megan caught her breath.

The chamber was awash with color, far more striking than shown on the live feed. A surreal sea and roiling sky bathed the space in bluish hues. Opaque material gathered in sapphire medallions embedded in the dome high above, like tears about to fall. As she watched, one stretched toward the floor, hanging from a thinning thread. Abruptly, the thread snapped, and the sphere spiraled lazily toward the luminescent fog covering the floor.

Megan leaned over the rail to study the drop as it drifted downward. Multi-hued arms spiraled within, and the more she stared, the more intricate the patterns became, the more fluid the movements, the more varied the hues. An upwelling from the haze swallowed the sphere with a subdued flash of green, pink, and violet. The sight was as mesmerizing as it was beautiful. She also heard music, a slow, haunting rhythm that rose and fell in a transcendent melody that took her breath away.

"Can you see this?" she whispered, fearing that raising her voice would scare it all away.

"I'm glad it's not just me," Obadiah said, his relief palpable. "The agents who removed the bodies saw only the haze."

"You hear it too, right?"

"The soundtrack of the transmission," he said. "The agents heard nothing."

Megan knelt, then passed her hands through the blue fog, creating little ripples which darkened into shades of violet. She bent closer and either saw or imagined infinitesimally small threads writhing through the haze. Puzzling, to say the least. Stephen had once told her the purpose of the Beacon was to enable communication, but Megan couldn't shake the feeling he had only told her what she expected to hear, which raised another question—why would he lie?

"I don't think this thing's a phone," she said.

"Notice anything else unusual?"

Megan stood up and looked around. "Are you kidding me? This is the definition of unusual."

"Close your eyes."

"Huh?"

"Just indulge me."

With a gasp, Megan realized that even with her eyes shut, the scene persisted—drops still fell, the haze still glowed. She opened and closed her eyes again. Nothing changed, except Obadiah flickering in and out of view. "This isn't possible."

"It occurred to me the phenomenon might be a side-effect of having been touched by, you know, one of them—Stephen and his child."

"What about Franny?" she asked, still blinking in disbelief. "Can she see this?"

"I didn't think to ask."

"Aren't you supposed to be in the intelligence business?"

An upward turn creased Obadiah's face, which Megan suspected might be the beginnings of a smile. "That's why I needed you."

Megan spun in a slow circle, tracking three drops as they lazily parted from the ceiling and fell to the floor. She checked her watch. "How long has this been going on?"

"Eight hours, more or less. Ever since Fisher died."

Megan divided the total hours by the time it took for a drop to fall, then multiplied the quotient by the frequency of formation. She guesstimated that at least two hundred of these drops had made the journey into the haze. "Did Melody or Fran offer any clue as to what's happening here?"

"They won't speak to me."

"I'm barely speaking to you myself," she half-joked, then her brow furrowed. "Hold on, is that the real reason you brought me here? To talk to them?"

"Partly. Are you offended?"

Megan rubbed the back of her neck, conflicted about his manipulation. Then again, she wanted to talk to the family anyway. Though their safety was her paramount concern, she also wanted answers. "When word spreads that Stephen's been murdered, the public is going to ask questions."

"True."

"The press will zero in on Fran and her daughter like a laser beam. There are dangerous people out there with strange ideas about what they represent."

"I'm well aware."

She wagged a finger at him. "You need to protect them."

"That might be problematic. Mrs. Fisher wants nothing to do with me or the government."

Megan blew out her cheeks, appreciating the conundrum. No way would Fran depend on the same people who had hunted down her family and killed her husband. Unless…

"That boss of yours is in quite the pickle," she said.

Obadiah watched another drop stretch from the ceiling. "President Martinez has spoken to me at length on that very subject. It's likely the United Nations will censure the administration, and our allies will be upset. A congressional investigation is a certainty. The President could get impeached and may lose the next election. I fully expect to be made the scapegoat."

That caught Megan off guard. "Really?"

"A political necessity. As you've already observed, this is quite the mess."

"Any chance I can speak with the President?"

Obadiah hesitated. "Possibly. What do you want?"

Megan let loose a dramatic sigh, having no desire to take on Dolores' burden. But if she didn't, nobody would, leaving Fran and Melody at the mercy of a government that had imprisoned the father. "It's not what I want, it's what Franny needs."

"Didn't you just accuse me of trying to provide cover for the

Administration?"

Megan clucked her tongue. "Now it's my idea. Plus, I have conditions."

With a disbelieving twitch of his eyebrow, Obadiah repeated, "You have conditions."

"In exchange for my help, yes. And they're non-negotiable. First off, Franny doesn't get charged with anything. A pardon would help. The rest I'm not prepared to share quite yet. I need to gather my thoughts."

Obadiah rubbed his jaw. "I could set something up, but you need to tell me what this is about."

"I have some ideas on how to navigate the situation. It's a bold move but will make partners of our allies and take the heat off the President. You're welcome to tell her that."

As Megan watched, another thread snapped, and they both followed the drop on its slow, spiraling descent toward the chamber floor. They watched as an upwelling of haze engulfed the sphere in a burst of prismatic color.

Obadiah bowed his head. "Thank you, Megan."

"The family comes first. Once they're safe, we'll talk to President Martinez. If that lady has any sense of self-preservation, she'll do exactly what I suggest."

CHAPTER THREE

Inside the temporary holding facility on the outskirts of Mercury, Nevada, Megan watched through the glass as an agent from the Department of Homeland Security tried to persuade Stephen Fisher's wife to remain in protective custody. Fran, pale, with half-closed eyes, rested her forehead on her hand, clearly still in shock. In her mother's lap, Melody sucked on two fingers while clutching a blanket to her chest.

Megan pursed her lips. "You're treating them like criminals."

"They were detained for their own safety," Obadiah said. "Rest assured, they spent the night in a comfortable room."

"With a guard at the door, no doubt. You need to learn how to make friends."

"Leadership needed to be consulted, processes followed—"

Megan interrupted, "You wanted answers."

He exhaled deeply. "Like I said, Mrs. Fisher isn't talking. Regardless, she's free to go, but I don't advise it."

"A better approach would have been to let them go home, then have a conversation."

"Unfortunately, the news of Fisher's death has already leaked to the press." Obadiah pulled out his cellphone and showed her the latest headlines: "Self-Proclaimed Extraterrestrial Found Slain," "From First Contact to Fatal Confrontation," "Top Official Suspected of Assassination."

"And those are from the responsible news outlets," he added. "You can imagine what's happening on social media."

Megan dismissively waved her hand. "It was just a matter of time before the news broke."

He pocketed the phone. "The point is, the threats to Mrs. Fisher and her daughter are growing. The press corps have surrounded their house and are harassing neighbors as we speak. Demonstrators are on the sidewalk, pushing whatever it is they believe, including a group that calls itself the Sword of the Lord. Despite all this, Mrs. Fisher insists on going home. I can direct Homeland Security to provide protection, anonymity, and whatever else she desires to keep her life private. But she needs to agree."

"A choice between two evils—the government or the mob. I'm not sure which is worse."

"You need to talk sense into her."

"Don't be so sure you know the sensible course," Megan said. "You said it yourself, you expect to become a scapegoat."

"I'm irrelevant. Protective custody will keep her safe."

"Maybe, but that doesn't solve the real problem. If President Martinez thinks sacrificing you or Franny will help her keep her job, then she'll do it."

"She is a politician," Obadiah conceded.

Megan was counting on that. "What about Stephen's brother Eric and his wife Tara? If the press tracked Franny down, they'll surely come for the rest of the family."

"Probably so, but first things first."

Megan watched as Melody sucked on her fingers while rubbing a ribbon attached to her blanket—an innocent child caught between forces she couldn't hope to understand or control. Just then, the child lifted her head, her eyes widening. She jumped off her mother's lap and ran to the window, where she pressed her hands and nose against the glass.

Megan turned to Obadiah. "Isn't this supposed to be a one-way mirror?"

"Ostensibly."

Melody pounded on the glass and waved, her gaze fixed on Megan.

"I better get in there," she said. "Can you get rid of that agent?"

"He already knows to leave when you arrive. Should I come with you?"

"Absolutely not."

"Please inform Mrs. Fisher that I have a plane on standby to take her and her daughter to a safe house. It's in a rural area, well away from danger, with a reputable school. They'll be secure there."

"Until someone decides to press charges," Megan said. Obadiah's face turned grim, signaling all she needed to know—he lacked the authority to protect the family. They needed a commitment from President Martinez. "Alright, time for a talk."

The moment Megan stepped into the room, Melody ran over and wrapped her arms around her waist. Without a word, the agent departed. "My Daddy's gone," Melody said, her voice too innocent to bear the weight of such words.

"I'm sorry, dearie." Lifting the child, Megan carried her to the table and took the seat the agent had just vacated.

Fran's weary eyes met Megan's. "They killed my husband."

Megan clasped her hand, filled with sorrow and fear for the family's future. "I heard."

In a subdued and broken voice, Fran recounted everything that had transpired since they had last seen each other: the failed attempt to destroy the Beacon, the activation of the alien machine, and the gruesome murder of her husband. She spoke little of Dolores, mentioning only that she had found peace. Struggling to contain her tears, Fran said, "I want to go home."

"I'll take you there myself," Megan promised. "But first, a question: Are you aware of what's happening?"

Fran's eyes blazed, a clear sign of the pressure she was under. "It's a circus, I know, but that man, Obadiah, wants to put me in a cage. I won't allow that, not for myself, and certainly not for my daughter."

"I wouldn't either," Megan said, picturing Obadiah's stricken face behind the mirrored wall. "Don't get me wrong, he's a good egg, but he represents an agency that's afraid of what you'll say and wants answers you either don't have or don't want to share. Even if he has your best interests at heart, others might not."

"I knew you'd understand."

"But, Franny, the crowds won't vanish. In fact, they're likely to grow. And unfortunately, so will speculation concerning—" Megan kissed Melody on the forehead.

Fran exhaled a weary sigh, deflating like a balloon.

Cradling Melody on her knee, Megan rested a hand on Fran's

shoulder. "Here's what we'll do: We'll go back to Santa Barbara, but not to your place. You and Melody can stay with me for as long as necessary. My house is huge, has plenty of rooms, and is in a quiet neighborhood. We'll figure things out together. To be honest, I'd appreciate the company. Besides, your daughter adores my dog. I suspect the little traitor prefers her over me."

Melody removed her fingers from her mouth and beamed. "I promise to feed Twinkles, walk her every day, and sleep with her every night."

A trace of a smile escaped Franny, the first Megan had seen in a long while. "Perhaps not every night, pumpkin."

"Great, we have a plan," Megan said. Glancing at the mirrored window, Megan gave Obadiah a thumbs-up. "And we already have a ride."

◆

Megan, Fran, and Melody accompanied Obadiah to a waiting military aircraft that would transport them to Vandenberg Air Force Base. From there, she planned to drive the family to her home, tucked against the foothills on the outskirts of town.

The mother and daughter settled around a small table across from Megan. Obadiah selected a seat near the cockpit, far enough away to give them a semblance of privacy, yet close enough to overhear. Stephen's body had been stowed in the cargo hold.

Once in the air, Megan retrieved a capsule from her purse and offered it to Fran. "For emergency use only."

"What's this?" Fran asked.

"Something to take the edge off. You're exhausted and can barely keep your eyes open. You haven't slept, have you?"

"Not a wink," she admitted, fatigue evident in a yawn.

Fran took the capsule, leaned back, and gazed out the window until her eyes finally closed. Melody delved into her mother's purse, extracting a box of crayons and a coloring book. Obadiah made a call and was soon engrossed in a conversation. And thirty thousand feet below, the desert brown transitioned to a verdant green.

"How are you holding up, dearie?" Megan asked.

With her tongue out, Melody pressed a crayon to the page. "I'm worried about Mommy. She's sad."

"It's okay for you to feel sad, too."

"I am, but my daddy's coming back. Mommy doesn't believe me, but she should."

Megan's hand moved involuntarily to her heart, her emotions swelling as a protective instinct surged. So young, yet this child had experienced more trauma in the past few weeks than an adult might in a lifetime. No wonder she hadn't accepted the loss. Then and there, Megan resolved to shield this young soul from the harshness of a world that seemed hell-bent on destroying her family. "Your dad was a good man, a good friend, and you're a great comfort to your mom. I can tell."

"I'm a helper."

Megan gently touched Melody's cheek. It seemed cruel to add one more burden to her loss, but Megan felt in her bones that what this child knew could change the course of history. "I totally understand if you're not ready to talk right now—"

"But you have questions," Melody cut in, her tone revealing a depth of understanding well beyond her years. For Megan, it was a stark reminder this child wasn't what she seemed.

"I know this is a terrible time, and—"

"It's okay. Go ahead."

Megan glanced at Franny, who was still sleeping. She had so many questions, things that had haunted her since the machine had been built. Questions for which answers had been guessed at by the greatest minds in the world. Megan didn't fall into that category, not by a long shot, but she sensed none had come close to understanding the true function of the Beacon. She started by confirming the obvious. "You're like your dad, aren't you?"

"We're from the same place, if that's what you mean."

"Right. I knew that. Just to be clear, you're not from the future, right?"

Melody looked up at her, lifting the crayon from the page. "Why would you think that?"

"Because you look like, um, us. People, I mean. Scientists a lot smarter than me have suggested it as a possibility."

Melody resumed her coloring.

Uncertain how to proceed, Megan clasped her hands together. "Okay, bear with me. You look human, and obviously, are human, but somehow, you're not from here."

Melody didn't raise her head. "I am from here."

"Let me rephrase that. How did you get to Earth, exactly?"

"The same way as you."

Megan ran her fingers through her hair, feeling like she was getting nowhere. Out of the corner of her eye, she noted Obadiah turning around in his seat. "Sorry, I don't understand."

"You have a mommy, right?"

Megan felt an unwelcome pang. Too short with a twisted back, her mother had believed that her child was a punishment inflicted by the Almighty. "A test of my faith," she would always say. Only after years of physical therapy was Megan able to correct her cursed genetics. But none of that helped her now. "My mother wasn't as kind as yours."

Melody placed her small hand on Megan's knee, as if she were the one who needed consoling. "I'm sorry."

"Thank you, dearie. But what does my mother have to do with anything?"

"She had a baby. My mom also had a baby. My dad had a mom. I never met her, but she had a baby, too." As if that explained everything, Melody went back to her coloring book.

Sensing she missed something obvious, Megan glanced at Obadiah, who had his elbows on his knees, intently studying the child. "Maybe," he began, speaking slowly, "Melody died where the transmission originated, and was born here. Transmigration."

Melody pointed the crayon at Obadiah. "That's right. But I don't know what that last word means."

Megan's mouth fell open, disbelief warring with the analytical side of her mind. Yet nothing else could account for the child's presence. Even if faster-than-light travel was possible, where was the vessel? And how could she take human form? Given time-travel was out—an outlandish theory to begin with—that had to be the explanation. Once she ignored her preconceptions, the answer was as obvious as the nose on her face. "How did you figure that out?"

"Lots of people believe in some form of afterlife. Besides, that conspiracy theorist, Max Mystery, discussed the possibility on his show. Just one of many, but it happens to fit."

Megan shook her head, stunned, both at the implications and the fact that Obadiah listened to that dumb show. "I can't believe it. Holy shit."

He angled his chin at the child, a reminder they had company.

"Oh, right," she said. "Sorry dearie. I was just surprised."

Melody's eyes sparkled. "My mommy says that word all the time: shit, shit, shit."

"I'm sure your mother doesn't want me teaching you bad words."

"Crap, crap, crap. She says that too."

"Wonderful, dear, but I think that's enough."

A chime on Obadiah's phone sounded, causing him to turn around and cup his hand over the speaker. Melody ripped a page from her coloring book and held it up. "Look what I drawed," she said.

A grinning octopus wearing a jaunty sailor's hat stared back at Megan. Within its bulbous head, Melody had drawn spiraled lines in the shape of a hurricane. "That's a lovely picture, with such vibrant colors. You're quite the artist…" Her words trailed off as her eyebrows shot up. Snatching up the page, she scrutinized it more closely. The intricate pattern and many hues mirrored what she had observed inside those drops falling in the Beacon's injection chamber. "What is this?"

Melody traced a finger around one arm of the spiral. "That's you."

"Pardon?"

"That. Is. You," she repeated.

"Me?"

Fran opened bleary eyes and stretched her arms over her head. "That's how she sees us, Meg. Inside of you, me, and every living thing. She's like her father in that way."

"You've been listening," Megan said.

Fran answered with a nod and a yawn.

"Is it true, the transmigration thing?"

"I know it's a shock. And to answer the question you're about to ask, the Beacon allows people to travel from here to there while retaining a memory of what came before. Stephen told me that. Without that machine, he says we're stuck here and will remember nothing of our previous lives." She tousled her daughter's hair.

"Except for little one and her father. They can travel anywhere and remember everything from what came before. They're special that way."

"I am special," Melody agreed.

Megan rubbed her temples, trying to wrap her head around what this implied. Stephen had told her the function of the machine was to communicate with the civilization that sent the transmission. It turns out that he had lied. But why? Whatever his reason, Megan knew that any sober-minded scientist would dismiss Stephen's claims anyway. Concrete proof was required, and the word of a young child wouldn't suffice.

"How come you don't already know this?" Melody asked.

"I guess I'm a little slow," Megan said, still grappling with the implications.

"No, you're not."

"How could I have predicted this, dearie?"

"Didn't you see the instructions?"

Megan wondered if she heard right. "What?"

"Maybe I didn't use the right word." Melody scrunched up her mouth. "What about directions? Do you have the directions on how the Beacon works?"

Megan glanced at Fran, who shrugged, indicating she hadn't heard this either. "There was a blueprint that we used to build the Beacon. But there were no directions, instructions, or anything that explains how the thing works. I'm sure of that because I helped to decipher the transmission."

"But it was part of the message," Melody insisted.

"There's only one message, dearie."

Melody gazed out the window, squinting at the clouds passing below the aircraft. "Maybe you should look again."

CHAPTER FOUR

In the hushed corridors of the White House, Megan felt the weight of uncertainty pressing against her chest. Muted light washed over the floral-patterned carpet, and the air was tinged with the scent of aged leather and turmoil. Obadiah walked beside her, a stoic presence in a labyrinth she'd only seen on television. Samantha Peebles, the President's Chief of Staff, led the way with brisk steps, her purposeful stride emphasizing the severity of the quagmire the Administration was embroiled in. As they passed the staff in the hall, hushed conversations turned silent, intensifying her apprehension.

"Megan," Obadiah said. "Address her as Madam President. Be professional and be respectful."

"Am I usually not?" she asked, hefting the strap of her bag more comfortably on her shoulder.

"You can be abrupt at times."

"Does she remember me?"

Obadiah slowed his pace to put some distance between them and Samantha. "Quite well. She's also aware you don't care for her or her policies. Tread lightly, especially given the political storm that's brewing. Best to let me do most of the talking. When you do comment, avoid placing blame or getting personal."

"Her decisions caused this fiasco," Megan mumbled so as not to be overheard. "You know that as well as I do."

"Maybe so, but we're in the realm of politics, not on a jury. Remember what you're here for."

Right. To assure Fran and Melody are protected and to pitch her plan. Secondarily, to stay out of jail. Given this one chance, she had no intention of blowing it. "I'll be on my best behavior. What have you already told her?"

"I briefed her about the blue haze, the infrared images you brought along, and my suspicion concerning Melody's origin. Also, the child's claim that instructions should have been found in the transmission. Beyond that, I didn't feel qualified to speculate. There's no proof."

"Nothing about what we perceive inside the chamber?"

Obadiah just shook his head.

Samantha waited for them by the door leading into the Oval Office. "Be warned," she said in a low voice, "President Martinez is not happy with either of you." With a brisk gesture, she ushered them inside, then strode across the carpet to take her place beside the Resolute Desk.

President Janise Martinez stood with her back to the room, gazing out the window into the Rose Garden. Near the fireplace, the Secretary of State paced. Obadiah acknowledged the Secretary with a dip of his chin, which wasn't returned. As Megan settled into her designated chair, the room seemed to shrink under the weight of unspoken words.

Silence lingered until the familiar voice of the President cut through the stillness. "My Secretary of Defense kills a man before he collapses from something physicians can't explain. For some reason, my National Science Advisor shoots herself in the head, and my Intelligence Director prevents none of this, despite being present. To make matters worse, what should have been restricted intelligence leaks to the media. As a result, Congress is threatening to appoint a special counsel, and the United Nations is moving to censure this country for not disclosing the existence of that goddamn alien machine."

Turning from the window, eyes like daggers impaled Megan before fixing on Obadiah. "Tell me why I shouldn't fire you and press charges against the perpetrators of a terrorist act, including the conspirator in this very room."

Megan swallowed hard, but not a ripple of emotion marred Obadiah's expression. "I serve at your pleasure, Madam President, and will tender my resignation immediately. However, charging the widow of the man who was murdered and the person who gave sanctuary to his family would be highly problematic. Stephen Fisher was a popular figure, and attacking his family would hurt your public standing. Not to mention the uncomfortable facts that would be exposed in any trial.

Embracing the truth might prove to be a better option."

"Agree on all points," Samantha said, earning a glare from her boss.

"The truth?" the President scoffed. "Whose version of the truth is that?"

Obadiah's smile remained fixed, his gaze unwavering. "Yours. Though the facts can't be changed, perceptions can be shaped. General Beckman went rogue, letting paranoia overcome good sense. Eyewitnesses will support that account of events. You've always been concerned about his temper and could say you were searching for a replacement. When it comes to Dolores, she was distraught, with only weeks to live. No need to explain her actions, only mourn her passing. Last thing, the existence of the Beacon has been an open secret since Max Mystery's interview with Fisher. Nothing has changed with this latest leak, other than substantiating claims people already believe. Besides, it was your predecessor who imposed secrecy on the project, not you."

"Not a bad interpretation," said the Secretary.

Samantha inclined her head. "I think we could make that work."

The lines on the President's forehead eased, and she took her place behind the desk. "Especially because it's true."

Megan clucked her tongue—an involuntary response to nonsense. President Martinez had no qualms about secrecy, and no plans to replace General Beckman. Those two were peas in a pod.

The President quirked an eyebrow. "Something to share, Doctor McCullough?"

Obadiah shot her a warning glance.

"Sorry for the interruption, Madam President," Megan said, berating herself for getting off on the wrong foot. "I'm nervous is all."

"I don't recall you ever having a problem speaking your mind. You obviously came here for a reason, might as well spit it out."

Megan straightened her shoulders. "Yes, Ma'am. Let's say you do everything Obadiah suggested. Further, he resigns, and you put me in jail. Nothing changes. Congress remains in the hands of the opposition, who will appoint a special counsel regardless of what you do."

"Aren't you an astrobiologist?" the Secretary of State asked, his foot tapping with barely concealed impatience.

"Let her speak," the President said, her tone permitting no argument.

Megan turned to the Secretary. "What you say is true, but in this case, science and politics are intertwined," and returned her attention to the President. "The crux of the problem is the Beacon, which hangs around your Administration's neck like a millstone. Since no one knows what it does, everybody has an opinion, and since the machine is operated by the government, you get the blame for any real or imagined problems. But conditions have changed dramatically, and there's an opportunity to make science your greatest ally. Turn the board around so you can play the same game, but with the pieces reversed."

Leaning back in the leather chair, the President's posture relaxed a fraction. "All right, Doctor McCullough, you've got my attention. Be aware that I've been told about the blue haze and speculation concerning the child, which I don't buy. Now tell me something I don't know."

Despite having rehearsed this a million times in her head, Megan felt awkward, like she had ten thumbs. Retrieving a binder from her bag, she accidentally dropped it, scattering papers over the carpet. Most of the mess landed at the feet of the Secretary of State, who made no move to help, only pinched his lips together.

Megan hastily snatched a picture from the ground and held it up to the President. The Secretary and Samantha craned their necks to see. Three ghostly red spheres stared back at them from the page: images produced by the infrared cameras monitoring the injection chamber. Though it lacked the spiraled pattern and colors she and Obadiah had seen first-hand, it proved the phenomenon wasn't a figment of their imagination. When she had asked Melody about these drops, the child had claimed ignorance.

"Sensors captured these spheres falling inside the chamber shortly after Stephen Fisher passed," Megan said, speaking too fast. "They stopped forming after seventy-two hours, leading me to believe the phenomenon is part of the machine's initialization sequence. To do what, we still don't know, but there may be a way to find out, direct from the source."

The President barely glanced at the image. "Another mystery

scientists can't explain. If you're alluding to this other transmission, forget about it. Nobody is going to take the word of a little girl, no matter her suspected origin. Is that all you've got, Doctor?"

Megan picked up another folder from the carpet and pushed it across the desk. "We have evidence supporting the existence of this new transmission, Ma'am. Dolores had suspected it existed all along,"—probably having heard about it from Melody—"and ordered NASA to analyze the raw telemetry coming from the newly upgraded gravitational observatory. Turns out, hidden among the actuation fluctuations and thermal variations, gravitational blips repeat at regular intervals, strongly suggesting another message exists at wavelengths too weak for the observatory to fully capture."

The discovery highlighted both the capabilities and limitations of current technology. Positioned in heliocentric orbit at a Lagrange point, the Astrometric Massive Interferometer Gravitational Observatory, the AMIGO, remained the largest and most sensitive scientific instrument ever constructed. But it wasn't sensitive enough to fully capture the signal.

"We need a more powerful observatory," Megan continued. "An interferometer that can detect gravitational waves that flow in minutes rather than seconds. A Mega-AMIGO, if you will, with longer arms and an improved configuration. That's where we'll find—"

"What I hear is a plea for more money and more time," the President cut in, pushing the binder back across the desk. "Both of which are in short supply and neither of which Congress is likely to grant."

"That's a certainty," Samantha said.

Concerned she was losing her audience, Megan spoke rapidly. "I thought of that. So, we propose an international consortium, pooling funding and resources to expedite the process at minimal or no cost to us. Every country and scientific institution in the world would jump at the chance to—"

The President lifted her hand. "While I'm sure this would make an interesting science project, it does nothing to help me navigate the current situation. Thank you for your time, Doctor McCullough. And don't worry, I have no intention of pursuing charges. Just keep your nose clean and don't cause me any further trouble." With a dismissive wave, she reached for a sleek tablet on her desk. Her fingers flew across the screen, the rapid tapping filling the sudden silence.

Megan fidgeted in her chair, unsure of what to do. She not only failed, but she also hadn't had the chance to raise the subject of pardoning Fran and her extended family, abandoning them to the whims of political forces that none of them could control. They were at her house now, with Twinkles, their hopes pinned on promises Megan had made but couldn't keep.

The President's eyes flicked up, sharp and cold. "That will be all," she said, her voice clipped

As Samantha opened the door to escort them out, Megan implored Obadiah with a look. For a split-second, a flicker of understanding passed between them. With a barely perceptible nod, Obadiah shifted in his seat and steepled his fingers. "Madam President, may I offer a suggestion before we leave?"

"I have yet to decide what to do with you, Obadiah," President Martinez said, not looking up. "But if you have more to say, make it quick."

"Put the blame squarely at the feet of your predecessor," Obadiah said in a monotone. "Everything—the secrecy, the mistreatment of Fisher, what we know of the Beacon. Full transparency. You had reservations about the former president's strategy from the very beginning, but as Vice President, it was your duty to support the Commander-in-Chief. Nobody will question that. Given the challenges you've faced since taking office, you simply haven't had the opportunity to change course. But now's the time. You announce a new direction. Publicly confirm what people already suspect and disclose the preliminary evidence of a second transmission. Then you call for an international consortium to investigate. The U.S. doesn't provide a cent of funding, as this country has already invested billions building the AMIGO and constructing the Beacon. Since no funding is required, congress is out of the loop."

"And hand the Beacon to the consortium," Megan added, surprised at the eloquence of the man she considered a sphinx. "Then it's no longer your problem. Further, you pardon Fran and offer protection for her extended family. In one stroke, you become the savior of a widow in need, gain the support of the international community, and undermine the argument from your domestic opponents."

Megan held her breath, uncertain how the President would react. After what seemed like an eternity, President Martinez laid the tablet aside and glanced at her Chief of Staff.

Samantha closed the door and returned to the desk. Crossing her arms and placing a hand on her chin, she stood in silent contemplation. "Coming clean would improve public perceptions," she said. "Certainly, it takes the steam out of Congress, who'll be reduced to complaining you should have done that in the first place. And who cares about the UN? I mean, if they censure this country, that'll improve your poll numbers."

Megan was still afraid to breathe, though she allowed herself a glimmer of hope.

"I can't think of any downsides," said the Secretary. "The UN aside, the international community would have no choice but to embrace the plan. I'll check with Legal, but I think you could do it with an executive order."

The President rhythmically tapped her fingers on the desktop, the sound aligning perfectly with the ticking of the grandfather clock against the wall. With a hard look at Megan, she pulled back the folder containing NASA's findings. "There's a hole in your strategy, Obadiah," she said, flipping through the pages.

"What's that, Ma'am?"

"Someone needs to lead the effort, a person with experience, credibility, and objectivity nobody dares question."

"Much will hinge on that decision," Samantha said, pulling up a chair. "The NASA administrator would be an excellent candidate. He's capable, well-known, and can handle himself. I've heard good things about the Deputy Director as well."

"Except both were complicit in efforts to keep the transmission a secret," the Secretary of State said. "If we're going to disown the former policy, we can't put the enablers in charge. In fact, it may be advisable to fire one or both of them to enhance the credibility of the Administration."

"That rules you out, Obadiah," said Samantha. "Not that you want the job."

"A fair assumption," he agreed.

"I can have a list of candidates prepared by the end of the day," Samantha said. "We'll look them over, and I'll set up a discussion with the contenders. For my part, I'll be looking more for political acumen than experience."

"Thoughts, Doctor McCullough?" asked President Martinez, not looking up from the pages.

Megan tried not to betray her elation. "I'd be happy to look over the list. I can suggest a few other names as well."

"The more I think about this," the President said slowly, her eyes lifting from the binder, "the clearer the choice becomes."

"Who do you have in mind, Ma'am?" Samantha asked. "I'll bring them in."

The President closed the folder, then pointed at Megan. "Her."

Megan's heart fluttered. She was a scientist, an educator. Not this. Never this. "Ma'am, I'm a team player, not a leader. This is a political matter for which I'm extremely ill-equipped."

"I concur wholeheartedly," said the Secretary of State.

Samantha pressed a finger against her lips. "I like it."

President Martinez kept her eyes on Megan. "You told me that politics and science are intertwined, which I'm starting to appreciate. If I recall, it was your insight that proved crucial to producing the alien blueprint, which makes you more than qualified. Since you left the project before things fell apart, your objectivity isn't compromised. That gives you credibility across the aisle and you already have it with the scientific community. Yes, you're the best candidate. You will also replace Dolores as my National Science Advisor."

"That's good," Samantha said. "Increases your credibility too."

Panic rose in Megan's throat. "Ma'am, I support the plan. I really do. But I have no experience leading this type of thing, know nothing about politics, and barely get along with my dog. I'm sure you can find somebody more qualified."

The President's mouth became a line. "This is an emergency, and I expect you to treat it as such. Now's not the time to indulge your insecurities, Doctor. I have confidence in your abilities. Clever to have Obadiah propose a plan I'm sure you came up with. You're better at politics than you think. You also care for that little girl and the mother. What better way to assure their safety than to become part of my administration."

Samantha's lips curled into a sardonic smile. "Congratulations, Doctor McCullough."

Desperately thinking of a way to get out of this, and failing, she looked to Obadiah for support. Not only did he not come to her rescue, but an upward twitch of his lips betrayed his agreement with the appointment. Megan's shoulders slumped, and in a resigned tone, she asked, "You'll pardon Fran and the family?"

"Unnecessary," the President said. "I've already spoken to the Attorney General. Charges won't be filed."

"Thank you. And you'll allow the Beacon to be transferred to a consortium?"

"I have a government to run and want this off my plate. Yesterday, if possible. Get it done. I'm also growing wary of what's happening inside that chamber. Find out what that goddamn machine does before I decide to vaporize it with a nuke. You hear me?"

"I do, Ma'am."

"Rest assured, you'll be granted full authority and independence to create this consortium. Do you have a name for it yet? I need to know for the press conference."

Heaving a sigh that seemed to come from the toes of her orthopedic shoes, Megan bowed her head. "ISBLIC, Ma'am, the International Space-Based Laser Interferometer Consortium."

CHAPTER FIVE

Nine months later

A tidal wave of pain caused the woman to shudder from head to toe, as if someone pushed forcefully against her spine while twisting her insides. She clenched her fists as each contraction pulled her further into a vortex of agony. Fire burned her nether regions.

"One last time," urged the midwife. "You're almost there."

Convinced she was about to die, tears streamed down her cheeks, mingling with the sweat that plastered her bangs to her forehead. The woman rallied with a desperate but waning strength. Then, after a full night of what she would later term "the exquisite agony," a child unlike any other came into this world.

The midwife cut the cord that bound mother to child, though not the connection. With practiced hands, she suctioned fluid from the baby's mouth and vigorously rubbed its body with a towel. But the child didn't cry. She flicked the soles of its feet to the same result. Concerned at the lack of respiration, the mid-wife checked the baby's color, which was good, and the pulse, which was strong. In growing alarm, she grabbed the mask from the adjoining table and was about to force air into the child's lungs when the newborn took a couple of fitful breaths. A surge of relief washed through her. Then, to her astonishment, the baby opened its eyes and locked them onto hers.

The fibers within the child's irises interwove and twisted around the black epicenter of each pupil. Colors coalesced among the strands, becoming currents that turned into whirlpools. A pang of unease prickled the midwife's senses, but she found she couldn't look away.

As if from a distance, she heard the mother say, "Please hand me my child."

In an instant, the colors and whirlpools vanished. The midwife blinked and shook her head, dismissing the vision as fatigue-induced imagination. She placed the newborn into the waiting arms of the mother.

"A baby boy," she said.

The mother held the child to her breast, feeling the beat of its small heart against her own. Caressing the baby's head, she turned to her husband, leaning against the weathered clinic wall. "'A great sign appeared in heaven'," she recited. "'A woman clothed with the sun, with the moon under her feet, and on her head a crown of twelve stars.'"

The man took a long drag from a blunt, his eyes veiled by half-closed lids. With smoke curling around the rope-like strands of his nutbrown hair, he slowly exhaled. "Be not so wise in your own eyes, wife. It was the Creator who fashioned the heavens and earth. I don't think He consulted you."

The midwife pointedly waved a hand before her nose, a not-so-subtle hint for the man to take it outside. But he paid her no mind, nor was she in a mood to object. Like the mother, she had been here all night. And as the only midwife within fifty miles of this rural speck of a New Mexican town, she had more patients to attend to this morning.

"You misunderstand, Hosea," the woman said. "My soul makes its boast to the Lord of Light, not you. Come, hold your child."

Another of Hosea's wives peeked through a crack in the door. He dismissed her with an impatient flip of his hand. "Having the kid was your idea, Joybelle, not mine."

"An angel came to me in a dream and proclaimed—"

"That you will conceive in your womb and bear a son," he finished, having heard this boast one too many times. "Yes, so you keep telling me. I slept with you is what happened. It didn't help that I forgot to take precautions. Having the boy was fifty-fifty. That's not divine intervention. That's biology."

Joybelle hugged her child close and whispered, "He knows not what he says, Jezreel. Forgive him."

Hosea took another drag from the blunt. "You have what you want. Now, I have a sermon to give."

"Your dozens of followers can wait for the return of their

prophet."

"When you mock me, you mock the Divine. Despite that, I'll share the good news with my flock. Blessings be with you, wife."

"The Divine is closer than you think, Hosea. Before you go, please, please, let my child know he has a father."

With a sigh, Hosea flicked the spent joint to the floor and approached the bedside. Joybelle kissed the baby on the head and extended the newborn to her husband.

As Hosea took the infant into his arms, his body stiffened, his eyes rolled back in his head, and he sank to his knees with his head lolling to the side. The midwife rushed forward to make sure he didn't drop the child.

Joybelle gave Hosea an icy stare. "Only now do the scales fall from your eyes. As you have prophesied from the pulpit, the Lamb came as Stephen Fisher to break the Seventh Seal. The gates of Heaven now lie open, and the alien machine does indeed herald the coming of Armageddon. But what you don't know, dear husband, is that it will be you who commands legions of believers in service to the Lord of Light. Soon, the blind will see, the deaf will hear, and the dead will live again."

PART II – THE CHURCH

And they worshiped the dragon, for he had given his authority to the beast, and they worshiped the beast, saying, "Who is like the beast, and who can fight against it?"

— Revelation 13:4

CHAPTER SIX
Six Years Later

Heads turned as Megan led the mutton-chopped senator and his female companion into operations control at the headquarters of the International Space Based Laser Interferometer Consortium, known as ISBLIC. Situated in Mercury, Nevada, within the former proving grounds of a nuclear weapon testing site, this was the organization Megan had envisioned when she spoke with President Martinez in the Oval Office.

The consortium evolved much as Megan had imagined. The U.S. National Aeronautics and Space Administration, the European Space Agency, the Japan Aerospace Exploration Agency, and the Indian Space Research Organization formed the initial core of the group, eventually being joined by emerging space programs from other nations. Megan had been elected Director General by acclamation. In a gesture of global cooperation, the consortium made public the blueprint deciphered from the extraterrestrial transmission. Despite this, China and Russia insisted on going their own way, building another machine in the Taklamakan Desert. Except theirs didn't work because they lacked two critical ingredients: Melody and Stephen.

True to the President's word, no charges were pursued against Fran and her extended family, now living under assumed names in a protected location. Control of the Beacon had been handed over to ISBLIC, and Megan was given broad authority to commit U.S. resources to the consortium. This occurred despite vociferous opposition from political opponents who accused them both of selling out their country. Regardless, these decisions had reduced the political hurricane to a squall, helping President Martinez win re-election—but just barely.

Scheduled for today was a key operational test of the new

observatory built by ISBLIC, an event Megan presumed the Senator had come to observe. She didn't know the woman who accompanied him, a slender figure clad in a form-fitting white tunic designed to accentuate her curves. With a high forehead, wide mouth, and cheekbones casting shadows on a complexion pale as newly fallen snow, the woman seemed designed to amplify Megan's own insecurities in height, weight, shape, and every other feature she cared to compare. She had no clue why the lady was here, though the possibility she was the Senator's mistress crossed her mind.

Megan exchanged nods and greetings with the assembled physicists, engineers, and technicians, all of whom represented the best minds in their fields. Among such accomplished individuals, she often felt out of place. Most of the team barely spared the Senator a glance, but some gazes lingered on the plunging neckline of his companion.

"Everybody," Megan said, raising her voice. "I'm privileged to introduce Senator Wigfall, the chairperson of the ISBLIC steering committee. He's here to observe the first engineering run of our new observatory. Since he's also responsible for our paychecks, let's give him a good show." Sporadic clapping and a few crooked smiles followed.

Until today, the Senator hadn't shown the slightest interest in the workings of the organization he purported to lead, having never contacted Megan or shown up for a meeting. Given he was a political appointee from a hostile congress, that didn't much surprise her, though it left her wondering about why he had come. Beyond winning one election and having coached a college football team (Megan didn't know which), the man had no qualifications whatsoever. He only chaired the steering committee because the Beacon sat on U.S. soil, and the other consortium members didn't wish to annoy their host.

Raising a hand to acknowledge the mostly indifferent audience, Wigfall told her under his breath, "I won't be doing this for long."

Megan didn't much care, other than hoping whoever replaced him wouldn't cause trouble. "Sorry to hear that, sir," she said, directing him and his guest to the back of the room.

As they walked, Megan filled the awkward silence with what she thought the Senator should know. "People have been working around the clock to prepare for today's run. The engineers are all set to test the laser oscillator, an instrument that detects minute changes in beams of light between the three spacecraft. It's a crucial component, able to measure relative displacements up to a resolution of ten picometers— a hundred times smaller than the diameter of an atom. A triumph of twenty-first-century engineering, if I may say so."

The Senator's fixed smile matched his glazed eyes. Not wanting to be rude, Megan added for the benefit of his lady companion, "Think of it as a buoy on a lake that detects ripples in the water, except the water is space."

The woman showed her pearly white teeth. "I understand. The new observatory detects low-frequency gravitational waves, where you hope to find another voice from the heavens. Those waves are an ideal means for interstellar communication, given they're unaffected by obstacles that would otherwise disrupt an electromagnetic signal. I have every expectation you will succeed and wish you the best of luck, Doctor."

Megan blinked. "That's right."

"You are the Herald who sounds the trumpet that will expose all earthly corruption and bring about the coming of New Jerusalem." The woman then made a peculiar motion with her hand, similar but not the same as making the sign of the cross.

"I neglected to introduce my guest," the Senator said. "Doctor McCullough, this is Joybelle Leroux, the Disciple in charge of the Grand Temple that sits in my great state. The people in her congregation are ardent supporters of mine and my party's nominee for president, William Stoughton. She requested this visit, and I was only too happy to oblige."

Megan's eyes fell to the pendant nestled in the woman's cleavage, recognizing the symbol of a movement she despised. Resembling a distorted ankh, the colored pearl inlay inside the teardrop-shaped loop connected to a stem with twelve curved arms rather than the traditional two, and a base that flared into three sharp appendages. A shudder passed through her as she recalled what the misguided convictions of another cult had done to her mother.

Noting Megan's attention, Joybelle gripped the trinket. "A symbol of my faith, awarded by our leader when he ordained me into the priesthood."

"You're from the Church of the Prophet," Megan said, voice flat.

"A refuge from sinners intent on driving this world into the abyss, yes."

"Are you channeling the Book of Revelation, or do you just make things up as you go along?"

Calmness radiated from Joybelle's every pore. "You're familiar with the story. Then you must recognize the Lamb has broken open the Seventh Seal."

Having been raised listening to this type of nonsense, Megan knew exactly to what she referred. "Stephen Fisher was no Lamb. The transmission is not a seal. And the Beacon is not a gate."

"You have doubts, I understand. I admit to having some myself. Consider my words a metaphor if that provides you comfort. The Prophet foretells the coming battle between good and evil and is searching for the Beast he must face. When it is found, everybody must choose a side."

Megan pointed an accusatory finger at the woman, striving and failing to keep her voice steady. "Members of your flock accuse me of experimenting with children. Those kids were on a field trip, for goodness' sake. I also have an inbox full of death threats, calling me a demon and worse for refusing to hand the Beacon over to you people. This is happening because of the hysteria your church is stirring up."

Joybelle's toothy smile didn't falter, only grew wider. "Excitable souls who mean well but are misguided. Rest assured, our leader reveres you and tells me you will have a crucial role in the end times. In part, that's why I'm here—to meet you. Trust in the Prophet with all your heart and do not lean on your own understanding, for that will surely lead you astray."

Noticing people surreptitiously glancing their way, Megan lowered her voice. "You traffic in unfounded conspiracies and nonsense, Miss Leroux."

"Now, now," the Senator cut in, wagging a hand. "Be respectful. A good number of voters belong to that church and believe in its teachings."

"Including you?"

"Politics is my religion," he intoned, solemnly dipping his head.

"And science is mine."

Wigfall patted her on the forearm, as if trying to calm an unruly pet. "Of course, that makes perfect sense. To each his own is my policy. Consider that a free nugget of wisdom. Say, if you don't mind, I'd appreciate an opportunity to say a few words to your team."

Taking a slow, deep breath, Megan reminded herself that the Senator remained the nominal head of this organization, and the woman was nothing more than a political pawn. Gesturing to the front of the room, she said, "Of course, by all means," fully expecting him to make a fool of himself.

"Can you remind me what this, um, observatory is called?"

Megan resisted the impulse to roll her eyes. How could he not know? Even the cult lady understood. "Officially, The Interstellar Gravitational Observatory Recorder. But everybody around here calls it IGOR."

"What does it do again? In language a farm boy might understand. Sorry, but these technical terms go right over my head."

"Think of it as a new sense to hear what the universe has to say. In this case, that's a literal interpretation of what we're doing."

"That's beautiful," Joybelle said.

Megan ignored her.

In a twang as gracious as it was false, the Senator said, "Indeed it is," and marched down the center aisle.

Busy chatter quieted into puzzled murmurs as Wigfall reached the small podium at the front of the room. He broke into a practiced smile. "I'm honored to join you on this historic day to witness the christening of our new observatory, what we call the IGOR. A good friend of mine characterized the instrument as allowing humanity to better hear what the universe has to say. That's a wonderful sentiment, isn't it? As chairman of this great organization, I look forward to leading you on a quest to answer the most awe-inspiring questions of our time. What is the Beacon? Who sent the blueprint? And for what purpose? Most of all, how can we use that knowledge to improve our lives here on Earth? I'm confident you'll find those answers. Be proud of your efforts. The long hours and missed meals with your family are minor sacrifices when compared to creating a legacy that can be handed down to your children and your children's children." He raised a fist. "God, in all his glory, will speak to us tonight. And we will be listening!"

Enthusiastic clapping ensued, along with a few hoots. More out of a sense of obligation than anything else, Megan tapped her fingers together in a half-hearted clap. To her relief, it turned out the Senator wasn't entirely full of fluff. He seemed a skilled orator, which the consortium would need given the potential change in the U.S. Administration.

Joybelle leaned in toward Megan. "The Senator is a vessel of the Prophet's will, nothing more."

"Pretty sure he's using you to get re-elected," Megan said, refusing to look at the woman.

"You believe I'm a simple-minded fool."

"Perhaps. And a fraud."

"In the times to come, you will discover we are more alike than you realize."

"We are nothing alike," Megan said with more vehemence than she intended. "I deal in facts and evidence, not fairy tales and doomsday prophecies. You remind me of somebody I once knew, another lost soul looking for simple answers in a complex world. Now, if you don't mind, this vessel has a job to do."

Megan slapped her hand on a nearby table and raised her voice. "Alright people, thank you for your attention and the kind welcome you gave to Senator Wigfall, but it's time to get back to work."

As the team prepared for the practice run, the Senator returned to Megan's side with a noticeable bounce in his step. "Good speech," she said, meaning it.

"My pleasure," he said.

Despite Senator Wigfall's indifference to technology, Megan felt obliged to brief him on upcoming events. "Our primary goal today is to ensure the end-to-end functionality of systems working with the laser oscillator. We're confident about the communication components, as those are direct descendants from the first observatory. The real challenge lies in the submicron-level optical alignment of the lasers. Assuming success," she gestured at a chart on the big screen, "there'll be a horizontal line along the x-axis. That shows IGOR is online and—"

"I didn't come to see your test," he interrupted. "I was hoping to speak to you privately about a special request."

Megan lifted an eyebrow. "Not interested in hearing what God has to say?"

"I always have an ear bent to receive the good word, but I have a flight to catch. This will only take a few minutes of your time."

As head of the steering committee, Megan had hoped the Senator would be more interested in this seminal moment in the organization's history. But apparently not. "No problem, but I need a few moments to ensure we're off to a smooth start."

"We'll wait, but don't be long," the Senator said. With a slight bow, he and Joybelle retreated toward the exit.

The operations manager, Michael, shot Megan a quizzical look, wondering if she wanted to say a few words. An inspiring speech had been her original plan, but Senator Wigfall and his guest had taken the steam out of that desire. She responded with a shake of her head and signaled for the test to begin.

Michael's voice cut through the room, "T-minus sixty seconds to initiate the test."

"Copy that," the lead mission controller said. "All subsystems reporting nominal."

"Instructions being sent now," the engineering station reported.

"Received. Status incoming. Power systems are stable, readings nominal."

"T-minus thirty seconds," Michael said. "Commencing final checklist."

"Laser interferometer alignment sequence initiated."

"Confirmed complete."

"Telemetry links established."

"T-minus ten seconds, five, four, three, two, one… Starting test sequence."

"Receiving telemetry," the communication station reported. "Stand by for preliminary results."

A tense silence fell over the room as data began streaming across multiple screens. Megan's eyes darted to the primary display, hoping for a clean signal as indicated by a horizontal line. Instead, the graph showed an irregular pattern of spikes and dips.

"We're seeing significant noise in the carrier signal," the mission controller reported, his brow furrowed. "Possible interference from an unknown source."

Megan felt a knot form in her stomach. While they had anticipated issues, this level of interference was unexpected. She couldn't shake the feeling that their unwelcome visitor, the priestess, had jinxed the test.

"Begin diagnostic sequence," Megan said, her voice steady despite her growing concern. "Let's isolate the source of the interference."

She strode toward the control station, finding the operations manager's gaze fixed on the console. Michael, an expert cryptologist and computer engineer, had played a crucial role in deciphering the original transmission. In typical fashion, he sported the same rumpled clothes from the previous day and had neglected to comb his hair.

"More noise than we expected," Michael said.

"Maybe the radiation pressure?"

He shrugged noncommittally, fingers flying across the keyboard. "If there's a signal hiding in that telemetry, it's going to take time to filter out the garbage, then weeks more to capture the entire message."

"It's there," Megan assured him, projecting more confidence than she felt. "The Senator wants to talk. If anything comes up, come get me, otherwise, I'll be right back."

"This is going to take a while, so no hurry."

"Understood."

After offering supportive words to the team, Megan re-joined her waiting guests. "My office is just down the hall."

"Lead the way," the Senator said.

◆

From Megan's sixth-floor office window, Wigfall fixed his gaze to the north, where just over the horizon, the Beacon's dome rose from the desert floor. He retrieved a tin canister from his suit jacket pocket, tapped the top, and extracted a cherry-sized pinch of tobacco that he placed behind his lip.

"As a courtesy," the Senator began, "I'm letting you know I'll be resigning as chair of ISBLIC next week. My party's nominee for president isn't comfortable with my role here."

Though Megan didn't know what 'special request' the Senator

wanted to discuss, she hadn't expected him to quit. "But the election isn't for months."

"Best to prepare for the inevitable. Stoughton has a double-digit lead in every poll in every state. I suggest you consider declaring support for the new order. Might help you keep your job, little miss."

Megan fought down her irritation, both at the moniker and the implied threat. "The Director General is elected by the ISBLIC steering committee, not dictated by one country among the ninety-two voting members. Even if your man wins, he can't change that. And don't call me 'little miss.'"

"You're a prickly one, aren't you? No offense meant. I say that with the purest of intentions. People don't trust what's going on here. That's not your fault, that's on the current president. More than most, you know that to be true. All those terrible threats and crazy stories are ridiculous, I agree, but they're symptoms of a larger problem." He waved at the horizon. "Martinez gave away what wasn't hers."

Megan recognized the talking point and knew Stoughton had exploited that to pander to his base's increasingly hysterical notions about Armageddon. Proof of that stood at the Senator's side. "Will your nominee follow through on his threat to withdraw from ISBLIC?"

"Oh, come now. That's just campaign talk." Wigfall expectorated into a dented thermos he took from another pocket. "Bill has the highest regard for this organization, despite your failure to learn much of anything about the alien machine."

Megan recoiled at the stench and the implication. "That's not true. The Beacon's ability to amplify gravitational waves upended our understanding of physics. All science begins with a question, the more puzzling the better. And once we find that second transmission, I expect we'll learn its true purpose."

"One who walks in darkness does not know where she's going," Joybelle said.

Megan ignored her, though that didn't stop the blood from rushing to her head. "I appreciate the heads-up about your resignation, Senator, and wish you the best wherever you go."

"Homeland Security, if you're wondering," he said.

"I was. Now, if you don't mind, I have a test to oversee."

"Sorry for rambling on, but that wasn't the reason I brought us here. My friend, Joybelle, has a request of you."

"I'd like to visit what you call the Beacon," Joybelle said. "And would greatly appreciate if you would accompany me."

The "no" already formed on Megan's lips battled with a morbid curiosity about this woman and the cult she embodied. Who were these people, and why did they believe such nutty things? What little she knew about the church she had learned from social media. They spread outrageous lies about demons and angels traveling through the Beacon to wage a final battle, in the form of children, no less. And that a Beast had emerged from the abyss to oppose them. Lies told with such earnestness that the primal part of Megan's brain understood the appeal: to be part of a cabal with access to hidden knowledge—the superpower of all cults. If it wasn't for the inexplicable popularity of this movement, Megan would've dismissed these people as nothing but a bunch of wackadoodles.

"Why?" she ended up asking.

"I have questions that need answering. I suspect you do as well, about a great many things. A visit will give us a chance to get to know one another and may help you understand what is to come."

Megan's eyes flickered with uncertainty, caught in a battle between distaste and desire to know more about the threat this woman posed. Absently toying with the edge of a paper on her desk, she abruptly decided a tour could do no harm. Access to the machine wasn't restricted, only managed, so time could be properly allocated to scientific groups running experiments judged to have the greatest merit. But on any given day, Megan could squeeze in a special request, however superfluous. One perk of being the Director General.

She looked to the Senator, leaning against the windowsill, sucking on his cheek. "I insist you accommodate the Disciple's request," he said without prompting.

"I was going to ask if you're coming along," Megan said.

"Oh. Is it dangerous? I heard something about radiation."

"At one time. But since the machine activated, the only radiation comes in the form of visible and infrared light. Perfectly harmless."

Wigfall winked. "Then I better come along to protect you ladies."

52

CHAPTER SEVEN

The cool ocean breeze ruffled my hair as I lay on the grass, looking up at the lights glittering in the night sky. My parents and Aunt Franny chatted at the patio table, laughing and clinking their glasses. Although the day had been filled with laughter and games, as it got later in the evening, a familiar unease crept over me. Bedtime approached, and with it came the sights, sounds, and smells of places I'd never been, with people I'd never met, and there were creatures I'd never seen. Some of these dreams turned into nightmares.

My cousin Melody lay beside me, holding a computer tablet over her head. She snapped a picture of the sky and showed me the screen, tapping one of the fuzzy white dots. "Do you know what this is, Stevie?"

I didn't need to look at the picture to know where she pointed—she brought it up all the time. "Is it that same star you keep talking about?"

"That's where we come from, home."

I took my paper plate from the lawn and sat up. After brushing off a few ants, I ate the last bite of cake. "That sounds made up."

"It's true," she said, her green eyes searching mine.

I shook my head and patted the grass. "This is our home now," though it didn't feel like it.

We had been forced to move twice in the last three years. Each time, I had to make new friends and learn a new last name. No one ever told me why, except for Melody, who said someone had recognized her mom in the grocery store. I understood we needed to stay hidden, but that didn't mean I liked it—especially when my parents argued about returning to our "real home," wherever that was.

Probably not around that star my cousin just pointed out.

Melody scratched the back of her leg with her foot, looking at me for a long moment before handing me the tablet. "My gift for your birthday. I picked it out all by myself."

"Really?"

"Mm-hm, I loaded it up with all the games you like. Now you don't have to borrow my computer anymore."

"Thank you!"

"You should thank my mom, too. She paid for it because I don't have any money."

I looked over at the patio table where Aunt Franny sat with my parents. Empty cups dotted the tabletop, and only crumbs remained of my mom's homemade banana cake, my favorite. Catching my eye, Aunt Franny smiled warmly and called out, "Happy Birthday, little Stevie!"

I held up the tablet, beaming. "Just what I wanted!"

"You're welcome, sweetie," she said.

Mom, sitting across the table, flashed five fingers at me—her signal that it was almost bedtime. I shook my head, not wanting the party to end. Dad, still wearing his pointy party hat, must have noticed because he talked to Mom, then flashed me a thumbs-up. I shot one back at him.

Melody propped herself up on her elbows, glancing at our parents before whispering, "Don't you remember we came here together?"

Tucking the tablet under my arm, I didn't answer, only wondered why she kept asking me that.

"I know you have weird dreams. They can be confusing. Mine were too."

She had never told me that. "You have weird dreams?"

"Not anymore, but I used to. That means it's time to wake up. And I hope you do it soon. Ever since we turned on the Beacon, travelers have been coming here. Now they're stranded, and I don't know what to do. I'm afraid they're going to be hunted down, like us, and it's getting worse—way worse. It's why our parents keep moving."

I kicked at a clump of grass. "I don't know what you're talking about."

Melody exhaled sharply through her nose. "And I don't understand why it's taking you so long. Those dreams are memories, Stevie. They came back to me when I was little, way littler than you."

"I'm not little."

"You're six, which is three years older than I was when it happened." She paused, searching my face intently. "Can you at least hear the music?"

How did Melody know about that? Sometimes I did hear music, playing softly in the background, where the shadows and whispers lived. Even thinking about it now made the sound echo in my head. "I don't know," I said, not wanting to talk about it.

Melody scrunched her mouth to the side. "The music only gets louder the longer you wait, Stevie. Let it out before the memories overwhelm you."

I bit my lip, torn between curiosity and fear of those dreams. "Did that happen to you?"

"No, because I didn't fight it. You shouldn't either. It's easy when you don't."

"How did it feel when it…happened?"

Her eyes glazed over, her voice distant. "It was like drifting down an endless river, the current of time pulling me backward through a blue mist. On the shore, I saw people I knew in places I had once been, the faces, shapes, and smells both strange and familiar. I know that sounds weird, but I felt whole after it happened. When you finally wake up, know that what you remembered was real and what you experienced was natural. You're the one who told me that."

"Did not."

"Did too. But that was before we came here. You also told me to anchor myself in the here and now so that I didn't get lost in those old memories. 'They're only echoes,' you said. Take your own advice, Stevie, and embrace who you are. Don't be afraid."

"I'm not," I said too fast.

She took my hand. "When you do wake up, be careful who you tell. Even my mother took some time to accept who I am. Your dad's going to be okay with it, I can tell, but I'm not sure about your mom. When she thinks I'm not looking, she studies me like I'm a bug or something."

I had seen that too. "I'll tell her to stop doing that."

"Don't worry, I'm used to it. Your dad, on the other hand, never treats me different. Uncle Eric is… well, you'll find out soon enough. Outside of our own family, don't tell anybody anything. People have weird ideas about my parents and me."

I nodded, because I knew what had happened to her dad. Sensing movement out of the corner of my eye, I turned to find a figure outlined against the moonlight. It was a crow, perched on the fence, as still as a statue and as silent as the night. It seemed to be staring at me, judging me, like it knew I hadn't told the truth. "Melody, I do hear music. I didn't want to tell you because I'm scared."

She dipped her head. "I thought so."

Glancing back at the fence, I found the bird was gone. Or maybe it was never there, like the voices in my head. "I also see shadows and hear whispers. When I told my mom about that, she said it was only my imagination."

"Set those shadows free, Stevie. When you do, you'll see them for what they really are—your life."

"In my dreams, one of those shadows does terrible things. I don't want to let that one out, ever."

Melody tapped her lips with a finger, then her eyes lit up. "That's why you're stuck. Before we came here, you told me, 'The longer I wait, the harder it is to wake up,' but you never explained why. I bet it's because there are things you don't want to remember. That's why you said that—because you might need help. I'm the helper."

"I don't know about that," I said, growing nervous.

Melody gently lifted my chin. "I helped you once before and you were way more stuck than you are now. You thanked me after. I'll tell you what. If you let me help, those dreams will stop."

That sounded good, actually. "Really?"

"Really."

"What are you going to do?"

She tapped the middle of my forehead. "We put our heads together. And then I give you a little nudge. You taught me how to do this, too. Don't worry, it's fun."

That didn't sound like fun to me, but I wanted those nightmares gone. "Okay. Let's try it."

She took the tablet from under my arm and laid it on the grass.

"Close your eyes."

"Why?"

"Just do it."

Trusting her, I did so.

"Now take a deep breath," she said, pressing her forehead against mine, "and let it out real slow. With each breath, allow yourself to relax. It helps to first focus on your toes, letting go of the tension, then move to your feet, your ankles, and then to your legs until your body becomes loose and limp."

"This is making me sleepy."

"That's good. Now imagine a peaceful place, a place where you feel safe and calm. It could be here, in your backyard, a forest, or anywhere that makes you feel good. Picture yourself there, feeling completely at ease."

I imagined myself at the beach, with my feet in the warm sand, watching the waves roll in.

"I'm going to count down from ten. With each number, you'll feel yourself drifting deeper into relaxation. Here we go. Ten, nine, eight, seven. As you relax, your mind becomes more open. You feel calm, peaceful, completely at ease. Six, five, four, deeper and deeper, the stress and tension melting away. Picture yourself floating on the surface of the sea, the sights, sounds, and sensations merely currents passing beneath you. Can you hear the music?"

"I do," I mumbled, my eyes closed, my body limp.

"Let the music surround you, run through you. Three, two, one. You can open your eyes."

Melody's face slowly came into focus. She said nothing, only smiled as streams of red, green, and yellow flowed from her eyes and began to spin, combining into a single whirlpool that grew to fill her head.

"It'll be like living through a dream," I thought I heard her say.

As I watched the whirlpool, the music got louder and louder, joined by whispers, smells, and images coming out from wherever they had been hiding. I fought down the fear, this time letting the sensations wash over me. Beginning to feel dizzy, I lay down on the grass, the world spinning around me.

A woman leaned over me. Though I recognized her face, I couldn't remember her name...or mine. She mouthed something lost in the growing roar of music. Confused, I could only gape in astonishment as her face dissolved, running down the edges of my vision like rain-soaked paint.

Abruptly, the ground dropped out from under me, and I fell off a cliff so steep that if time were wind, it would have whistled past my ears.

CHAPTER EIGHT

M egan led Senator Wigfall and Joybelle through the underground corridor into the control room monitoring the Beacon's injection chamber. Tables were littered with candy wrappers, soda cans, and half-empty bags of chips—remnants of the research team's hasty departure to accommodate the tour.

At the control panel, Megan pointed out various dials and switches, explaining that gravitational energy was collected in the nested domes above, then amplified and redirected into the chamber. She emphasized that though the physicists at ISBLIC couldn't explain how this was accomplished, the effects were measurable.

Joybelle paid close attention while Wigfall fiddled with his tie. "I hear the Chinese Government invited your team to examine the machine they constructed in the Taklamakan Desert," Joybelle said. "Would you mind sharing your findings?"

Megan hesitated, thrown off guard by the perceptive question. Though not a secret, the results of their visit hadn't been made public. "There were no surprises. We detected low-level radiation, comparable to a dental X-ray, and a measurable increase in gravitational energy, exactly what we recorded in our own injection chamber before the change." She fixed Joybelle with a pointed stare. "Any particular reason you're asking?"

"The Prophet sought confirmation from a trusted source," she said, then her voice shifted to a disconcerting sing-song tone, reminiscent of sugar and spice and everything nice. "You are indeed the Herald who portends the Kingdom of Heaven is near."

"Good lord," Megan muttered to herself, already regretting having brought the cult-lady here. She tapped in the security code to unlock the controls, then flipped the lever to part the shield that encased the chamber, allowing gravitational energy to flood inside.

Amber lights flashed, and a computerized voice began the countdown: "T-minus sixty seconds, fifty-nine, fifty-eight..."

Megan directed her guests to enter the lift on the opposite side of the room. Though it happened years ago, she kept her eyes forward to avoid the grim reminder of bloodied footprints. "What do you hope to find in there, Miss Leroux?"

"Please call me Joybelle. I hope to find proof that the gateway to New Jerusalem lies open. The Prophet provided specific guidance about what to look for—beginning with the blue haze. The Senator mentioned you've observed other phenomena. I'd love to hear what you perceive, Megan, if I may call you by your given name."

An alarm bell rang in Megan's head. What she and Obadiah perceived inside the chamber was a closely held secret. As a member of the Senate Intelligence Committee, Wigfall had access to that information. She glared at him, pinching her lips. Senator Wigfall merely shrugged, tacitly admitting his culpability, then spat into his thermos before entering the lift.

"I see what everybody sees," Megan said, wondering what other secrets Wigfall had spilled.

The lift ascended through the aperture in the ceiling. With a pneumatic hiss, the cabin doors opened into the heart of the injection chamber. They stepped onto a circular platform, about three meters in diameter, and raised one meter above the floor. Lights embedded in the surrounding railing blinked on.

Wigfall turned in a full circle. "Darker than a moonless night on the ranch. What exactly are we supposed to be looking at?"

"You'll get an eyeful in a moment," Megan said. "Any recording you may have seen doesn't do it justice."

The countdown continued its inexorable decline: "Five, four, three, two, one."

The gears engaged, parting the heavy shield and causing the floor to vibrate. Sapphire medallions embedded in the domed ceiling high above cast a soft glow over her guests. The blue mist materialized, creeping over the ceiling and blanketing the floor, rising to the edge of the platform.

"Son of a gun," Wigfall said, kneeling to wave his hand through the haze. "It's cold."

"Six degrees Celsius," Megan said. The Senator cocked his head, so she translated, "Forty-two degrees Fahrenheit."

"Ah." With a grunt, he lifted himself from the floor. "Where does this stuff come from?"

"The interference pattern observed in the interferometer passing through this space suggests a massive increase in the strength of the gravitational field, but physicists can't agree on whether the haze is the cause or an effect."

Senator Wigfall did a couple of knee bends. "I don't feel any heavier."

Megan suppressed a sigh. "Gravitational waves disrupt the fabric of space-time, like ripples on a pond. They're not caused by the displacement of matter."

He gave her a blank look.

"It doesn't make you any heavier."

"Why didn't you say so in the first place?" The Senator leaned against the railing, tucking another pinch of tobacco behind his lip. "What about it, Joybelle? You're the one who wanted to come here. Happy?"

Joybelle touched her forehead, then the middle of her chest, and made two loops around her shoulders, as if trying to mimic the cross, but with a cultish twist. "Absolutely gorgeous," she said. "I especially love the music."

Megan's eyes widened, then narrowed as she realized the Senator must have spilled the beans about the music. It made sense Joybelle would pretend to share this ability to hear what others couldn't; after all, that's what charlatans did—claim to possess special powers denied to mere mortals. "You might want to get your hearing checked, Miss Leroux."

Joybelle arched an eyebrow before peering up at the ceiling, where a drop grew heavy within a single medallion. This phenomenon had become a rarity now, having decreased precipitously in the days following Fisher's death. Stretching into a thinning thread, the drop parted from the medallion, spiraling downward in widening circles until the haze swallowed it up in a flash of green, pink, and violet.

"Like an angel falling from the sky," she said, again making that weird motion over her chest. "Or was it a demon? I can't tell, though we disciples have a method of detecting children touched by the Beast."

The Senator searched the ceiling, trying to figure out what Joybelle was talking about. If Megan didn't know better, she could swear Joybelle saw the sphere. But that was something only the infrared sensors could detect—and Megan herself. Just another pretense, she decided, though the priestess lucked out on the timing.

"Do you toss kids into a river to see if they float?" Megan asked. "I hear that works for finding witches."

"Now, now," said Senator Wigfall, whom they both ignored.

"Let's be honest with one another, shall we?" Joybelle said. "I'll start. Now that I'm here, I realize it wasn't the Prophet who needed a sign, it was me. Before I left the Grand Temple, he told me, 'You will know the truth, and the truth will set you free.' You see, he knew I had doubts. I realize only now that he sent me on this pilgrimage to satisfy my own questions rather than answer any of his. I feel ashamed. What about you, Megan? Do doubts keep you awake at night?"

Not usually, she thought, though a growing suspicion about this woman might keep her up tonight. Did Joybelle really hear the music? Did she see that drop? Or was it all an act? If an act, the timing strained coincidence. If not, well, she wasn't sure of the implications.

Megan returned honesty with honesty. "After I met Stephen Fisher, my world changed, as did my perspective. That doesn't keep me up at night, though the questions raised by his existence motivate me to learn more about this machine. What drives you, Joybelle? Is it fooling others into believing you're something you're not?"

A flicker of annoyance marred the woman's otherwise radiant countenance. "Doubt is like a wave of the sea that is driven and tossed by the wind. While you may find me unconvincing, I expect that won't be true of another. The Prophet tells me it takes two to bind the gateway between Heaven and Earth. That means the Lamb came here with another. We search for that companion now."

Megan's blood ran cold, the allusion to Melody unmistakable. The child had told her it took one to find a world and two to bind them together, something she had never shared with anybody, not even

Obadiah. So, how did this so-called prophet know? Another coincidence? "You're talking nonsense."

"Have I become your enemy by speaking the truth?"

The Senator took another pinch from his can. "Friendly advice, little miss, whatever the Prophet says, you can hang your hat on."

From within the folds of her tunic, Joybelle produced an envelope which she presented to Megan. "I was bidden to give this to the Herald."

Megan turned the envelope over in her hand, plain white and adorned with a seal in the shape of the pendant the priestess wore around her neck. "What is it?"

"An invitation."

CHAPTER NINE

As I fell, I tried to grab onto something, anything, but there was only empty air. Up and down lost all meaning, like being tossed underwater by a monstrous wave. Shadows danced just beyond my fingertips and voices whispered in my ear, but I couldn't understand what they were saying. Fear gripped me, but there was nowhere to hide, only to fall. Everything kept fading as I plunged into the void until the shadows themselves disappeared. What remained wasn't just black; this was pure emptiness, a place where even darkness got lost.

Unable to recall who I was or where I had come from, I cried out in a panic, "Help me, please!"

From somewhere within the black came a voice, clear and sharp: *Head toward the light.*

I latched onto those words like a drowning man to a buoy. "Where is it?"

At the bottom, said the voice.

A tiny white dot appeared, getting bigger as I fell. I didn't know if seconds or hours passed when the light finally swallowed me up.

I found myself standing on a narrow strip of land atop a high cliff. Crystal trunks grew from the ground, with glassy leaves hanging from brittle branches. They threw little rainbows over a floor littered with what looked like broken glass. Below me, a green sea stretched to the horizon under an orange sky. Looking over the edge, I watched in wonder as a swell emerged from the deep sea, grew impossibly large as it approached the shore, then exploded onto sharp rocks in a shower of spray.

The ground trembled beneath me. When I tried stepping back from the edge, I found I couldn't move. Confused, I looked down... then froze. Instead of legs, I saw a curled tail connected to a muscular body that shone under the light of not one, but two suns. Hardly breathing, I raised one of two long arms. Three slim fingers came into view, shaking as I held them in front of what I assumed to be eyes.

"What's happening to me?" I asked—or tried to ask—because no sound came from my mouth, only lights flashing behind me. When I looked over my shoulder, I saw stalks protruding from my back, their ends glowing bluish green.

"We've always liked this place," said a voice, the same that had spoken to me on the way down. "Peaceful."

I spun around to find a shadowy figure next to one of those crystal trees. As I watched, the form came into sharper focus. It had messy hair, a long face, and a thin body. The word "human" came to mind—an adult male.

"Who are you?" I asked, my voice silent, though the lights blinked.

The man brushed a hand over the glass leaves, making a soft chiming sound and scattering light on the ground. "The better question is: Do you know who you are?"

I frowned, or at least thought I did. "I'm…" I began, but couldn't finish.

"Lost," said the figure. "In my time, I was too. Until my child helped me find a way back. Her name was Melody."

The name rang like a struck bell, though I still couldn't place it. "Do you know where we are?"

"I brought you to a place we once called home. And to answer your first question, I put you in a body that I hoped you'd find familiar. We spent many lives on this world before coming here. But in reality, we're in your head, balancing between the conscious and physical planes of existence."

"I don't understand any of that."

"You will."

My eyes were drawn over the edge of the cliff, where I saw shadows swimming beneath the green water. One of those shadows rose to the surface, a massive head glaring at me with four bulbous eyes. It looked like a cross between a blimp and a jellyfish, with small arms around an egg-shaped body and two long tentacles trailing behind. I shuddered. "What's that thing?"

"You tell me."

I knew the answer without having to be told. "A memory."

The man nodded. "The sights, sounds, and sensations you've been experiencing are echoes of the past. Similar to memories, but more like disassociated identities that strive to live again. You could call them ghosts, I suppose. But unlike ghosts, they live within you. Some are more lucid than others, including that creature in the water. That thing did terrible things, killed innocents and enabled the oppression of entire civilizations. But that being is no longer you, though it's the reason for your nightmares. It's also the reason you're here, with me. We don't like to be reminded of what we once did."

"Are you a ghost?"

"More like a manifestation of your previous life. Another way of thinking of me is as your subconscious, which knows what you need to do, but your conscious self is afraid to face. That's okay, I had a hard time as well. Somebody I called the Stranger helped me navigate my own memories, much like I'm going to help you. In other words, you're waking up."

"I don't feel like I'm waking up. This feels like another dream."

"That's about right, except for one big difference—I'm here. Can you tell me your name?"

I searched for an answer that wasn't there. "No."

"Then you know what you need to do," the ghost said, looking around. "It's created by us, flows around us, and binds the conscious and physical planes so that life can flourish. That interrelationship is what we call music. I can hear it, and so can you. But you need to concentrate."

I closed my eyes, hearing the music playing softly in the background. As I concentrated, it grew stronger, louder, the notes offering unexpected comfort. My name came to me in a flash. "Stevie," I said, opening my eyes.

The ghost nodded. "A vessel for the accumulated hopes, fears, and burdens of an existence spanning eons."

"I know who you are."

"Then you understand why we came back. You also know how to get out of here."

My heart raced, afraid of what waited beneath those waters. But if

I wanted to see my family again, I needed to face it. "Is there any other way?"

"Not if you want to wake up," the ghost said, dissolving before my eyes. "Think of it as another metaphor, like me, representing your embrace of all that you once were. It's a choice, Stevie."

"Please don't go," I said, my plea reflected in the flicker of lights along my spine.

I'll be there when you most need me, said what was now nothing but a whisper. *Better get on with it. Your parents are worried.*

With a sigh—if this body was capable of such a thing—I squirmed to the edge of the cliff. Without looking down, I jumped. My body spun head over tail toward rocks jutting up from the sea floor like black knives. Unable to watch, I closed whatever passed for eyes.

The moment I hit bottom, the floodgates burst open, unleashing a torrent of images, scents, tastes, and sounds that engulfed me in a chaos of sensation—like pouring an ocean into a thimble. Though I couldn't make sense of it, I knew I had lived through it all.

At that moment, I truly understood what Melody had said about floating on the sea. The swirling currents beneath me were memories of all I had once been. But I didn't have to drown; I could simply rise and fall with the swell. Peace replaced fear.

Whatever I had done, whatever burdens I carried, they were but ripples in a vast ocean. At my core, I remained Stevie—and was ready to wake up.

CHAPTER TEN

Megan retreated to her office, having returned from operations control where she'd found the team of scientists and engineers still huddled around screens analyzing the raw telemetry from the test run. They had adjusted mirrors, fine-tuned suspension systems, and recalibrated optical cavities on the spacecraft. Despite their efforts, the surge of noise persisted, drowning out any potential signal. Megan had lingered there, offering moral support until Michael suggested the triage effort would take days or even weeks to identify the root cause.

Exhausted by the long day, the problems with IGOR, and the questions that plagued her, Megan collapsed onto her worn desk chair, a piece of home she had brought to add warmth to the sterile office at ISBLIC headquarters. The Senator and Joybelle had already departed—he to catch a flight, and the priestess to chant spells back at her temple.

Megan's thoughts turned to the note burning a hole in her pantsuit pocket. She tore open the envelope that Joybelle had given her, revealing a sheet of ivory bond paper. As she smoothed it across the desk, her eyes scanned the imprinted words:

> *To the Herald of New Jerusalem,*
>
> *The honor of your presence is requested at a service of worship where we confront mortality and shed the illusions of this world before the Lord of Light. A rite of passage for new adherents will follow. Come join the community of faith and open your eyes to a new reality.*

Sunday, two p.m. at the Grand Temple of the Prophet.

Written in flowery cursive below was a personal note: "Please join me for a private talk afterward, where we both may find enlightenment—Your friend in worship, Joybelle Leroux." A tiny heart adorned the name, evoking memories of grade school.

Megan stared long and hard at the message, replaying the conversation with the priestess. Deciding she had questions best not ignored, she pulled out her cell phone and dialed the number etched into her memory.

Fran picked up on the second ring. "Hi Meg, is there a problem?"

"No, no, not to worry. Sorry for the late hour, but I have a concern that can't wait for our weekly call. Any chance I can have a quick chat with Melody?"

"Sure, but only for a minute. We're about to go visit Stevie at the doctor's office."

"What? Is he okay?"

"He fainted and when he came to, seemed disoriented. I'm hoping it was just stress from the move. Tara and Eric are having him checked out right now. Hold on a sec."

A muffled cry and rustling ensued, suggesting Franny had pressed the phone to her chest. After a moment, Melody's voice rang through the speaker. "Hi Aunt Megan!"

"Hello, dearie," Megan said, one ear ringing from the outburst. "Hope your cousin's going to be okay."

"He's fine. I told his parents he didn't need to go to a doctor, but nobody ever listens to me."

"That's not true. I'm all ears. Tell me how school was today?"

"Boring. The teacher says I talk too much. She's right, but what else am I supposed to do? I know this stuff already. Mom's going to talk to the principal about me skipping another grade, but I don't know about that. The good news is I blocked two goals after school, but my team lost anyway. We're terrible. Did you find the instructions? I know you turned IGOR on. Did it go okay? Can I see what you found?"

Accustomed to her barrage of words, Megan addressed each point in turn. "I'm sure your teacher means well. She's just not used to such an exceptional student. Congratulations on blocking those shots!

Sounds like you're getting good at being the goalie. I'm sorry about your loss, but that's how it goes sometimes. Regarding IGOR, we have to work out a few bugs, but nothing major. We'll find those instructions, and when we do, you'll be the first person I call. Now, can I ask you a question about a different topic?"

"What is it?"

"Is it possible there are others here, like you and your dad?" she asked, thinking of Joybelle and this prophet. "Aliens, I mean."

"I'm not green and don't have antennas, Aunt Megan. We call ourselves travelers. I told you that."

"Sorry, dearie. You're a beautiful young woman, not a cartoon character." She rephrased the question. "Did other travelers come here with you and your dad?"

Silence followed, and Megan pictured Melody wriggling her nose in contemplation. "Nobody came with us. I'm pretty sure."

"Does that mean it's a possibility?"

"Who are you thinking of, anyway?"

"Probably just posers pretending to be something they're not," Megan said, thinking the timing of the falling drop could have been a coincidence. Then again, how did that lady know it took two to bind worlds? A lucky guess seemed like a stretch. If it looks like a duck and swims like a duck…

"Are these people old, new, or somewhere in between?" Melody asked.

Megan pondered Joybelle's perfect complexion and the few pictures she had seen of the Prophet. "Let's say early thirties."

Another pause, longer than the first. "My dad told me we were the only ones here."

The tightness in her chest loosened. Joybelle's words were nothing more than a coincidence combined with a lucky guess. "All right. Just to be clear, there are no travelers here other than you. Is that right?"

Again, the pause, causing Megan to believe the call had dropped. "Hello?" she said.

"I can ask again."

Megan winced. This wasn't the first time the child had alluded to her father being alive. Megan could understand; it had taken her a long time to accept her own mother's death, despite their difficult relationship. As for her father, Megan had none, though she suspected the cult leader might have been the sperm donor. But Melody still hadn't directly addressed the question. "Is that a yes or a no? In your own judgment."

"Um, I can't be sure," Melody said after another delay. "I have to go now."

"Thank you, dearie," Megan said, the tightness around her chest returning. "I hope your cousin is okay. Say hi to Uncle Eric and Aunt Tara for me and thank your mother for letting me speak with you."

"I will. Talk to you later, Aunt Megan. Have a good night."

Megan hung up. Instead of allaying her suspicions, the child had only raised them. Feeling restless, she abruptly stood and paced before her office window.

Stars filled the cloudless night, their twinkling a secret language only they understood. Much like the invitation lying on her desk. Over the horizon, she sensed the brooding presence of the alien machine—once again the eye of a growing storm. Not content waiting for it to hit landfall, she dialed Obadiah's personal number.

The first attempt went directly to voicemail, as did the second. Megan paused before dialing a third time. Per their agreement, three consecutive calls signaled an emergency, requiring an immediate response.

She made the call.

True to their arrangement, Obadiah answered on the third ring. Before he could speak, Megan jumped in, "What do you know about Joybelle Leroux?"

"I'm in an important meeting, Meg. Any chance this can wait?"

"If it could, I wouldn't have used our secret code. What are you doing at work, anyway? It's ten-thirty in the evening."

"I have a twenty-four-seven job and tonight's one of those nights. What is it?"

"Senator Wigfall paid me a visit."

"I warned you he was coming."

"But you didn't tell me he'd bring along a sorceress from the cult of some prophet."

After an audible sigh, he said, "Hold on, I need to find a private space." Megan heard distant voices and shuffling on the other end. A full minute passed before Obadiah returned, his voice clipped. "That doesn't qualify as an emergency, Meg. Members of that church are major contributors to the Senator's reelection campaign. I expect he brought a guest along in return for that support. Anything else?"

Megan's grip tightened on the phone as she briefed him on what had happened inside the chamber. "I swear, this woman heard the music and saw one of those drops fall from the ceiling. She also insisted another traveler accompanied Stephen Fisher, clearly alluding to his daughter, though she didn't identify the child by name."

"You sure about this?"

"I'm about sixty-forty right now," Megan admitted. "I suppose Joybelle could have been putting on an act, but if so, it was a convincing one." She then read back the invitation. "What do you know about this church?"

Obadiah didn't speak for a time, though Megan could hear him breathing on the other end. "You need to keep this to yourself," he finally said.

"I always do."

Obadiah's tone became somber. "Dozens of children have gone missing. That type of thing rarely comes to my attention, except for the tie that binds these cases together—either one or both parents are members of the Church of the Prophet. The parents tell investigators it's 'The Lord of Light's will' and claim to know nothing more, despite how hard they're pressed. Some parents are clearly distraught, while others seem unnaturally calm. But there's no evidence directly tying the parents or the church to the kids' disappearance. Could be the children ran away or were taken by a relative that didn't approve of how they were being raised. Too early to know. At the moment, the Justice Department is focusing the investigation on a militant sect affiliated with the same church. You've heard of them."

"The Sword of the Lord," Megan said, recalling the group that had tried to assassinate Stephen Fisher.

"That's the one. They've turned themselves into the church's private militia, not only in this country but worldwide. That said, there's no reason to think the Senator's guest knows anything about that group or those kids. What was the name of your sorceress again?"

"Joybelle Leroux," Megan said, though she couldn't imagine that woman hurting a child. On second thought, extremist beliefs often spawned extreme deeds. Her dead mother was proof of that.

"I've not heard the name but can make inquiries."

"Thank you."

"Be careful about going to that temple, Megan. Better yet, don't go at all. I shouldn't have to remind you that being the Director General of ISBLIC makes you a target. Let my people do their job, don't do it for them. Anything else?"

Megan traced her finger over the embossed ankh-like symbol on the invitation's letterhead. "She called me a herald."

"I don't know what that means, but I know you won't take my advice." Obadiah's voice hardened. "If you insist on doing the unadvisable, then I'm assigning you a security detail. Don't argue. It's for your own good. Hold on..." Megan heard muted voices in the background. "I've gotta go, Meg. You're welcome to call anytime, but when you pull me out of a cabinet meeting, it needs to be a life-or-death situation. This could've waited."

"One more thing," Megan said.

Obadiah emitted a long, audible breath. "What now?"

"Senator Wigfall spilled the beans about what you and I perceive inside the chamber. You should see this woman. It's like she stepped out of a fashion magazine. Tall, thin, young, blonde, the whole package. The man is smitten, I tell you. Take my word for it; anything he knows, she knows." A sudden thought struck her. "Any chance the Senator has learned where you sequestered Melody? He's on the intelligence committee, after all."

"I personally made the arrangements to relocate the family. The only other people involved I trust with my life. Since the family has been moved, any inquiries about their location have to go through me. And I've not approved a single one. Rest assured, the Senator knows nothing."

Megan felt a weight lift from her shoulders, not realizing how wound up she'd been. "Good to hear. One last thing, I want Buzz on my security detail, just him. Too many guards will draw unwanted attention."

Obadiah exhaled. "If I agree, can I get off the phone?"

"Yes."

"I'll make the arrangements," he said, ending the call.

Megan leaned back in her chair, glancing once more at the invitation on her desk. Despite Obadiah's warnings and her own misgivings, she knew she had to attend. The answers she sought—about the travelers, Joybelle's cryptic knowledge, and especially this prophet—lay within the walls of that temple.

CHAPTER ELEVEN

Drenched in sweat, I lay curled up in an unfamiliar bed, my knees pressed against my chest. It took a moment for my memory to catch up — collapsing onto the lawn, sensations pouring into me like a flood tide, and the voice of my previous incarnation guiding me back to the present.

As my breathing steadied and my heart slowed, I grappled with the disorientation of awakening to full consciousness. No longer was I the carefree child free from the burden of knowledge, but a vessel containing a multitude. As time stretched endlessly before and behind me, the past settled on my chest like a dead weight. I felt old, of an age not measured by the spin of a planet but by the lifetime of a star.

Hearing voices, I cracked open my eyes, blinking away the daggers of light that pierced my skull. As my pupils adjusted, I beheld three rippling silhouettes beyond the foot of the bed. The music still echoing in my head faded, allowing their features to come into sharper focus. A white-coated doctor tapped away at a keyboard, while my mom and dad hovered over his shoulder, a greenish-yellow current of anxiety flowing through them both.

As I gazed at them, a mixture of familiarity and strangeness washed over me. Bonds forged in the past persisted beyond death, especially the feelings for those I had once cared for. In my past life, my dad had been my brother, my mom a friend, Aunt Franny my wife, and Melody my daughter. Though I knew this to be true, it didn't seem real, nor did it matter much, for I remained my parents' son and loved my family even more because of our shared history.

My father caught my eye, then tapped the doctor's shoulder. Following his gaze, my mom rushed to the bedside, squashing my face between her hands. "How are you feeling, honey?"

In truth, I felt drained from the effort to contain the cacophony of voices that threatened to escape the corridors of my mind. But I had no intention of sharing that with my parents. So, I answered as the child my mother imagined me to be. "Tired. I just want to go home."

Mom planted a kiss on my forehead before reaching into her purse. From it, she retrieved a worn blanket, transporting me to the first day of kindergarten when I handed it over, declaring myself to be "big." I couldn't believe she still carried it around. Sensing my hesitation, concern creased her forehead. More for her sake than mine, I took what felt like a relic from another life. Surprisingly, I still found solace in the musty smell and faded colors.

My dad crowded next to the bed. "You gave us a scare, champ. What do you remember?"

What to tell him? That this happens every time I wake up the past? Hardly the answer he would expect. "Having cake," I said.

Dad softly brushed my hair back, worry clear in his eyes. "And afterward?"

"Nothing, really. Where's Melody?"

"In the waiting room with your aunt," Mom said. "You kept mumbling… things. Did you have a nightmare?"

Fortunately, the doctor intervened before I had to reply. He asked me several questions: where did I live, what was my name, my birthday, and what did I recall eating? I answered promptly, not wanting to give him a reason to keep me here.

Shining a bright light in each of my eyes, he moved it up and down, then from side to side. He poked and prodded various body parts, listened to my heart, then tapped a finger against his lips. "Your son seems perfectly healthy, but I'd like to see the results of the blood test. I recommend keeping him overnight for observation."

"There's nothing wrong with me," I said.

Mom gestured for them to step out of earshot, but I heard the conversation anyway. The doctor asked my parents about previous episodes of fainting. Diabetes came up, along with epilepsy, both of which I had to search through old memories to understand. When the doctor suggested a brain scan, my father winced.

I raised my voice. "I feel fine."

Ushering my parents farther away, the doctor turned his back and lowered his voice. That's when Melody crawled from beneath the curtain.

"Are you back finally?" she asked, keeping her voice low. But not low enough. My mom spared her a glance before rolling her eyes, not at all surprised she had sneaked into the emergency room. But she let us be, returning her attention to the doctor.

I sat up and stretched my arms, my mood lifting. Though Melody might be my cousin, I would always think of her as my child, regardless of age, place, or the forms we inhabited. "It's good to see you."

She leaned in closer. "Do you remember everything now? Like where we came from and stuff?"

I returned a tired smile. "Sorry it took so long."

"Your parents think you're sick or something. I kept telling them you just needed to sleep, but nobody ever listens to me. It didn't help that you kept talking to yourself. I had no idea what you were saying, like you were speaking a different language or something. Freaked everybody out. What the heck happened?"

Melody didn't understand because she had never done terrible things. Hopefully, she never would. "I got confused and had to find my way back home," I said. "How long was I out?"

"An hour maybe. We just got here. Can't believe you passed out. That never happens to me."

I didn't have the energy to explain. "I'll tell you about it later."

"I'm just glad you're okay."

I reached out to caress her cheek. Though Melody could travel anywhere without the aid of a beacon, I always feared she might lose her way. That fate had befallen many other travelers, for without a beacon to anchor their consciousness, it became difficult to maintain a sense of self in the vast anonymity of the conscious plane. That's why I had returned: to guide Melody back home, as any father would.

"This life will be our last on this world," I said. "We'll return together."

She frowned. "Maybe I don't want to go. I like it here. And what about the other travelers? They're stuck with no way to get back."

"We can't interfere, Melody. At least, not any more than we already have. Travelers understand the risks."

"That's not fair—" she started, then cut herself off as her mother, my Aunt Franny, and former wife, entered the room, impatiently gesturing for her daughter to leave. Melody complied, but not before patting my head and announcing at the top of her lungs, "He's feeling much better!"

Aunt Franny offered me a reassuring smile before guiding her daughter back to the waiting room.

My parents and the doctor returned to the bedside. Mom squeezed my hand. "Hey."

I suppressed a yawn, wanting to be back in my own bed, where I could sort through the jumble of memories in peace. "Can we go home now?"

"Soon," Dad said.

The doctor crouched to my level, his expression soft yet firm. "Stevie, we're going to keep you overnight for observation. Just to make sure everything's okay."

"It's only a precaution," Dad added.

I sighed, deciding there was no chance of talking them out of it.

"Your parents can stay with you until you fall asleep," the doctor continued. "We'll make sure you're comfortable for the night. If anything comes up, anything at all, the nurse will call them immediately."

"And we'll come right over," Mom said.

The doctor assured me I would be fine, then excused himself, leaving my parents at the bedside, their concern palpable.

As Mom found some chairs to arrange around the bed, Dad asked, "Stevie, what did you mean about finding your way back home?"

A jolt of surprise shot through me. He had heard that. I scrambled to collect my thoughts, unsure what to tell him. Of all the people in my family, aside from Melody, my father had the most experience dealing with travelers. But now was not the time for that discussion. Not yet. Maybe not ever.

"I just had a bad dream," I said, keeping my voice steady. That was partly true, at least.

"But you told Melody you were confused."

"Leave him alone, Eric," Mom said, sensing my discomfort. Or maybe her own. She handed me a cup of water, offering a welcome distraction. "He's tired and needs some sleep. I'm sure Stevie will feel better in the morning."

My dad nodded slowly, his gaze never wavering from mine.

CHAPTER TWELVE

Megan stood at the edge of the stage, surveying the packed Dolores McCann Auditorium at ISBLIC headquarters. The air buzzed with palpable energy, generated by the diverse crowd drawn from all corners of the globe for the unveiling of the second transmission. Journalists jotted down notes, media personalities gathered in small groups, and even a few prominent politicians had made an appearance. Members of her project team lingered near the back, behind the television cameras broadcasting the event.

The ISBLIC steering committee occupied the first row, including Senator Wigfall, who remained chairperson because the other committee members had refused to seat a priestess from the Church of the Prophet as his replacement. The lady in question, Joybelle Leroux, sat beside him, her gaudy pendant glinting between barely concealed breasts. Catching a whiff of her perfume, Megan wrinkled her nose in annoyance.

At the lectern, Elizabeth, the Public Relations Director, gestured for silence, her crisp voice cutting through the murmur of conversation. "Ladies and gentlemen, if you could please take your seats…"

While people settled into their chairs, Megan flipped through the speech Elizabeth had prepared for her last night. The formal tone and fancified language sounded nothing like Megan, and the speech didn't even mention the tremendous effort her team had expended to detect and decipher the transmission. But she didn't blame Elizabeth, only Wigfall. He was the one who insisted on the live press conference, overruling her judgment that the project team should have time to study the output before releasing the results to the public. But no matter, it was done. Never comfortable speaking to a large crowd, let alone millions of viewers, Megan decided to scrap the script. It would only make her nervous…more nervous.

As Elizabeth introduced her, Megan ascended the stairs, feeling self-conscious amidst the notables in their expensive suits. Reaching the lectern, she noted the step stool discreetly placed behind it— Elizabeth's foresight, no doubt. Grateful, she stepped up, now able to comfortably reach the microphone. Megan turned to face the audience, hoping her words would inspire the public to embrace science rather than the nonsense Joybelle embodied.

"Good morning, everyone," she said, clearing her throat. "Evidenced by your attendance today, you're already aware that the Interstellar Gravitational Observatory Recorder, the IGOR, detected a second transmission. I'm pleased to report that our engineering team has fully decoded the signal, uncovering what we believe to be a raw data stream intended to be fed into the alien program deciphered from the original transmission. This is a tremendous achievement, especially given the compressed timeline the team has been working under. I'd like to extend my personal thanks to the many people involved in planning, designing, building, and launching the observatory, allowing us to reach this historic milestone."

Enthusiastic applause followed, which Megan joined. Once it died down, she continued, "If all goes according to plan, we are about to hear more from our alien friends." She gestured to the timer displayed on the projection screen—a wholly unnecessary dramaturgical device conceived by the public relations director. "When the countdown reaches zero, the operations manager will feed the input into the program. The output will be displayed here in real-time."

She made a show of crossing her fingers. "Please keep in mind that we're operating on a number of unproven assumptions. To be candid, we're uncertain what to expect or if the program will work at all. There will be no refunds." This prompted a few laughs from the audience and a frown from the Senator. "With that, I'll turn the podium over to the chair of the International Space-Based Laser Interferometer Consortium, Senator Wigfall."

As the Senator took over the lectern, Megan noticed the symbol of the Church of the Prophet pinned to his lapel. Her cheeks flushed as she fought the urge to reach over and rip the thing off his jacket. Instead, she forced a brittle smile and stepped aside.

"Thank you, Doctor McCullough," said the Senator, his gaze fixed not on her, but on the camera. "The purpose of this alien machine continues to confound even the brightest minds of our generation. Some call it a Beacon, but I say it's an enigma wrapped in a riddle, shrouded in mystery. Is it a gateway to another dimension? A cosmic telephone to ring up little green men? Or perhaps, as many believe, it's the harbinger of the End Times, the final trumpet blast before the apocalypse." He bowed his head toward Joybelle Leroux, who nodded in fervent agreement.

"Maybe it's all the above, or maybe it's something beyond our wildest imaginings. The truth is, ladies and gentlemen, we don't know. And that, my friends, is precisely why we've constructed the most advanced space observatory in the history of humankind. Not because it was easy, but because it was hard, because that goal served to organize and measure the best of our energies and skills, because that challenge is one we were willing to accept, one we were unwilling to postpone, and one we intended to win…"

Megan edged off the stage, shaking her head at the Senator's blatant plagiarism of Kennedy's "Choose the Moon" speech. The moment she was off camera, she headed straight for the exit, politely acknowledging the whispered congratulations from various council members but ignoring the shouted questions from the press. On the way out, Elizabeth wagged an exasperated finger at her for not following the script.

After making her way down the hall and into the control room, Megan let out a sigh of relief. The space was free of press and cameras, occupied only by a core team of physicists, engineers, and technicians—the people she had worked alongside since the founding of ISBLIC. Her eyes found Michael, hunched over a laptop at the systems engineering station, probably obsessing over every detail before running the program.

Obadiah stood over Michael's shoulder, his typically placid demeanor revealing nothing of his inner emotions—whether it be anxiety, excitement, or something else entirely. Megan had invited him as a special guest, recognizing that his support had made this achievement possible. The rest of the team was at their stations, though there wasn't much required of them at the moment. The hard work had been done, all to prepare for this pivotal moment.

Megan looked around at her colleagues, noting their wide grins and the eager gleam in their eyes. Perhaps making this a public unveiling hadn't been such a bad idea after all. They deserved the recognition.

"Alright, folks, it's showtime," Megan said. "Don't worry about what's happening in the auditorium, that's just a sideshow. If the program works—and I have every confidence it will—I want you to pause, take it in, consult with each other, and prepare your notes for further analysis. Despite the press attention, this isn't a race; it's a marathon. Whatever we choose to communicate to the public needs to be well-considered. There will be plenty of armchair astrophysicists out there second-guessing our work. That's okay. It's expected. Maybe it'll even help." She broke into a crooked smile. "Probably not. Regardless, you should all be proud of getting us to this point. Because of your hard work, we're about to see what this second transmission is about. Great job!"

The team exchanged meaningful glances and subtle smiles, their expressions a mix of pride and nervous anticipation. Years of dedication had led to this moment, and while they refrained from overt celebration, the atmosphere was charged with a sense of shared accomplishment.

Megan approached the engineering station, where Michael's fingers flew across a computer keyboard. Despite the powerful array of equipment surrounding him, the alien program required no more processing power than what was available on a standard cell phone— a testament to the elegance of the technology. Clearly, whoever had sent this transmission valued simplicity above all else.

"Feels like only yesterday we deciphered that first message," Megan said.

Michael looked up, his bloodshot eyes revealing his lack of sleep. "A shame Dolores isn't here to enjoy the moment."

"I heartily agree. Is everything ready on your end?"

Michael tapped the screen, drawing Megan's attention to various charts and metrics. "These monitor system performance—processing power, memory, input/output, that sort of thing. To avoid any interference, I've pulled the wireless card and disconnected the computer from the network. There's no external connectivity, with two exceptions: output from the program will feed directly to the display in the control room, as well as the projection screen in the auditorium." He scratched at the stubble of his beard, seeming to reconsider his next words.

"Spit it out," Megan said.

"Well, given we don't have an opportunity to interpret the output, there's a risk the public will misunderstand what's being communicated. Are you sure you don't want us to review the results before we share them publicly?"

"I had no choice in the matter, unfortunately. The best we can do is mitigate any confusion with cold, hard facts."

"Got it."

Obadiah handed her a headset. "Good job at the podium—short and to the point."

Megan arched an eyebrow. "Did you just call me short?"

The faintest hint of a smile played at the corners of Obadiah's lips. "Your PR director is on the line. She insists on speaking with you."

Megan donned the headset. "Hi Elizabeth. I know you're upset."

"I wrote that speech for a reason," Elizabeth said, her voice brittle. "You didn't bother to acknowledge the Council or the countries that pay the bills. I'm the one who's going to hear about it, not you. Please stick to the script next time, Megan."

"You know I'm no good at speeches. Our chairperson, on the other hand, is quite verbose."

"The Senator is an excellent public speaker. You could learn a thing or two from him."

"He steals from the best."

"Forget about that and forget about the Senator," Elizabeth said. "What I need from you is to keep me updated on what's happening, especially when I'm on camera taking questions. I'll be wearing an earpiece. Can you promise me that?"

"Sure," Megan said, her eyes darting to the display. The timer caught her attention, its digits rapidly ticking away. "I'll keep you informed of any developments."

As the countdown neared its conclusion, the team's unified voice rose: "Five, four, three, two, one!"

Michael looked up at her, awaiting her signal.

"Let's make history," Megan said.

"Feeding the data stream into the program now," Michael said.

Intermittent cheers rang out, dying down as seconds turned into minutes. Team members abandoned their stations to gather around Michael's computer, the only sign of activity being the figures bouncing around the charts and graphs.

"Two percent of the data stream has been processed," Michael reported. "The program hasn't crashed yet, so that's a good sign." He looked up from the screen. "It just accessed the blueprint, just as you predicted, Doctor McCullough."

"Seemed logical," Megan said, unsurprised. Melody had told her the program would require the "pictures," which Megan interpreted as meaning the Beacon's schematic. So, she ensured Michael loaded the full blueprint onto the computer's default drive.

With the program running, Megan turned her attention to the screen on the front wall, which displayed a live feed from the auditorium. Elizabeth walked onto the stage, accompanied by Patricia, an engineer who was also a skilled communicator. When they reached the podium, Elizabeth introduced Patricia, who then stepped up to the microphone.

"Hello there," she began, flashing a warm smile. "I'm here to distract you while my hard-working colleagues are doing the real work down in the control room." That elicited a few chuckles from the audience. Megan smiled along with them. "You're probably wondering—where exactly is this IGOR observatory we keep hearing about? I'm glad you asked. It's at what we call a Lagrange point. Think of it as a cosmic parking lot, just a short hop from Earth, about a million and a half kilometers away. A nice, safe place to detect gravitational waves, which are ripples in the fabric of space-time, produced by massive cosmic events like black hole collisions."

She gestured to the sky, her enthusiasm infectious. "Somehow, our extraterrestrial friends have figured out how to generate these waves artificially. We're not sure how they do it, but we know why it works so well–gravitational waves can pass through obstacles that would disrupt normal electromagnetic signals. Of course, detecting these waves requires an absurd level of precision. The first space-based interferometer, AMIGO, could measure displacements in spacetime down to 20 picometers—that's less than the width of a single helium atom. But the IGOR is far more sensitive. It can pick up movements of just one picometer..."

A chirp from the headset interrupted Megan's thoughts. She pressed the speaker to her ear as Elizabeth's voice came through. "Can you hear me, Megan? Come on, you promised. If you don't answer, I'm coming down there. What's happening?"

"I'm here, I'm here," Megan said, shifting her focus from the presentation to the computer screen. "The program's working, which validates our assumption the transmission is a data stream. Feel free to share that news. But you need to be patient. This may take some time. I'll let you know when there's more to report." Before Elizabeth could object, Megan tossed the headset onto the table.

Turning back to the task at hand, she asked, "How are we doing, Michael?"

"The program's already processed forty percent of the input," Michael said, his eyes fixed on the monitor. "It's speeding up now— just hit fifty percent, now seventy-five. Uh oh, the I/O fell off a cliff. The program probably crashed." He squinted at the screen. "Hold on, the GPU just spiked."

Images spilled across the display, a mesmerizing series of beautiful, almost artistic forms. Megan leaned in, her breath catching in her throat. The sheer beauty of the patterns unfolding before her was unlike anything she'd ever seen—intricate, flowing designs that seemed to pulse with energy.

Cheers erupted throughout the control room, punctuated by high-fives and fist bumps. Michael thrust his arms skyward. A profound sense of relief washed over Megan—it had worked, all the years of effort finally paying off. Up on the livestream, she could see the audience leaping to their feet, pointing excitedly at the projection screen.

Then the display went dark.

"What just happened?" Megan asked.

"The program's done," Michael said. "The output was redirected to a file. I'll bring up the video and slow it down." He tapped some keys. "All right, here we go."

Spherical forms appeared on the computer monitor, simultaneously displayed on the screens in the auditorium and control room. Megan watched intently as some orbs expanded while others shrank. One burst, its remnants growing into smaller spheres of their own. Her gaze was drawn to one particular bubble, which magnified until it dominated the display. Delicate, shimmering walls seemed to beckon her forward, creating an illusion of depth on the flat screen.

Suddenly, the view shifted, as if the camera had pierced the bubble's surface. The display now showed a myriad of pinpricks and smudges of luminescence against a black background, as if they were viewing the interior of the sphere. Megan leaned closer to the screen as these lights began to rotate and coalesce until....

"Galaxies," Michael breathed.

She squeezed his shoulder. Even to the untrained eye, the resemblance was unmistakable—clusters of stars and swirling clouds of gas with distinct central bulges and spiral structures with long curving arms. Other formations were smooth and elliptical, while some were irregular blobs. The magnification increased, focusing on a single galaxy, and continued until one star dominated the screen. Tornados of fire danced along the surface while fiery loops of plasma burst from the edges, shining so brightly it made Megan blink.

"A sun," said a hushed voice.

"And those bubbles," someone else said. "Those could be other universes."

Megan had repeatedly asked Melody what to expect from the transmission, and her answer of "galaxies and stuff" didn't nearly do this justice. Seeing the images unfold before her eyes was breathtaking, making her feel as if she were an infinitesimal speck within a vast multiverse, which apparently was a real thing. Perhaps that was the intent of the message—to convey a sense of perspective.

She mused about how many other specks existed in their cosmic bubble, a question she had never thought to ask Melody. This prompted another thought: If the Beacon allowed one to be reborn on another world, what was its range? Between stars seemed obvious, but what about between galaxies? Or even universes?

As these questions swirled in her mind, the display shifted once more. The star on the screen shrank to the size of a dime, and another spherical object rose from the bottom. Based on its shape, the crescent of illumination, and the wisps of vapor moving over blue water and landmasses, Megan presumed this to be a planet.

Obadiah peeled away from the crowd around Michael, coming to stand beside her. "What do you think this means?"

Megan backed away from the screen and lowered her voice. "Melody told us the output shows how the Beacon works. Maybe this is like a travelogue. 'Oh, the places you'll go' type of thing."

"What?"

"Doctor Seuss. Didn't your parents ever read to you?" Before she could elaborate, movement on the screen drew their attention.

A three-dimensional schematic of two beacons appeared on each side of the display, drawing gasps from members of the team. The devices resembled giant lollipops, with the gravitational wave collector serving as the candy and the amplification tower as the stick. At the tail end was the bulbous injection chamber—the place where teardrops fell.

Inside the chamber of the leftmost beacon, an anthropomorphic form materialized. It had an oblong-shaped "head" trailing three lines—two of equal length flanking a central stem that oscillated from side to side. A swirling vortex of color filled the oblong. Suddenly, the vortex shattered into fragments and all movement ceased.

On the right side of the display, the head of the second figure filled with an identical vortex, and its appendages began to move. The scene now showed two beacons and two figures separated by the planet. One figure was full of color and moving, the other still and dark.

Voices rang out, speculating on the nature of the images.

"Those are microorganisms," someone said. "See, the line on that figure moves like a flagellum."

"Could be a spaceship."

"Or the Beacon is a homing signal, pointing the way to a habitable planet."

"Maybe they're already on the way."

"No. It's a message, and those patterns represent information. Did you see how it moved from one place to the other?"

"I think it's an Ansible."

Megan only listened, understanding the meaning and wondering how they didn't see it. Those figures were lifeforms. One had died only to be reborn at the location of the second beacon, the consciousness having transferred from one place to another. Melody had told her as much, though she still found it hard to believe.

"How could they not understand?" she said, voice low.

"You have an inside source," Obadiah said. "Besides, some have guessed transmigration is at the heart of the matter, including those from that church you're so determined to visit."

Megan scowled at the reminder. The leader of that cult claimed that demons and angels came through the Beacon to walk among us. Not exactly the same as transmigration. But before she could object, movement on the screen silenced their conversation.

The celestial elements faded along with the beacons, leaving only the anthropomorphic figures behind. The two figures then moved to the center of the screen and merged into one. The body elongated into a central stem, adorned with intricate patterning. Multiple curving appendages sprouted symmetrically from this stem, resembling tentacles or flowing ribbons. The upper limbs curved gracefully upward, while the lower pair swooped down and inward. Atop the figure, a circular emblem containing a star-like symbol crowned the design.

A murmur of unease rippled through the room. Obadiah clenched his jaw while Michael chewed on a cuticle. Megan felt as if someone had punched her in the gut. Remembering the livestream audience, she looked up at the display.

The camera inside the auditorium panned from the lectern. It focused on Joybelle Leroux. The woman rose from her seat, using one hand to smooth the white robe that draped her frame. With the other hand, she reached up and unclasped the necklace around her neck, dangling the pendant before her piercing blue eyes.

Megan's blood ran cold—the pendant was in the exact same shape as the merged figure on the screen.

Joybelle's lips stretched into a beatific smile as she addressed the millions of people watching the livestream. "May the blessings of the Prophet grant you everlasting life."

CHAPTER THIRTEEN

The lilting drawl of my teacher commanded the classroom as she aimed her laser pointer at the world map hanging on the wall. Mrs. Craven, her silver hair pinned in a bun, called on students one by one to identify the country where the red dot landed. I sat at my desk, following along closely, my eyes tracking the darting red light across continents and oceans.

"Stevie," Mrs. Craven prompted, the dot settling on a landmass.

I straightened in my seat, having no idea where she pointed. But I knew who would. Brushing aside the shimmering curtain where the ghosts lingered, I searched through the memories of my last incarnation.

Knowledge of the *before-time* carried forward as general concepts and feelings based on bonds forged in the past. Details were lost but could be recovered by reliving those experiences, transferring information from the conscious plane into my head, much like a computer moves data from long to short-term storage.

A vivid recollection surfaced: walking in the rain with my wife toward a needle-like tower piercing the clouds. In that life, she had long hair and no tattoos.

"The country is Canada, in the Ontario province," I said. "That's Toronto."

Mrs. Craven's eyebrows shot up. "That's right," she said, sliding the red dot to another location. "How about here?"

Sensory impressions flooded my mind—streets of water, the distinctive scent at low tide, and the murmur of idling crowds. Venice, Italy, where I'd spent my honeymoon in my last life. But Since I hadn't been the most attentive student, I hesitated to identify the location. A sudden display of geographic knowledge might draw unwanted attention. So, I purposefully fumbled the answer, causing the teacher to move to the next student in line.

The lunch bell rang, and I drifted toward the playground, my eyes scanning the faces of friends with a sense of detachment. Despite their cheerful invitations to play, I couldn't bring myself to join them. Ever since I'd unearthed memories of the past, an invisible barrier had risen, separating me from those who had once been my peers. Their laughter and joyful banter now felt distant, almost foreign. As I watched them play their games, a bittersweet ache gripped my heart—another reminder that I had left childhood far behind.

I settled into a swing to wait for Melody. We always had lunch together, a routine that would help anchor me in this new life. Soon, I caught sight of her striding across the field, exchanging waves with other kids. Any trace of loneliness melted away. Melody was my faithful companion, bridging the gap between past and present.

She took the swing next to mine and offered me half of her peanut butter and banana sandwich. I declined, as I always did and would continue to do so throughout this life and into the next. After taking a large bite, Melody picked up the thread of the conversation she had started back at the doctor's office. "What are we going to do about the travelers?"

That very subject had been weighing on my mind. Specialists in first contact, this cohort of travelers was tasked with forging connections between civilizations. If the world proved ready, additional beacons would be built. But that assumed people saw visitors as opportunities for growth and wisdom, rather than as a source of fear and conflict. Considering the fate of my previous incarnation, I knew the answer to that question. But that wasn't my primary concern. What troubled me more was that the *First Cohort* had arrived with no way to get back home.

"Have you told anybody about them?" I asked.

"Only my mom, and she won't tell. She knows what would happen."

"Do you think Aunt Megan figured out they're here?"

Melody chewed thoughtfully on her sandwich before answering. "She's pretty smart and has already asked if other travelers came with us. I told her no, but I'm not sure she believed me. May not matter anyway. Lots of people have guessed what's happening since Megan showed the second transmission."

"I agree," I said, rummaging through my lunch bag for a pack of crackers.

"I met a traveler once, here in the playground. Her name's Tina."

"What? You never told me that."

"Because you weren't you yet and wouldn't have known what I was talking about." Melody tossed the remains of her sandwich to a waiting squirrel. "She asked about you. I told her you weren't here yet but would be soon. She gave me her phone number."

"That's dangerous, Melody. You're leaving a trail that others could follow."

"But she really wanted to talk. I couldn't say no. She's stuck here, Stevie."

"Nothing is certain," I said, trying to sound optimistic.

Melody pulled a chocolate bar from her bag and offered me a square. I declined, holding up my last cracker. "Maybe Aunt Megan can help," she said, chocolate smudging the corner of her mouth. "She could sneak Tina and the other travelers into the Beacon. Then they can go home."

I shook my head. "Sending kids into the chamber can't stay a secret, especially when they leave their bodies behind. Megan would get in big trouble, assuming she'd even try it. And imagine how their parents would feel. The travelers need to stay hidden, like us."

Melody sniffed her disapproval. "But we can get home without a beacon. Other travelers can't. We need to help them."

"They need to—" I began, but the voice intruded.

Pay attention, Stevie. Another approaches.

Closing my eyes, I tuned out the sights and sounds around me to focus on the music within. As it grew in volume, the shackles of the physical dimension loosened, allowing the conscious plane to bleed through. A hidden world unfolded before me.

Spindly trunks of pine and oak glowed a warm ochre, their branches vainly reaching for the sky. Tiny streaks of luminescence flitted within the canopy; birds chirping praise for the afternoon sun. Dappled sunlight flickered through pine needles that shone neon green, creating ever-changing patterns on the living soil. On the playground, multi-hued whorls spun within the minds of my classmates, for it wasn't just people I perceived differently, but the entirety of the living world.

Then I sensed the presence of another, moving a couple of blocks away. And that mind was not like the others.

I turned to Melody. "You called Tina, didn't you?"

"Maybe," she said, fidgeting with the hem of her shirt.

"That puts us all in danger, her most of all."

"She won't tell."

"But Tina has parents, and those parents have friends, and those friends have families."

Melody whipped her head around. "Is she already here?"

"On the way. You know there's nothing I can say or do that will change things."

"She just wants to talk. That's all. Will you? Please. For me?"

I rolled a pebble under my foot, then kicked it aside. "Looks like I have no choice."

Melody hopped off the swing and kissed me on the head. "Thank you. I have a feeling she'll want to talk to you alone, so I better go. You're the best!"

"Pretty sure your friend won't agree. I'll see you after school."

"Love you!"

As Melody skipped across the grass, a car pulled into the parking lot. Sensing trouble, like a dark cloud on the horizon, I shielded my mind, a trick I had learned long ago.

A girl, not much older than me, stepped out of the vehicle and walked onto the playground, her eyes darting from side to side like a hunted animal. The two adults remained in the car, their gaze fixed on me. She took the swing beside me and lazily kicked her feet. We didn't speak for a while, which I ascribed to the uncertainty swirling through her mind. Given that I'd shielded my thoughts, I assumed she remained unsure of my identity. To remove any doubt, I greeted her: "May you live an undying life."

"Are you the Undying One? It's hard for me to tell."

"People here call me Stevie. Are you Tina?"

The girl dipped her head. "The envoy from Lumina Minor. Some travelers believed you to be another. I'm glad to find they were wrong."

"How did you find Melody?"

"I stumbled upon her by chance, though I've kept my distance since. Safer not to advertise our presence."

"Then why come back now?"

Tina brought the swing to a halt. "I have questions that need answering. Such as, why did you give them the key to unlock the blueprint for a beacon? And why activate it? You know this place isn't ready."

"I would have known had I been myself," I said, dragging my feet in the sand. "But I wasn't. It's a long story and telling it won't change the ending. I'm sorry for bringing you here, truly."

"Is it true you were murdered?"

"Not all of them are like that."

Tina wrinkled her nose. "But enough are. When I tried explaining to my parents why I was here, they wanted to take me to a head doctor. But after some talk and tears, they grew to accept I wasn't making it all up."

"Mine didn't believe me either," I said. "Not the parents I have now, but the father I had before. I'm glad yours came to accept who you are." I tilted my head toward the car idling in the parking lot. "Is that them?"

Tina didn't look, but her shoulders tensed. "They're still unsure what to believe. Had I known what was going on, I wouldn't have told them anything."

"That might have been wise," I said, waiting for the real question she had come to ask.

Tina looked up at the clouds, their billowing forms wandering in the breeze. "How do we get back?"

There it was, and though I knew it was coming, I had no good answer. "For now, all we can do is hope people grow to understand and accept us."

Crystalline shards formed within the currents of her mind. "Easy for you to say. But unlike you, I can't get home without a beacon. From what I've seen, the people here would rather imprison us than help us."

I averted my eyes and gazed at the trees. Such a beautiful world, lush and blue, but for Tina and every other traveler, it had become a prison. Without access to the Beacon, the girl was destined to lose all memory of who she was and where she had come from. Worse, she was stranded, with no means to get back home. "I'm sorry."

"You already said that."

"There's one who might help," I said, thinking of Megan.

"The Prophet?"

"Who's that?"

"A man preaching about everlasting life and angels coming through the Beacon. Some in the First Cohort thought he might be you."

"I would never expose a traveler, especially here."

"Non-interference, I know. Your gospel. But good intentions fade when your very existence is threatened. Some travelers sought out this Prophet."

"You should have warned them."

"How? They're scattered all over the planet. I know, like, maybe a dozen. And even if I talked to them, what could I say?"

"To live life to the fullest. That's all we can do right now."

Her mind flared scarlet. "Live life? And after that, what? Be forever unable to recall family, friends, and generations of existence? Other travelers warned me you could be cruel. It seems they weren't exaggerating."

"That's not how I meant it."

She lifted herself from the swing and looked down at me. "The same forces that once murdered you have grown stronger. We're being hunted, each and every one of us. Though the public doesn't know for sure that we're here, others have guessed. Nations are trying to find us, hoping to extract what we know. Some would kill us just for not being part of their tribe. People make a habit of that, which is the reason a beacon never should have been built. Not all travelers will sacrifice themselves on the altar of non-interference. Some will do anything to get back home."

"Every member of the cohort knows the dangers of first contact," I said, immediately regretting it.

Tina only stared at me, a swirling finger of crimson sprouting from the dark heart of the storm raging inside her mind. "When you get back, tell those I left behind that I love them and kept them in my thoughts before I passed into oblivion. Will you do that?"

With nothing left to say, I could only nod.

Tina departed the school grounds without a backward glance. I understood her anger. Ignorance awaited her in the next cycle, stripped of all memories of those she once knew and loved. Unless she could find her way to a beacon, she was doomed to live out this life as if it were her last.

That troubled me, but not as much as the possibilities that desperation breeds.

CHAPTER FOURTEEN

Megan marveled at the massive, white-domed temple that radiated like a second sun under a crisp, sapphire morning sky. Streams of people crossed the courtyard and climbed the grand stairway leading to the arched entrance of the sanctuary within. Well-dressed parents clutched their children's hands as they hurried up the steps to find their seats before the service began. Elderly couples leaned on handrails, helped along by the young, all to the rhythm-driven beat emanating from hidden speakers. Many congregants slowed their ascent to admire the sculptures set under an open-air rotunda halfway up the stairs. For Megan, the temple complex seemed a mishmash of Saint Peter's square, an Aztec Temple, and Greek orthodox dome topped with spires ripped off from the blue mosque in Istanbul.

Escorted by Buzz, Megan stopped at a four-sided wooden kiosk positioned at the heart of the courtyard. She eyed the posting on the signboard:

A Prayer Dedication

The Church of the Prophet has at its heart the great commission to redeem souls and make disciples of the worthy.

As a patriot of faith, I attest allegiance to the teachings of the Divine Prophet. I am a shepherd, ambassador, and sword given sacred power to be a watchman over this world and a steward to its children.

Because of this covenant, I am anointed by the Prophet to identify heretics and stop the advance of the Beast. In recompense for my sacrifice, I will be granted everlasting life.

Megan snorted. "Who do you think this Beast is, Buzz?"

"Anybody who doesn't agree with them, Ma'am," he replied distractedly, eyeing people who came too close.

"That sounds about right."

Placing her hands on her hips, Megan contemplated the mountain of stairs rising before her. The base of the stairwell stretched fifty yards, tapering as it ascended to an open area before the gated entrance, like an over-sized narthex. Just contemplating the climb made her knees ache.

Engraved on the vertical face of each step were verses, the first of which proclaimed: "And he dreamed, and beheld a ladder set up on the earth, and the top of it reached to heaven." Jacob's Ladder, she knew, the allusion casting congregants as angels ascending to the temple, their earthly heaven. Not very subtle, but then again, this place seemed designed to overwhelm.

Buzz touched her forearm, eyeing the passing crowd, many of whom stared boldly at her, some in an unfriendly fashion. "We should get inside, Ma'am."

Megan's lips tightened as she surveyed the scene. "Agreed," she said.

Since the second transmission became public, Joybelle had proclaimed that the merged anthropomorphic figure represented the leader of her church, a self-declared prophet. She asserted the message was a sign of the coming Armageddon. Due to the figure's resemblance to Joybelle's pendant, the church had experienced a huge increase in followers, so many that tickets were needed to attend today's service. Reactions from other faiths ranged from indifference to claims of divine intervention.

The impact of the second transmission extended far beyond religious circles. Conspiracy theories ran rampant. Some fringe groups dismissed the transmission as a hoax, while others claimed the figure represented a secret society governing the world from the shadows. One theory even connected the Beacon to the building of the pyramids. Ridiculous, but the more outrageous the idea, the more attention it garnered. Politicians followed the herd, amplifying whatever their base wanted to hear, with Senator Wigfall being the prime example.

To Megan's disappointment, the scientific community dismissed claims of the Beacon being a means to transfer consciousness and instead landed on the idea that it was some sort of communication device. Not new, and not a bad theory, but completely wrong.

Regardless of the source, one thing all these groups had in common was that Megan was at the center, lauded or despised, depending on one's perspective. The increase in attention and growing threats had forced her to change her phone number.

Megan pulled down the brim of her floppy hat, shielding her face from onlookers. "Lead on."

With her protector at her side, Megan ascended the stairs, stopping at the rotunda to study sculptures set between Greek-style concrete colonnades. Buzz kept his bulky body between her and the highway of people making their way up to the temple. Anybody who wandered too close, he dissuaded with a grim stare.

The first statue was a carved figure of Jesus with arms outstretched. A golden, cross-legged Buddha sat between the next two columns, followed by a dancing Krishna playing a flute, the four-armed and elephant-headed Lord Ganesha, the six-pointed star of David, the Islamic star and crescent, and other symbols and figures from the world's major faiths. An equal opportunity cult, she mused. Some figures she didn't recognize, including a lion with eyes on the front and back of its wings. Surreptitiously, she snapped a picture of the thing, intending to identify it later.

"Heads up," Buzz said, bending his head toward a knot of people winding their way through the courtyard below.

Megan followed his gaze and swore. In the middle of the group, a rotund man greeted admirers and signed autographs, obviously enjoying every moment. With the jet-black goatee and handlebar mustache, his profile was unmistakable. Max Mystery, the addled host of a nonsensical show, and the biggest conspiracist of all. Inexplicably, his show attracted millions of credulous fans. More inexplicably, Max's rantings about the Beacon occasionally rang true, which why Megan listened to his broadcast every week.

"Let's get out of here," she said.

Buzz gave her a sideways glance. "He's already on the way up. Just keep your head down."

Blood rushed to Megan's cheeks, wishing she could disappear. The thought of encountering Max brought back a flood of uncomfortable memories.

Megan had met him at an astrophysics conference in Amsterdam late last year. She had given the keynote, presenting a paper exploring how gravitational waves could be artificially produced. What Max was doing there, she had no idea, but that hadn't stopped him from pestering her for an interview. She had refused, as any respectable person would, until Max invited her to dinner. Strictly out of a misdirected desire to talk sense into the man (a fruitless effort, it turned out), she had agreed. And regretted it. The following week, Max had crowed about their dinner date on his stupid show. Only in retrospect did she realize that dinner was a stunt to garner him much-needed credibility. She felt as much a fool now as she did then.

From the periphery of her vision, Megan watched as Max's pylon-shaped legs laboriously pushed his enormous bulk up the stairs. A group of people followed close behind. To her dismay, Max stopped at the rotunda to catch his breath and squinted in her direction. Megan hurriedly turned toward the winged lion, her heart beating in her throat.

"Carved into stone is the wisdom of your faith," she heard Max bellow to his fans. "I hear all are welcome in your church, though few are selected to become members. I pray your glorious prophet deigns to take in another humble follower." He paused and into that space came scattered applause. "If you would allow me a moment of peace, I will ponder my many faults and even greater sins. Though I will try my utmost, I can't promise success at remedying any of them."

Megan peeked over her shoulder. Rather than scoff, as any right-minded person should have, heads solemnly nodded all around. Some even made that weird sign of the cross. After Max mugged for a few selfies, the crowd began to disperse.

Buzz gripped Megan's elbow in a move to escape, but they weren't quick enough.

"Doctor Megan McCullough," Max said, tipping his fedora. "I was hoping to find you here. How are you, my darling?"

Torn between ignoring the man or confronting the scoundrel, Megan chose the latter. Stepping from behind Buzz, she stabbed an index finger into Max's generous gut. "You're a two-faced jerk."

Before she knew what was happening, he grabbed her hand and gave it a sloppy kiss.

Buzz lunged forward, but Megan quickly placed a restraining palm on his chest. "It's okay," she said. "Max is harmless, at least for those who know better."

With a distrustful glare, Buzz turned his back and shooed away a curious fan.

"I probably should be offended," Max said, pulling a red rose from his suit pocket. "In honor of our first date."

Megan gave the flower an investigatory sniff. "It's fake."

"It's silk, and you are a vision of beauty. Why haven't you returned my calls?"

"Maxwell Bartholomew Cooper, I'm not foolish enough to fall for another of your publicity stunts."

Max slapped a hand over his heart. "Our dinner was no stunt. Come now, I crossed an ocean to see you. In my excitement, I shared our little tête-à-tête with my audience. A mistake for which only passion is to blame. From the bottom of my black heart, I apologize and beg forgiveness. And what happened to Maxy? I adore that nickname."

Megan glanced at Buzz, hoping he wasn't listening. Fortunately, he was busy shooing another fan away. "What *are* you doing here?"

Max puffed out his chest. "The mistress of this fine establishment extended me a personal invitation. I'm the first journalist allowed to visit the Temple of the Prophet. An exclusive! Judging by the exquisite craftsmanship on the outside,"—he patted the winged lion—"it's bound to be beautiful on the inside. Are you available for dinner tonight? We can compare notes."

"Calling yourself a journalist is quite the stretch. Did Joybelle tell you I'd be here? And no, I'm not going to dinner with you."

"You unfairly disparage my credentials, Madam," Max said, pretending to be hurt. "But it's true insofar as I'm not just a correspondent. I make the news, not just report it. Sue me for giving my audience what they demand. Call me journalist or fabulist, you can't deny my sources are the best. I am the envy of the media world." To prove his point, Max gestured at the white dome. "To answer your question, I heard through my own sources that you'd be coming to—what did you call this place? Oh yes, an asylum for gullible halfwits. I like that. Anyway, that's the reason I didn't assign one of my lackeys to cover the story. Though I admit to being curious about what brings you here. And why not have dinner with me?"

Megan smoothed her frock with a hand. "Maybe I don't like you. Just to be clear, I'm here strictly as a favor to our chairperson, Senator Wigfall. He urged me to accept the invitation. Nothing more and nothing less. An obligation."

"You sure it isn't related to that little trinket Miss Leroux wears around her neck? Funny, but it bears a striking resemblance to the image produced by your transmission. I noted that pendant when I first met Joybelle. Thought it was odd. A journalist instinct, you could say."

"When did you meet her?" Megan asked too quickly.

Max smiled in that smarmy way of his. "Not to worry, my dear. I met the good lady when she sanctified the new temple being built in Melbourne. They call it the Trans-Pacific hub of faith, the only one in Oceania. I crashed the ceremony."

"Typical."

"A fortuitous event that led me to you. Strangely enough, Joybelle seemed to be expecting me. Handed me an envelope with the invitation. I accepted on the spot."

"So, your being here has nothing to do with me. You smelled ratings…which is fine. As it should be."

Max's smile broadened. "Love and ratings make the best companions, my dear."

Off balance and more than a little embarrassed, Megan turned on her heel and ascended the stairs. Buzz caught up with her, remaining mercifully silent as he kept pace by her side. Huffing behind them came Max, making so much noise she half-expected him to keel over with a stroke.

Three quarters of the way to the top, Megan stopped at a free-standing wooden rack stuffed with envelopes and pamphlets. Curious, she perused one handout.

Signs of the Beast

Symptoms—Does your child, or a child you know, talk to themselves, or speak in tongues? Do they have seizures and describe dreams of living on another world? Is your son or daughter an outcast at school? Are animals unusually attracted to him or her? If your child is under six years old and shows one or more of these symptoms, contact the church for an immediate consultation.

Raising Awareness—Be alert for signs of danger. A demon that slinks through the gates of heaven to possess a child will look and act human. They will claim to be no different from you. But their very existence is the embodiment of a lie. Be sober-minded; be the watchmen; be the Sword.

Megan's mood darkened. Yet another crackpot conspiracy, this one particularly ominous because it came wrapped in the teachings of a church. It didn't help that the warning contained a kernel of truth. Yes, people are reborn, but not as mythical beings, demons or otherwise. More disturbing was the sheer number of followers this church attracted. Megan would never understand why anybody believed this stuff. She threw the handout onto the steps, earning an offended mutter from an elderly congregant, who picked it up and carefully tucked it back into the holder. Megan kept climbing.

At the top of the stairs, she and Buzz passed under a free-standing jewel-encrusted arch, entering the spacious narthex that fronted the temple. An ornately carved red marble tub rested atop six golden legs in the center of the space. Heavy iron gates stood open at the far end, a heavy thrum of music booming from within the temple.

A bell sounded, and two blue-robed, barefoot men clanged shut the gates, leaving at least a couple hundred people stuck outside, including them. The crowd erupted in shouts and banged on the gate, waving what looked like tickets. Grim-faced guards streamed from doors on either side of the narthex, forming a line in front of the temple entrance. They shoved back the unruly crowd with things that looked like cattle prods, causing one person to fall and be trampled by another. An old woman held out a wad of cash, only to have a guard throw it to the ground.

Megan sidled closer to Buzz, grateful that Obadiah had insisted she have a protector. "What now?"

"We leave," Buzz said, sounding relieved.

But curiosity got the better of her. "Not before I see what's inside that tub."

"Unadvisable."

"I'll only be a minute."

Megan threaded her way through the agitated throng and stood on her toes to peer into the tub. Inside lay darkness. Not exactly black, more like a hole in space. She reached out, encountering a solid surface that seemed to suck the heat from her body. Where had they gotten this?

Max sidled up to her, wiping brownish beads of self-tanner sweat from his brow with an embroidered silk handkerchief. "Draconium," he observed, gesturing toward the object.

Megan's eyes narrowed as she considered the implications. Four different agencies regulated the material, including the Nuclear Regulatory Commission. Turn off the power, and the tub would become a pool of radioactive goo. She rapped her knuckles against the composite, producing a muffled clang. "How'd they get it?"

"Courtesy of the man you claim to be doing a favor."

"Who?"

"Senator Wigfall. He's a deacon of the church and managed to get an exception from the NRC."

Of course, Megan thought, unsurprised. It explained his subservience to Joybelle. "You sure about that?"

"My sources are the best, my dear. But the better question is why they want it in the first place. Draconium is considered holy to members of this church, not to mention a symbol of wealth. On the black market, the going price of *draco*—that's what they call it—is ten thousand American dollars an ounce. That tub represents ten million dollars of big magic."

Megan looked at Max anew, forced to acknowledge he had a brain. "A demonstration of the church's power," she said. "Both political and monetary."

"Exactly," he agreed.

A blue-robed man peeled himself from the temple doors and approached. He had a wide forehead, an untrimmed beard, and a mouth puckered with distaste. Sewn onto his robe was a cross with two daggers turned at right angles to a long blade. Megan's blood ran cold. This was the symbol of the Sword of the Lord, a group of fanatics the Church of the Prophet had adopted as their private militia. Suspicious eyes glittered from beneath the man's hood.

"You have a ticket?" he demanded.

Megan pulled an envelope from her purse and waved it under his nose. "Personal invitation," she said.

The man barely glanced at it. "As the head Sword for this temple, the Disciple bids me to escort you to the visitor gallery." He directed a withering stare at Buzz. "Only you."

"Buzz is my plus-one," Megan said. "And we can seat ourselves, thank you very much. Just tell us where to go."

The Sword shook his head and gestured toward the staircase. "You abide by the rules of the temple or leave the grounds."

"Joybelle's your boss, right?" Megan asked, or more accurately, stated. "She claims I'm a herald, whatever that means. I don't know the lady very well, but I have a feeling she doesn't like being crossed. You're welcome to test that theory. I'll wait while you check."

The Sword shifted his weight from one foot to the other, his gaze darting between her and the temple doors.

Max stepped from behind Megan and inflated his chest. "Do you know who I am, good sir?"

The Sword turned to face Max, his expression more concerned than hostile now. Recognition slowly dawned, and the confrontational lines on his forehead faded into acquiescence. He pulled the hood from his head. "I didn't mean you should leave, sir. Your presence at our temple is a great honor. I listen to every one of your shows. We all do. You're welcome here anytime, Mister Cooper. I mean that."

Max slapped the man so hard on the back that he lost his balance. "Only my lawyer calls me Mister Cooper. You may call me Max, as do all my close friends. What's your name?"

"Malachi is my chosen name, appointed by the Prophet to judge the unworthy."

Max wrapped a meaty arm around the Sword's thin shoulders. "I'm sorry to hear that, Malachi. Come along, there's not a second to lose. Sounds like the festivities have already commenced. I don't want to miss another minute. Lead on!"

Malachi nodded, leading Max to an entrance on the north side of the narthex. Megan and Buzz exchanged a glance before falling into step behind them. As they passed through the entrance, another blue-robed fanatic shut the door, but not before Megan noticed the envious stares from the thinning crowd outside. Never had she encountered people who wanted to go to church so badly.

They reached a steep, spiraling staircase carpeted in blue velvet. Megan huffed as she and Buzz climbed behind the wheezing Max, who grumbled about the lack of an elevator. Soon, they arrived at the entrance of a luxury suite overlooking a stage. As Malachi opened the glass door, loud music burst forth, rattling Megan's teeth.

Max entered the balcony alongside Malachi, who whispered something in his ear. Beaming with enthusiasm, Max took an offering envelope from a pew and scribbled on the back—an autograph, Megan presumed. He handed the envelope to his new best friend, who pressed it to his chest as he departed.

Buzz signaled for her to wait at the door. He checked every corner inside the suite and then returned. "All clear. I'll take up station outside."

Megan thanked Buzz and entered the suite, staring at the scene below in astonishment.

The temple's interior seemed larger than suggested by its external appearance, a cavernous space housing at least thirty thousand people. Tiered seating surrounded a raised central stage, encircled by large overhead screens. Blue-robed zealots patrolled the aisles, their movements purposeful and vigilant.

But what truly captured Megan's attention was the spectacle on stage. Musicians unleashed a barrage of heavy metal riffs and intricate guitar solos, punctuated by ethereal synthesizer melodies. Accompanying the thunderous music, a dizzying array of multicolored lasers pulsed and flashed, their seizure-inducing patterns synchronized to the pounding beat.

Max bobbed his head out of rhythm while sipping from a silver flask that had materialized out of nowhere. He motioned for her to sit beside him and offered her a drink. "You seem a little stressed, dear. This will take the edge off."

Megan initially shook her head at the offer, but after a moment's hesitation, conceded he had a point. As she sipped, the whiskey burned a fiery trail down her throat, and for the first time since her arrival, she felt her fears melt away.

The song built to a thunderous crescendo before fading into silence. The musicians stepped to the edge of the stage and took a bow, met with a smattering of applause. Megan found the muted response strangely at odds with the band's fame—even she had heard of them.

"Damn glad I came," Max said, taking another swig.

Suddenly, the lights went out.

An oppressive silence fell, as thick as the darkness enveloping them. Megan could discern nothing but Max's labored breathing beside her. She felt his hand fumbling for hers, which she shook off. As the seconds crawled by, her uneasiness grew.

Then a golden hue bathed the audience, the illumination coming from hundreds of fist-sized medallions embedded in the domed ceiling. Hearing the audience stir, Megan dropped her gaze to the floor of the temple.

The entire congregation got to their feet and extended their palms toward the now-empty stage. A low humming issued from thousands of mouths, rising and falling in a haunting rhythm that took her breath away. Megan placed a hand over her mouth, recognizing the sound of the transmission and realizing what should have been obvious about this place from the very beginning. The ceiling, the medallions, the floor, and stage resembled the inner chamber of the Beacon, but ten times the size. She half rose from her seat, intending to flee.

Max held her elbow. "I know what you're thinking. First thing I noticed too. But you came here for a reason, eh? Come, sit. We'll experience this together. Remember, your bodyguard is outside."

Megan allowed herself to be eased back into her chair. "I have a bad feeling about this."

"I, on the other hand, am quite content. What I've experienced already contains enough material for a week's worth of shows. And, quite possibly, my first Pulitzer."

Megan didn't bother to scoff, only pointed.

Light blazed through an opening in the center stage, causing her to shield her eyes with a hand. From it, an angel clad in a flowing white robe and golden sash rose into the air with a slow flap of outstretched wings. The congregation bowed their heads. Hovering over the audience, the angel stretched two arms to the heavens and boomed,

"Give glory to the Prophet, for the hour of judgment has come! You are the Chosen, redeemed from the bowels of earth to lead the battle against the Beast.

CHAPTER FIFTEEN

The brightly lit angel hovered above the stage, its wings flapping gently as it slowly descended back to earth. As the lights dimmed, six screens encircling the stage like a giant halo flickered to life. A face appeared, framed by long blonde hair, with a high forehead, wide mouth, and a complexion as pale as freshly fallen snow. Joybelle Leroux. Megan had expected as much.

"Our host," Max said, sipping from his flask. "What a great opening."

"What the hell was that about?" Megan wondered aloud.

Max chuckled. "Money, my dear. It's always about the money. Someone has to pay for this beautiful temple, so they put on a show in exchange for the twenty-five percent tithe they demand from their flock. The church even prepares their members' tax returns to ensure compliance. I, for one, am captivated."

"How did you know that?"

"I'm preparing a series of podcasts about the Church of the Prophet. Really dug into the inner workings of the organization, like how they choose disciples. Did you know they're all women? About time, I say." He took another sip from the flask. "Anyway, that's how Joybelle heard of me. She must have been impressed."

"Uh huh," Megan murmured, wondering why he had really been invited. "That's a pretty steep price for a concert and a spectacle." She returned her attention to the temple floor, watching as a young woman unhooked the wire harness from Joybelle's back.

What had she expected to find here? Evidence of otherworldly activity? She wasn't quite sure, but hadn't expected a circus. Now, more than ever, Joybelle's claims of witnessing the drop inside the chamber and hearing music appeared to be just another act in a grand performance, indistinguishable from dressing up as an angel. Joybelle's guess regarding a second traveler might be just that—not unreasonable, considering the blueprint featured two anthropomorphic figures. Then she remembered the pendant. For that, there was no satisfactory explanation.

On the stage, Joybelle gathered her voluminous robes and ascended to the altar. Gazing upward, her voice resonated throughout the temple:

"O great Prophet, exalted messenger of the divine, ever-present yet beyond our reach. Bless us gathered here as we consecrate this sacred ground. Let your wisdom permeate this sanctuary, and within these walls, may you gift the worthy with perpetuity of being."

Her voice intensified.

"Yet the fearful and unbelieving, along with the demons that seek a human chalice to corrupt the souls of men, shall be cast into the abyss that seethes with fire and sulfur. Believe in the extraordinary and embrace the impossible, for the chaos of this world can blind us to the truth. Heed the Prophet's teachings as if they were an impenetrable shield, and you will stand against the wiles of the Beast. This is the promise of our blessed Prophet, the giver of undying life."

Megan's stomach churned, the rhetoric sounding all too familiar. Promote the belief your group is special, isolate the members, incite fear of the Other, enforce conformity, and then exploit them financially. Her mother had fallen victim to a similar fanatical movement, losing her daughter, wealth, sanity, and ultimately her life.

Max, however, clapped with gusto, drawing stern glances from the congregants below. He had clearly never set foot in a place of worship—if one could indeed call this temple that.

Overwhelmed with memories and disgusted by the performance, Megan rose to her feet. "I'm leaving."

"Wait, we just got here," Max said, pulling on her arm.

Before Megan could respond, flares shot toward the ceiling, so bright she had to shield her eyes. As her vision adjusted, she saw Joybelle had vanished, replaced by the dark silhouette of a man. Within the shadowy form, a mass of appendages undulated like writhing serpents. The shape morphed, its two arms becoming four, and its head transforming into the likeness of Ganesha, then a smiling Buddha, continuing to shift through the religious statuary Megan had seen under the rotunda. A dazzling rainbow arched over the ever-changing forms, accompanied by flashes of light and peals of thunder.

Intrigued, Megan sank back into her seat, marveling at the volumetric display. She'd never seen holographic technology this advanced. The cost must have been astronomical.

Once the parade of iconography ended, a lean, nearly naked man stood alone on the stage. Dreadlocks fell to his waist, and feral eyes burned above an unkempt beard. Tattoos covered him from head to toe, interrupted only by a loincloth slung around his hips. Rings adorned every finger, and what looked to be a joint smoldered in his hand. He took a luxurious drag, blowing out a long plume of smoke which weaved trails above his head.

The audience clapped like maniacs and shouted cries of adoration. Megan shook her head, wondering how much money they'd thrown at this man who looked more deluded than she'd imagined.

"I take it that's their Prophet," she said.

Max grinned broadly. "The one and only."

"Pretty sure that's a joint he's smoking."

"To each their own," Max said, extending the flask of whiskey. She took a measured sip, an attempt to steady her fraying nerves.

The Prophet surveyed the crowd for a long while, puffing contentedly amidst a growing cloud of smoke. Megan's gaze landed on Senator Wigfall in the front row, his presence surprising, yet not shocking. After all, these were his voters.

After tossing the spent joint onto the ground, the Prophet sauntered off the stage, followed by a videographer who live-streamed his path across the temple floor. Megan's attention shifted to the projection screen, where she studied the tattoos on his face. Claws wrapped around his forehead, and teeth traced his nose and jawline, conjuring the image of a man consumed by a dragon. He turned, revealing a large, many-armed, distorted ankh emblazoned on his back, the same eerie symbol generated by the alien program. A sharp, inexplicable fear pierced Megan. Was it her imagination, or did those arms just move? Must be the whiskey, she told herself.

"The man is certainly committed," Max said, oblivious to her inner turmoil. "Say, isn't that the same symbol from your transmission?"

Megan offered no reply, her attention captured by the scene unfolding on the temple floor. A woman, cradling an infant, rose as the Prophet neared. His voice, amplified by speakers, boomed throughout the temple, "Tell me your greatest desire."

"My daughter is ill," the woman choked out, tears carving paths down her cheeks. "I want you to expel the Beast."

The Prophet laid a hand on the infant's head, his eyes closing in a solemn gesture. As he did, Megan noticed two additional eyes etched on his lids—their vertically slitted pupils seeming to stare directly at her. "This is not the work of a beast, mother, but the natural progression of disease. Though your child's time in this world will soon end, the essence within shall endure." He moved on, leaving the sobbing mother to her grief.

Megan's heart ached for the woman, her anger rising at the cruelty masquerading as wisdom.

The Prophet paused again, this time before a man whose face was marked by time. "Why are you here?"

The elderly man swallowed, his panicked face filling the overhead screens. "I… I came to experience the wonder."

"You came to be entertained? Is that what we are to you, an actor on a stage?"

"No, no, I meant that—"

"We know what you meant. Tell your truth, then face our judgment."

After a long pause, the man hung his head. "I have one month at the most and want the eternal life you promised."

The Prophet scrutinized him. "You speak as though you are but a child. Fear of death is born from the love of life. Surely, that's no reason to be afraid." Turning to the camera, the Prophet's grim visage filled the screens, seeming to look down upon the congregation. "What you people fail to realize is the only thing to fear is yourselves. While fleeing the inevitable decay of your bodies, you strip this world bare to fatten what will ultimately become a corpse. That's why we have come here: to save you from yourselves. To do that, our church needs shepherds, not sheep."

With a snap of his fingers, two blue-robed Swords hastened to escort the elderly man away. After a moment of stunned silence, the congregation hurled epithets at the retreating figure.

The Prophet continued his circuit around the temple floor, with followers eagerly reaching out to touch him and others recoiling in fear. Every so often, he would single out an individual, who was then swiftly ushered away. Megan observed this unsettling ritual in horrified fascination, while Max, absorbed in his own world, feverishly typed notes into his phone, muttering under his breath, "This is good stuff."

"He pretends to be a savior," Megan said. "In reality, he's just a bully."

Max set the phone aside and stroked his goatee. "Maybe so, but these people adore him."

As the Prophet passed by the front row on his way back to the stage, Senator Wigfall abruptly rose to his feet, blocking the path. "I'm here to bathe in the glory of your church," he said, his voice carrying across the hushed crowd.

The Prophet pulled another joint from his loincloth and lit it up. After languidly taking a few deep puffs, he leaned in close and blew a thick cloud of smoke directly into Wigfall's face. "A lying tongue, poisoned by the desire to be king."

Senator Wigfall flushed, his face magnified on the screens. "No sir. I'm a humble servant with no pretensions of grandeur."

The Prophet took another long drag. "You worship the illusion of power. But like sand slipping through your fingers, the harder you grasp, the more elusive it becomes. And when you finally open your hand, there is nothing there. Dust returns to the earth, as does the fruit of petty ambition. A lesson you've yet to learn."

In a sudden motion, the Prophet slapped him hard across the face.

Megan gasped, her hand reflexively rising to her own cheek, as if feeling the sting herself. Nearby congregants scrambled away. On the overhead screens, Megan saw the shock and humiliation in Wigfall's widened eyes as he nursed his jaw. For the first time, she felt a scintilla of pity for the man.

Not Max, who grinned. "My audience is going to love that."

They weren't alone. The crowd pelted the Senator with crumpled paper, pencils, bottles, even a shoe as he fled for the exit, head down and shielding his face. They hooted gleefully at his retreat.

"I'm getting a little scared," Megan said, glancing toward the exit, reassured by Buzz's presence outside the balcony suite.

He patted her knee. "Now, now. You're here by invitation of the Disciple herself. Nobody would dare lay a hand on you. Not to worry."

"Thank you, Max."

"My pleasure, dear. Have you changed your mind about dinner?"

"Another time, okay? I just need to get out of here and decompress."

"Well, you came to see the Prophet. Might as well stick around and see what other craziness ensues. Either that, or you'll have to listen to my show."

Megan laughed, feeling her burden lighten.

The Prophet returned to the stage, accompanied by a thumping rhythm that rattled Megan's teeth. A line of young kids emerged from the back of the stage, forming a ring around the tattooed man. The Prophet snatched the microphone from the altar, holding it high over his head as he swayed to the beat.

"This promises to be entertaining," Max said.

Megan could only nod, finding the whole scene surreal. Then, to her utter astonishment, the Prophet began to rap,

> *Unshackle your mind from preconception's chains,*
> *Cast off expectations, and truth remains.*
> *Prejudice and bias, blinders of the soul,*
> *Discard them now, let clarity take control.*

> *Behold the world anew, with vision unfeigned,*
> *Witness reality, raw and unchained.*
> *Beyond the veil of illusion, where new perceptions play,*
> *Grasp the silent truth, where words fade away.*

> *For the chosen few, the devoted and bold,*
> *A path to enlightenment shall now unfold.*
> *In the radiance of mysteries unwritten,*
> *I unveil the secrets that lie hidden.*

> *Through the annals of time, a beacon I shall be,*

Guiding those who seek true wisdom's key.
Open your mind, let your spirit soar,
As I reveal the truths that were concealed before.

The crowd surged to their feet, clapping and shouting. Even Max joined in. But Megan's heart pounded, a sense of impending panic seizing her for reasons she couldn't fathom. As the music faded and the crowd quieted, Megan's pulse didn't subside.

The Prophet casually puffed away at the joint, staring at his toes. Occasional muffled coughs from the audience only reinforced Megan's uneasy anticipation. She caught Max's eye, who merely shrugged, and extended the flask.

With a guttural grunt, the Prophet cleared his throat and spat on the floor, eliciting a gag from Megan. He then lifted his head, and for a fleeting moment, she could swear he looked directly up at her before turning, taking in the entire congregation.

Licking his lips, he asked the hushed crowd, "Are you ready to experience a miracle?"

CHAPTER SIXTEEN

Megan shook her head in disbelief as the entire congregation slipped from the pews and fell to their knees at the Prophet's promise of a miracle. Their blind adoration sent a shiver down her spine, for these people had willingly replaced their own intelligence with the ravings of a lunatic. Megan had little sympathy for zealots committed to such demagogic nonsense. What would this prophet do, anyway? Handle venomous snakes, babble in tongues, or saw a lady in half? He seemed capable of anything. Whatever the stunt, this horde of credulous followers would undoubtedly lap it up without questioning.

"This is pure gold," Max said, taking another sip from his flask. "The material I've already seen will fill a show or three."

"Your listeners are the perfect target for this type of nonsense," Megan said. "I expect that's why you were invited."

"Hey!" he protested.

"It's true."

Max handed her the flask, from which she took a generous sip, justifying it to help with her growing anxiety.

"That doesn't mean you should say it out loud," he said.

Megan rolled her eyes. "Okay, Max."

A cloying waft of perfume announced Joybelle's presence even before Megan turned to see the priestess enter the suite.

"She's right, Mister Cooper," Joybelle said, squeezing between them, her voluminous robes failing to conceal her shapely figure. "Or shall I call you Mister Mystery?"

Max sprang to his feet, unable to keep his eyes off her bosom, surprising Megan not at all. "Your temple is beautiful, Madame, simply breathtaking, as is the lady of the house. Please call me Max, as do all my close friends." With an elaborate swirl of his hand, he bowed.

Joybelle unleashed the full wattage of her smile, her pearly whites gleaming in the dim light. "I'm so glad you could join us, and pray you find inspiration from the ceremony. You chose a fortuitous day to visit, as the Prophet rarely graces us with his presence. Perhaps you could spread the good word on your show, encourage your listeners to join our community?" She leaned in, as if confiding a secret. "I hear you have quite the following these days."

"Forty-two million rabid fans and growing," Max preened, puffing out his chest. "Perhaps your Prophet would agree to a live interview. That would surely motivate my listeners to visit this beautiful temple, and your gorgeous self."

"And boost ratings," Megan added.

"That too," Max said, oblivious to her sarcasm.

"Alas, the Prophet rarely grants an audience to outsiders," Joybelle said. "He prefers solitary communion with the divine, as do I. But thank you for your consideration." Turning, Joybelle enveloped Megan's hand in a warm, two-handed grasp. "I'm gratified you accepted my invitation, Doctor McCullough. I hope you find our sanctuary a welcoming environment."

Megan pulled her hand away. "Let's see, one of your guards knocked over an old man at the door and your so-called prophet assaulted a congregant. The Senator is annoying, but surely, he didn't deserve that."

"People get overly excited when the founder of our church speaks—"

"You mean cult," Megan cut in, voice sharp.

Joybelle ignored the gibe, continuing as if not interrupted, "—and the Prophet oftentimes succumbs to his passions."

"This Prophet of yours, where exactly did he come from?" she asked.

"Albuquerque, New Mexico, where he was raised by a single mother who was never touched by the hands of a man."

"Infertility treatment," Megan said. "Good for her."

Joybelle's smile tightened. "Seeing they do not see, and hearing they do not hear, nor do they understand."

Megan countered with a verse of her own: "Woe to those who are wise in their own eyes, and shrewd in their own sight."

"You know the Book. I'm pleased."

"And you know the Prophet. But how well, I wonder?"

Joybelle placed a hand on her belly. "The Prophet shares his love freely with all his disciples."

Megan's gaze fell to the slight swell of Joybelle's abdomen. Memories washed over her, of her mother falling for the charms of another charismatic leader. "You're being exploited, dear," she said softly.

"The body is merely a vessel for the soul."

"His vessel's been busy," Max chortled, earning a withering glare from Joybelle.

"I hope you don't mind if I have a private word with Doctor McCullough, Mister Cooper," Joybelle said. "A Sword waits at the bottom of the stairs to give you a tour of the grounds."

"I didn't mean any offense, good lady."

"Offense is rarely given, only taken. Before you leave, I have a question for you, Mister Cooper."

Max spread his arms in a grandiose gesture. "I'm as open as the sky is wide and the oceans are vast."

"Who helped Stephen Fisher?"

Max tilted his head, tapping his pouty bottom lip. "You must be talking about his wife, Francine. A fine-looking woman and a good friend of mine. We met when I interviewed her husband. I'm sure you heard about that. Propelled me to fame, well, more fame. She's a feisty lady and prone to take offense at the most innocuous comment."

"You don't know," Joybelle said, voice flat.

"Excuse me?"

Joybelle gestured toward the exit. "Your escort awaits."

"Um, yes, but I don't want to miss the miracle. Can we do the tour after?"

"Goodbye, Max," Joybelle said, her usual sing-song tone replaced by something harder, more insistent.

Noting his hesitation, Megan patted his thigh. "It's okay. We'll talk later."

Max lifted his generous bulk from the pew. "I'll keep you to that promise," he said, and bowed stiffly to Joybelle. "A pleasure, Miss Leroux. I do hope we can stay in touch."

As Max lumbered away, Megan fixed the priestess with a pointed stare. She was about to ask another question when Joybelle placed a finger on her lips and shifted her eyes into the temple. Megan followed her gaze.

Seven angels holding seven trumpets descended from steel beams crisscrossing the vaulted ceiling, their robes fluttering in the gentle breeze created by the air vents. One hovered just above the balcony suite, close enough for Megan to see the heavy makeup, fake wings, and tennis shoes peeking out from beneath the hems. She wondered if the person felt as ridiculous as they looked.

From the stage, the Prophet said, "Create the circle of life," his voice carrying through the arena.

The people in the audience grasped the hands of their neighbors, bridged by blue-robed guards in the aisles and rows. The kids surrounding the Prophet made a line from the stage to the first row of congregants, forming an unbroken chain that wound around the temple floor.

Raising his hand over the nearest child, the Prophet said, "To rid yourself of delusion, close your eyes and open your mind to perceive what lies beyond the illusion."

The congregation obeyed, except for Megan, who glanced at Joybelle, finding her palms pressed together.

"Know that we are the way, the path, and the keeper of eternity," the Prophet said, dropping his palm onto the child's head.

Audible gasps erupted from thousands of throats, leading Megan to wonder what they saw—or imagined. As she stared, four elliptical pupils materialized inside the figure, appearing to gaze directly at her. She rubbed her eyes in disbelief.

"May you live an undying life," the Prophet intoned, lifting his hand from the child's head.

The congregation burst into expressions of ecstasy and adulation, with shouts of, "Praise the Lord of Light!", "Hallelujah!", and "Word of the Prophet!" Bodies gyrated, feet stomped, shoulders shook, and tears fell. Some congregants collapsed where they stood, while others writhed on the floor.

Lighting up another joint, the Prophet gazed serenely about the arena, the tattoo no longer moving.

"What the hell," Megan muttered. Had she been part of a mass delusion? Or was it the whiskey?

"The Prophet split open heaven for all to see," Joybelle said, resting her arm on the pew. "A pity you couldn't partake, for you might have found wisdom. But only the Chosen are so honored, for that is the Prophet's promise, that they may ascend with his blessing."

"Your Prophet is a con artist who tells people what they want to hear, leaving them to imagine their heart's desire. I don't mean that pejoratively, but as advice from somebody who has experienced this firsthand."

Joybelle lifted her gaze to the ceiling of the suite. "You don't believe. Then let me put it in a language you'll understand. There is another dimension—or universe—that overlaps and interacts with our own. The rules are different there, and space and time don't quite work the same... if at all. The Prophet calls it the conscious plane. I call it the home of our immortal souls. Or is that a concept you also deem worthy of contempt?"

Megan's mind reeled. The conscious plane, the term Melody used to describe the exact same phenomenon. "Who are you, really?" she asked, her voice barely above a whisper.

"I'm an eternal soul clothed in a person named Joybelle Leroux. But enough of that. I have a few questions of my own. Stephen Fisher activated the Beacon, but he couldn't have done it alone. There had to be another."

A chill ran through Megan's veins, again wondering how this lady knew that. Feeling extremely uneasy, maybe a little panicked, she glanced at the glass door. But Buzz wasn't there.

"Your bodyguard took a break," said Joybelle. "Was it Stephen's wife, Francine Fisher? We have reports Obadiah Wallner was present as well. Was he the companion?"

Megan strove to keep her expression neutral. "I don't know what you're talking about."

Joybelle rolled her fingers on the top of the pew. "Unlike you, I speak the truth. And I tell you up front that one of my gifts is the ability to detect falsehood. I've always known when people lie, and the

Prophet strengthened that organic talent. It's not hard, really, once you learn to perceive the subtle turn of a mind. That's why I accompanied Senator Wigfall to ISBLIC headquarters. I needed to learn what he knew. Turned out to be not much. Given his access to confidential information, I found that surprising. You, however, know of what I speak."

"That was quite the show," Megan said as she prepared to leave. "Very entertaining. Thanks for the invite, priestess, but it's time for me to go."

Before Megan could get to her feet, Joybelle clamped a hand around her wrist. "You won't be leaving just yet. But it's only polite I provide answers to your questions before asking my own. First, this temple. The Beacon is a holy artifact, and the design of our house reflects that. Surely, you noticed."

Because of Megan's small stature and having been raised in an unstable environment among unstable people, she had always taken an interest in self-defense. Over the years, she had trained extensively in marital arts, focusing on techniques that could help a smaller person overcome larger attackers. Recent threats had only redoubled her attention to her training.

"I suggest you remove your hand," she said.

Joybelle only fingered the ankh-like charm hanging around her neck. "This symbol of the church was created by the hand of the Prophet himself. It's no coincidence it looks like the image produced by the alien program. That may lead you to wonder if the Prophet comes from the place that sent the transmission. He says no, though I assure you he is not of this world. But what does it matter the origin of the Lord of Light? You may wonder if I'm from the same place. Hardly, though I strive to become more than what's encased by this lonely vessel. What else? Oh yes, the children on the stage. They came through the Beacon. Travelers, they call themselves, who hope to return home by the power of the Prophet. Any other questions, Doctor McCullough? Now is the time."

The hairs on Megan's neck stood on end, though not because of the hand which bound her, but the word "travelers," the same term Melody used to describe herself and her dead father.

"Who came with Stephen Fisher?" Joybelle asked again. "I assure you, we mean them no harm. And remember, I can perceive the turn of your mind."

"My mind's turning right now. I'm picturing a gesture that involves a finger. Can you guess which one?"

A glint shone in Joybelle's eyes. "Are you Stephen's companion, Doctor McCullough? You seem the most likely candidate, though reports don't place you at the Beacon during that time. But reports can be falsified."

Megan met Joybelle's gaze head on. "Assuming any of your bullshit is true, why do you care?"

"The minions of the Beast often disguise themselves as servants of righteousness. And now I know it isn't you. The Prophet told me as much, though I had to ask. How about your friend Dolores? She killed herself inside the Beacon, which is how travelers return to their world. Was it her?"

"You should really let me go."

Joybelle redoubled her grip, her nails digging into Megan's skin. "So, not Dolores, not the wife, not Obadiah, not you. It couldn't be General Beckman, and I understand that Eric Fisher, the brother, wasn't there. True?"

"You're out of your mind."

"Not him either. Hmm. That only leaves his child…"

"Last chance," Megan warned again, her muscles tensing.

Joybelle's eyes widened. "That is a surprise. Not just for me, but for the Prophet himself. He didn't think that was possible for a child so young. A truly capable being she must be. Where is Melody, Megan? The Senator revealed the family lives somewhere in Washington state but didn't know the exact location. Are they near Seattle, or farther afield? Tacoma, Spokane, Bellevue, to the east? Not there, I see." She blew out a breath, her eyes raised in thought. "Maybe off the coast, on one of the islands?"

Megan's eyes hardened.

"Ah, she's there," Joybelle said with a smile.

With a quick tug, Megan pulled her captive hand inward, drawing Joybelle off balance, as her other hand struck upward, connecting sharply with the underside of Joybelle's pert nose. Blood spattered over the woman's robes.

Megan sprang to her feet and ran out of the suite, descending the velvet stairway two steps at a time. Malachi, the blue-robed creep, lurked below. With a confused double-take at Megan's appearance, he sprinted up the stairs. Megan zipped past him.

Once outside the temple and in the courtyard, she grabbed her phone and dialed Obadiah's number. He picked up on the second ring.

"Move the family!" she yelled, her heart racing as she fled the temple grounds.

CHAPTER SEVENTEEN

I slid into the backseat of the car beside Melody, still unsettled after my talk with her friend Tina. One way or another, I needed to find a way to help these travelers get back home. That meant getting them into the Beacon, which would prove difficult if not impossible. Apart from urging patience, I had no better suggestions right now. I mean, what could two kids really do, other than grow up?

Aunt Franny greeted me from behind the wheel, for she taught fourth grade at our school and drove us home at the end of the day. As the car ascended a gentle rise, a sweeping view of Friday Harbor unfolded before us. Boats glided through the tranquil waters, their wakes disturbing the reflection of the island's pines on the glassy surface. A swarm of tourists boarded the mainland ferry, accompanied by a few vehicles snaking down the ramp. Seagulls wheeled above, while below, children walked home with their parents. Despite the beauty of this place, a prickle of unease crawled down my spine.

Like many, I could feel when I was being watched. Usually, this was nothing more than a fleeting glimpse of somebody at the periphery of my vision—a sixth sense channeling the interconnectedness of all living beings. Everyone possessed it to some degree. Yet, for me, this intuition was amplified a hundred-fold, allowing me to detect disturbances well beyond the visual field. It had never failed me. However, as I scanned my surroundings, I couldn't pinpoint the source of the disturbance.

Melody nudged me, angling her head toward the front of the car.

"Sorry, what?" I asked, then noticed my aunt peering at me through the rear-view mirror.

"I asked how your day was, Stevie," Franny said.

"Oh, just fine. Melody introduced me to a new friend."

"That's great to hear," she said, in that mildly dismissive tone adults often used when speaking with young children. Funny how things remained the same, yet felt utterly transformed.

We veered onto the two-way highway leading toward our hometown on the north side of the island, Roche Harbor. Leaving the coastline behind, we found ourselves flanked by oaks stripped of leaves by the winter chill. A golden field dotted with grazing cows stretched toward low hills covered with pine. Melody gazed straight ahead, seemingly lost in thought. I suspected she was worried about the fate of her friend.

Unable to shake the feeling of being watched, I twisted around in my seat. Three vehicles trailed behind us—two cars and a black pickup. Letting the music fill my head, I focused on the disturbance. Like a flame flickering in the darkness, I perceived another traveler inside the truck, accompanied by an adult, presumably the driver. Could it be Tina? Hard to tell, as this one tried to shield their mind. If it was Melody's friend, she had switched vehicles. Or perhaps another had followed her here, which was exactly what I feared—the breadcrumb trail come to life. If true, they had likely arrived on the ferry, leading me to wonder what they wanted with us.

I nudged Melody.

"What's wrong?" she asked.

"Concentrate," I told her.

Melody's eyes dilated, a sign she had opened herself up to the conscious plane. Drawing in a sharp breath, she exclaimed, "Somebody's following us!"

"What?" Aunt Franny said.

Melody repeated herself, adding, "They're behind us right now."

My aunt stiffened in her seat. "You certain about that?"

"For sure, absolutely, one hundred percent."

Franny cursed under her breath. As we rounded a curve, she slowed the car while studying the rear-view mirror. "Two kids and what looks to be the mother are directly behind us. In the second are two adults. The truck's too far away for me to see. Which one is following us?"

Melody shot me a glance, unsure where these people were. Not wanting to arouse my aunt's suspicions, I remained silent. "Hard to tell," she said. "But I think one of them is like me."

"Meaning one of them is a traveler?"

"I told you they were coming."

"Any idea what they want?"

"I don't know," Melody said, her voice edging upward. "It might be my friend, Tina."

"I told you not to encourage that girl." My aunt took a deep breath. "All right. I'm going to take a detour through the middle of town just to be sure they're following us. No way am I going to lead them back to our house."

Melody vigorously nodded. "Good idea."

Aunt Franny blindly reached around the front seat to pat me on the knee. "Stevie, don't you worry about a thing. We're just being cautious, and we'll be home before you know it."

I nodded absently, my attention fixed on the people in the pickup. The traveler remained hard to read, like trying to discern patterns through murky water. But the adult, a man, was an open book. His mind swirled with a fiery orange intermingled with shades of gunmetal gray, indicating a hardened resolve. The rough and uneven texture, akin to shards of shattered glass, reflected his hostility. Though I couldn't perceive thoughts, I could read emotions, which hinted at intention. And this man readied himself for conflict.

As if to confirm my suspicion, another car, carrying yet another traveler, appeared on the road a half mile ahead of us. This wasn't a coincidence; this was a hunt. And I suspected they searched for Melody, though the reason still eluded me. The only thing I was certain of was my ignorance.

Given the urgency of the situation, I felt compelled to intervene. After all, among all the people I'd encountered in this world, Franny was one I trusted most.

"The people in the black pickup are following us," I said. "A child and an adult. The car that just pulled in front of you holds two more. Probably working with the others. I don't know who they are. I don't know what they want. And I don't think we should find out."

Aunt Franny went rigid, gaping at me. The tires thudded over the center divider, prompting her to steer the car back into its lane. "Melody…is little Stevie a traveler?"

Melody glanced at me. I returned a shrug. "Maybe," she said.

"It's true," I admitted.

Aunt Franny bit her lower lip. "All righty, then."

"You're not surprised," I said.

"Let's just say I'm not shocked."

"How did you know?" Melody asked.

"I raised you, dear, and you can't keep a secret to save your life. Especially from your mother. Forgive me for saying this, but Stevie, you've always seemed…kind of odd. Too mature for your age, like my daughter."

"My parents don't know," I said. "I didn't know myself until recently."

Franny caught my eye through the mirror. "On your birthday?"

"Yes."

"What you tell your parents is up to you. But I have a feeling your dad's going to figure it out before too long. Remember, his brother was also a traveler. Anyway, can you tell if these people are dangerous? Either of you?"

I'd known travelers who'd intervened on newly discovered worlds, seeking to save what couldn't be saved. In a few instances, aged travelers leveraged their knowledge and command of the conscious plane to manipulate beings in positions of power to further their own agendas. But that didn't explain what these people were up to, though I suspected they weren't pleased about being stranded here.

"Hard to tell," I said. "They're supposed to help."

"Could've fooled me," Franny said, her eyes darting down a side road. "I'm going to call Eric." Before she reached for her phone, it chimed with an incoming call. She activated the speaker. "Eric, we've got a situation here—"

"I know," my dad cut in. "Tara and I are already at your house. You have the kids?"

Franny's mind quickened, belying the calm she tried to project. "In the back seat. What's happening at your end?"

"A friend of mine at the hardware store called to let me know our pictures are being shown around town. I'm guessing it's the press, maybe some reporter who came over on the ferry. Do you want me to get on the road, meet up with you somewhere?"

"You and Tara stay put. I'll be home in ten minutes. I have a feeling we're going to be leaving."

"Let's not get ahead of ourselves. Could be somebody just sniffing around. That's happened before."

"Just be prepared."

"Understood. I'll see you shortly. Take care, Franny."

"Always."

Once we reached the intersection at Roche Harbor, Franny abruptly turned left when we should have gone right. Pulling into the lone gas station, she kept her eyes fixed on the truck in the rear-view mirror. The pickup behind us slowed, and I caught my first glimpse of a bearded man staring at us through darkened windows. As the truck moved on and vanished from sight, my aunt got us back on the road, accelerating to twice the speed limit until trees concealed us. But it didn't matter. I could shield my thoughts. Melody couldn't. Her mind stood out like a lighthouse on a foggy day.

"We're taking the scenic route home," Franny said, trying to sound calm. "You kids sit tight."

After a few roundabout miles and many turns, we pulled into the gravel driveway of Aunt Franny's house. An unpainted picket fence enclosed a tidy lawn with a flagstone path leading to the front door. An expansive field separated this property from the nearest neighbor. In the backyard, the ocean lapped against a rocky beach. While isolation may have once provided protection, now the place felt exposed. My parents awaited us at the gate, their vehicle parked nearby. Sensing a prickling sensation on the back of my neck, I glanced over my shoulder. Sure enough, another truck rounded the corner.

The moment Aunt Franny brought the car to a halt, my dad rushed over and opened the front door. "I've already called the Marshall."

"We're being followed," Melody announced.

My dad let fly an expletive and hustled us into the house. Once inside, Franny flipped the deadbolt and disappeared into the bedroom, reemerging with a rifle. Dad grabbed a poker from the fireplace, and my mom fetched an iron pan from under the sink. We heard a vehicle screech to a halt in the driveway, sending rocks pattering across the ground. Mom herded Melody and me into the kitchen, where I peered over the counter at the front door.

Aunt Franny loaded a shell into the chamber of the gun. "What did the Marshal have to say?"

Dad looked through the gap in the curtains. "He said he'd send a sheriff to track down the person asking questions. Megan also called and told me to expect a visitor. Maybe this is them."

There was a sharp rap on the door. Dad let the curtain fall back into place and stepped away from the window.

"How many are out there?" Mom asked.

"One guy, clean-shaven. Looks to be in his fifties."

"Nobody else?" Aunt Franny asked.

"Just the one."

My aunt turned to her daughter. "Is this one of the people who followed us?"

Melody's eyes glazed over, concentrating on the mind on the front porch. "Not the same."

Dad approached the door. "Who are you?" he shouted.

"Agent Lars from the Special Security Force," the man shouted back.

"What do you want?"

"To tell you to pack your things."

My dad looked at my mother and my aunt. "I'm going to open the door."

Aunt Franny nodded, raising the rifle. My mom raised the skillet. With the metal poker firmly gripped in one hand, my dad unlocked the deadbolt and opened the door with the other.

A stocky figure filled the entryway. Taking an involuntary step backward, the man slowly raised his hands. "Now, take it easy, Miss."

"Show me identification," Dad demanded.

Keeping his eyes on the rifle, the man motioned to his chest with his chin. "Leftmost pocket."

My father reached into the man's jacket and retrieved a wallet. After a quick glance inside, he showed the badge to Aunt Franny and my mom. "He's who he claims to be."

Franny lowered the rifle a hair. "That can be forged."

"Doctor McCullough believes your location has been compromised," the agent said. "Director Obadiah Wallner sent me to fetch you. Can I put my hands down now?"

Franny let the gun drop. "You should have started with that."

Dad returned the wallet, which the man tucked into his pocket. "I heard about the pictures being shown around town," the agent said. "Anything else I should know?"

My aunt briefed him on events, leaving out any mention of travelers and the part Melody and I had played. The agent requested a description of the vehicles, which Franny provided in surprising detail. He then excused himself, made a call from inside his vehicle, and returned to the front porch.

His voice dropped to a low, urgent tone. "Listen carefully. We need to move. This isn't a drill or a precaution—it's imperative we take immediate action." He glanced over his shoulder before continuing, "We have protocols for situations like this, and I'm here to get you to a secure location."

"We've moved two times in the past three years," Mom said. "We can't keep doing this. The kids are still in school."

"Once this location is secure, we can consider returning. Until then, I need to keep you safe."

"Where do you propose taking us?" Dad asked.

"For now, a military facility on the mainland. After that..."—he shrugged—"That information is provided on a need-to-know basis, and I didn't need to know. Gather your passports, medication, personal items, and enough clothes to last a few weeks. How much time do you need?"

My mom pointed at three bags by the fireplace, as our family was always prepared to leave at a moment's notice. "If we have to go, we're ready."

"Same here," Aunt Franny said.

"We'll take two cars," Agent Lars said. "Three can fit in my truck, and the rest have to follow. Given what I've heard, we need to move quickly."

As my parents and aunt loaded the vehicles, I kept my antenna tuned for any hint of surveillance. Though I didn't detect any immediate threat, the absence didn't bring me comfort. They were out there; I could feel it.

Dad drove with my mom up front and me in the back seat. We trailed behind the agent's vehicle, with my aunt and Melody accompanying him. Passing through town, the watchers reappeared in the same two vehicles, following us from behind. Once again, I let the music fill my head.

Concentrating solely on the two travelers, I pierced the veil they used to shield their thoughts. Amidst the chaotic swirls within their minds, flashes of vibrant reds and pulsating oranges hinted at an underlying fear that drove their intensity. That puzzled me. What did these travelers have to fear from us? Even more confusing was that their attention focused exclusively on our car, completely ignoring Aunt Franny and Melody.

That's when it dawned on me: These visitors weren't interested in them; they were looking for me.

CHAPTER EIGHTEEN

Megan stepped out of Max's flying palace and paused at the top of the airstair. His jet stood as a monument to excess, its sleek exterior coated in an iridescent black finish that cast shimmering rainbows across every curve and angle. A gold dragon emblazoned along the fuselage glinted like a million tiny jewels, its head complete with a grinning maw of dagger-like teeth, reptilian eyes, curled horns, and a handlebar mustache. Sparkling crystals crafted into the owner's initials—MM—adorned the massive engines.

She gripped the railing and descended the stairs, her eyes falling upon the family waiting on the tarmac. Melody had sprouted a foot since their last in-person meeting, a testament to the years spent in hiding. Little Stevie clung to his cousin's hand, the spitting image of his father. Behind the children stood Eric, his dark, tousled hair resisting all attempts at taming. Beside him, Tara looked much the same, her graceful beauty untouched by time's passage.

But it was Fran who had undergone the most dramatic transformation. With cropped hair, purple bangs, and dark sunglasses obscuring her face, Megan found her nearly unrecognizable. A wise strategy, she mused, given the media's fascination with the widow of the self-proclaimed extraterrestrial messenger. Near the waiting turboprop stood Lars, the agent Obadiah had tasked with extracting the family to safety.

As Megan's feet touched the tarmac, Melody bounded over and flung her arms around her neck. "Aunt Megan!" the girl exclaimed, her face alight with joy.

Megan returned the embrace, surprised to find herself blinking back tears. With no spouse, no children, her best friend dead, and having been raised by a woman who cared more about her bizarre beliefs than her child, she often felt like an outsider. But here, enfolded in Melody's exuberant hug, she felt a sense of belonging. This was her family now, and Megan intended to help them.

"Hello, dearie. Oh my goodness, look how you've grown."

"Four foot eleven and a half inches," Melody said, using a hand to compare their respective heights. "Taller than you now!"

"But not wider," Megan said, patting her midsection.

Fran stepped forward to wrap Megan in a warm embrace of her own. "It's good to see you, Meg. You look great."

"Liar," Megan said fondly, noting the worry lines etched into her friend's brow. "Relax, you're in good hands now."

Fran's gaze slid to the garish jet. "I don't know about that."

"You look well too, Franny. I like the new hairdo."

"No, you don't, and you can't distract me. I'm not getting on that plane."

"An emergency measure, which I'll explain in a moment." Megan moved to greet Eric, a physicist and former professor who shared his late brother's brooding look. If not for the family's need to remain hidden, Megan would have gladly recruited him and his wife for ISBLIC.

Tara kissed Megan's cheek, then gently nudged her son forward. "Stevie, this is your Aunt Megan."

The boy stepped out from behind his mother and stared up at Megan, solemn and intent. She'd never met Stevie in person, only glimpsed him hovering in the background of video chats with the family, watching but never speaking.

"Your name is Megan McCullough," the boy said.

Megan crouched down to his level. "That's right. And you're Little Stevie, named after your brave uncle. He was a good man and a dear friend."

"He wasn't as good as you think."

Megan straightened, unsettled by the boy's words and unnerved by the maturity in his voice.

Tara flashed her an apologetic look. "Sorry," she said. "Stevie's been a little off lately. All the excitement, I suppose."

A biting wind swept across the tarmac, causing Megan to rub

warmth into her bare arms. "Totally understandable."

Eric jerked his chin toward the jet. "Does that belong to who I think it does?"

"Let's first get Melody and Stevie out of the cold," Megan said, not wanting to upset the kids with what might become an argument. "There's food, drinks, and even a TV on board."

"But I want to hear," Melody protested.

Tara, catching Megan's unspoken message, guided the children toward the aircraft. "Come on. Let's get inside."

Once the kids were out of earshot, Fran crossed her arms. "Well?"

"A few things," Megan began. "First, your location's been compromised. Senator Wigfall divulged what state you were living in to a lady from the Church of the Prophet. He'd have given her your exact address if he knew it. There's more to tell, but I'll save the details until we're in the air. I want Melody to hear." She glanced over at Lars, who stood with his hands in his pockets, leaning against the turboprop. Per Obadiah's order, he would stay with them until they boarded.

Lowering her voice, she continued, "Second, Obadiah doesn't feel he can guarantee your safety for much longer. The current administration's not the issue; it's what happens next. The opposing party's nominee for president is leading every poll in every state, and he's beholden to the church."

"I was wondering about that," Eric said.

"It gets worse. One of the Prophet's disciples—this same lady—is angling for my job. And Wigfall's slated to become Director of Homeland Security. He can be clownish sometimes, but he's smart and about to be armed with a flamethrower. Obadiah expects to be fired, and his replacement will be a loyal stooge who will use the intelligence agencies to help the Church wage their holy war against a mythical Beast."

Fran swore under her breath. "I think people from that church tracked us down."

"Very likely. Which is why we need to get you out of the country, pronto."

"Still doesn't explain that," Fran said, pointing at the jet.

"Obadiah wanted no trail that others could follow, which ruled out government and commercial transport. Max was the least bad option.

If it helps, I think he offered his 'chariot' to apologize for releasing your late husband's interview before you had a chance to leave the country."

"Apology not accepted. He screwed us once. He'll do it again."

"Seconded," Eric said.

Megan held out a placating hand. "I understand, truly. I wouldn't ask Max to babysit my plants."

"There have to be other options," Fran said.

Megan hesitated, knowing she shouldn't divulge this. But the family needed to leave these shores—the sooner, the better. "Remember those times Obadiah made you move?"

"How could we not?"

"It was because of threats Max uncovered. He's a government informant, with an audience of unsavory characters who apparently tell him things. I don't know why he does it. Maybe he feels guilty. Maybe Obadiah gives him intel he wouldn't otherwise learn. Whatever the reason, you can count on Max to follow his self-interest. For now, that means helping you."

"We agree on the self-interest part," Eric said dryly.

"I'll share more on the plane," Megan said. "Brace yourself, it's weird. All I ask is that you trust me."

Fran shouldered her bag with a sigh. "Weird describes our life. You've never steered us wrong, Meg. I don't like it, but I do trust you. Where are you taking us?"

"Australia," Megan said.

◆

The engines roared to life, and the aircraft taxied to the runway, soon lifting off into the air. As the jet reached altitude, the lush greenery of the Pacific Northwest gave way to an endless expanse of ocean, shimmering in the fading light of the sun.

A steward entered the spacious lounge, his black blazer expertly tailored and creased pants pooling ever so slightly over polished black shoes. The interior of the plane was no less extravagant than the exterior, with plush velvet upholstery covering every surface, intricate gold filigree adorning the walls, and ornate oil paintings lining the aisles. It all reflected Max's absurd wealth, self-indulgence and, as Megan had told him when she boarded, utter lack of taste.

With practiced efficiency, the steward laid out an assortment of juices and yogurt along with a selection of hors d'oeuvres for the adults: caviar tartlets, smoked trout croquettes, and more.

Megan and Fran took seats on stools at the bar, while the kids claimed the plush velvet chairs. Megan ordered a gin and tonic, heavy on the gin, and Fran a piña colada. Melody fiddled with the controls of the mechanical footrest, while Stevie continued to stare at Megan in that unsettling way of his. Eric sank into the leather couch, his eyes already drooping, with Tara resting her head in his lap. Nobody commented on the chrome stripper pole in the corner.

As the sun dipped below the horizon and the sea turned to a muted gray, Megan deemed it time to ruin the peaceful mood. But before she could open her mouth, Max sauntered into the lounge, waving a cocktail with a little umbrella.

"Welcome aboard, noble asylum seekers!" he bellowed.

Eric startled awake. Tara lifted her head. And Megan cursed. She had begged Max to stay out of sight for the duration of the flight. Fran sprang from the barstool, wagging a finger in his face. "You're a fake, fraud, and liar," she fumed. "As for this stunt, I'm certain you'll betray us at the first opportunity."

Max backed away, waving his hands and slopping his drink onto the shag carpet. "Dear lady, it was only with the best of intentions I agreed to the interview. Slay me for being generous, but my motivations were pure, though my memory proved faulty. To be honest, I don't recall discussing the interview's release. I thought you wanted it out as soon as possible, and I simply obliged."

Fran registered her displeasure with a torrent of words that scorched even Megan's calloused sensibilities. Melody's eyes widened, and Tara leaned over the couch to cup her hands around little Stevie's ears. Megan rubbed a spot over her left eye, feeling the first twinge of a headache.

"You cost my brother his life," Eric said, his voice dangerously calm.

Max placed a hand over what passed for his heart, his eyes darting between Fran and Eric. "I deeply regret any harm I inadvertently caused. In recompense, I've supplied you with a chariot to flee these hostile shores. Melbourne is a gorgeous city, and I've set you up with a palatial estate to keep you safe. There's a private cinema, two pools, a waterfall, and a pond with ducks. Also, a gym." He patted his rotund middle. "Not that I've seen the inside of one."

"I'd sooner live in a cardboard box," Eric said, rising from the couch. Tara placed a restraining hand on her husband's forearm.

Max bumped into the table as he retreated. "Now, now, good sir." Melody tugged on Max's coat. "Where's Melbourne?"

Max turned to face her. "Australia, little princess. You'll love it there."

"Are there kangaroos?"

"At the golf course, yes. Too many. They're like rats."

Fran returned to the bar and grabbed her half-finished piña colada, eyes flashing. Fearing what was about to happen, Megan popped out of her seat and herded Max toward the exit. "You're a piece of work," she muttered.

"I am a saint that offers sanctuary to the oppressed."

"I told you; they need time to get used to the new...you. Come along, back to your bedroom. You promised me."

"I'm a man of my word," Max said, studiously ignoring Eric's scoff. With a hand on the door, he bowed to Fran. "I remain your servant, my lady. If you or your family need anything, just ask the steward. Farewell!"

After Max retreated, Megan shut the door. "Sorry, I begged him to stay in his cabin."

Fran mumbled something incoherent, which, for the kids' sake, was probably for the best. Eric went to the bar, murmuring about needing a drink. Tara lay back down. Little Stevie stared at the door where Max had fled. To her surprise, he asked, "Where was Max before he came here?"

"At some temple we visited," Megan said, unsettled by the boy's intent stare. "Speaking of which..." She took a seat at the table opposite Melody. "That experience wasn't at all what I expected."

Fran joined Megan at the table, handing her the gin and tonic she'd left behind at the bar. Eric rummaged through the mini-fridge, retrieved a beer, and popped the cap off before returning to the couch.

He settled in next to Tara, putting his arm around his wife.

"What happened?" Melody asked.

Megan rubbed the back of her neck, uncertain where to begin. Did Joybelle really read her mind? It sounded far-fetched, even ludicrous, but she'd felt certain of it at the time. After taking a deep breath, she recounted the religious iconography under the rotunda, the draconium in the tub, the rapping Prophet, the children dancing on stage, the congregation's reaction, and finally, her interrogation by Joybelle. She omitted the details about Buzz, whom she'd found wandering outside the temple complex, claiming he woke up in a dumpster. She also didn't mention Joybelle's bloodied nose.

Incredulous gazes intersected one another as she relayed the story. Fran asked her to repeat certain elements more than once. Tara compressed her lips, occasionally making little horrified noises. Eric cringed at the mention of the Sword of the Lord, a reminder of the fanatic who tried to assassinate his brother. Melody bit her bottom lip, bouncing her knee up and down.

Little Stevie abruptly stood up. "I need to use the bathroom."

Megan waved at the door. "Down the aisle on the left," she said, keeping her attention focused on Melody. After visiting the temple, a familiar suspicion had grown in Megan's mind, which had first taken root when pondering the anthropomorphic figures produced by the alien program.

"My dear," she began, "you told me that when someone dies inside the Beacon, they're reborn at wherever the second machine is located. But Joybelle claimed those kids on stage were travelers. Is it possible the Beacon works both ways, allowing your people to come here to Earth?"

Melody averted her eyes, the sound of collective breathing only amplifying her silence. Megan took a slow sip of her drink, determined to wait her out.

Finally, Melody sighed so pathetically, it nearly broke Megan's heart. "I didn't want to tell you."

"So, it's true," Megan said, leaning back in the chair. Though she had suspected as much, it hadn't prepared her for the reality. She recalled the infrared images of drops falling inside the chamber—one thousand three hundred and sixty-four within forty-eight hours of the

Beacon becoming active. After that, only a few each month.

"She wanted to protect them," Fran said. "Her father was murdered because of who he was."

"And the same would happen to those poor kids," Tara added.

"You need to turn that damn machine off," Eric said. "Better yet, destroy it. Stop anybody else from coming here."

Megan puffed out her cheeks, surprised but not shocked that they all knew. "Too late for that."

"We never should've activated the Beacon," Melody said, her voice a pained whisper. "Travelers aren't any different from other people, you know. Some are good, and some…" She shrugged, as if struggling to find the right words. "It's like turning on a light in a dark place. Others can be attracted to that light."

"But that still doesn't explain the Prophet," Megan said. "The Beacon's only been active a few years. Because of that, you told me he's too old to be a traveler, right?"

Melody bobbed her head. "I didn't lie about that."

Megan's gaze wandered out the porthole, where the fading sun cast a pink glow over wisps of clouds on the horizon. She had seen this Prophet, felt his presence, and was convinced he was not of this world. But regardless of where he came from, the man remained a threat. And nobody stood in his way—be it through indifference, acquiescence, or fear. Silence only empowered the powerful, she knew. Her dead mother was a testament to that harsh truth. But Megan was no longer a child, nor was she helpless.

Leaning across the table, she squeezed Melody's hand. With quiet determination, knowing what she had to do, regardless of the consequences, she said, "Thank you, dearie."

CHAPTER NINETEEN

As Megan recounted her experiences at the Temple of the Prophet, a sense of foreboding gripped me. The Disciple, Joybelle, whom she had encountered, spoke of the conscious realm and knew it took two to activate the Beacon—knowledge only another traveler should possess. But when she mentioned the Chosen, the hazy veil of the before-time parted, and I was transported to a world long dead.

The sky roiled with angry clouds, and the air thrummed with the weight of impending doom. Across a ruined landscape, I watched the last vestiges of a once-mighty force gather around their besieged capital. At my command, sonic weaponry unleashed its deadly song, vaporizing soldiers and innocents alike. Moments later, the atmospheric bubble protecting the city shattered, exposing the inhabitants to the storms raging over the planet's surface. I then ordered my forces into the city to either convert or recycle the survivors. The thrill of battle coursed through me, certain I was the Lord of Light's instrument to defeat the empire that had once enslaved me. That entity had called itself Dalkhu, and I was one of their Chosen.

As the last echo of the before-time faded, a cold sweat broke out on my forehead. The similarities between that distant time and what Megan had just described troubled me, yet they didn't necessarily mean Dalkhu had returned. Except for what I perceived spinning within Max's head when he barged into the lounge.

People born into this world shared similar characteristics. Their minds moved in a singular direction, like wind-rippled water flowing over a bed of stones, quite unlike travelers, whose minds flowed counterclockwise in a myriad of textures and patterns. Max's mind was typical of those born here, except for one thing: powerful emotions spawned eddies that defied the main current. Eventually, these eddies dissipated, along with the emotion that triggered them. But not for Max. The eddy spinning within his mind refused to disperse, flowing counterclockwise with the texture of one reborn elsewhere. I had seen this before, in the minds of the other Chosen from that long-dead planet.

Rising to my feet, I announced, "I need to use the bathroom."

Megan waved toward the exit where Max had retreated. "Down the aisle to the left," she said, and carried on with her story.

I walked out of the lounge, passed the bathroom, and paused in front of a closed cabin door. After glancing over my shoulder to ensure nobody was watching, I entered.

Pictures adorned the walls, mostly of Max posing with people I assumed were luminaries of one sort or another. The desk was a chaotic mess of papers and piles of books—a fitting reflection of the man. Various knick-knacks decorated the shelves, most of them sexual in nature, mirroring the content displayed on the computer screen: naked ladies cavorting with other ladies. On the opposite side of the office was another door. The sluggish meander of Max's mind emanated from within, confirming his presence.

I crossed the room and tried the door. Locked. I knocked, but there was no answer. I knocked again, harder this time. Still nothing. Determined to speak with him, I went to the desk and rummaged through the contents until I found a set of keys. The second one worked.

Gently easing the door open, I called out softly, "Hello?" No response, though I could hear muffled voices. When I stepped inside, I found myself in a spacious bedroom. Max lay sprawled atop the rumpled sheets of an enormous circular bed, wearing nothing but underwear and headphones. A tall drink teetered precariously on his mountainous, hairy belly. Facing away from the door, he watched a large wall-mounted screen, absently munching on chips from an open bag at his side. To my surprise, my family and Megan served as the entertainment. Cameras must be hidden somewhere in the lounge, I assumed.

"Hi there," I said.

Max's head whipped around, causing the drink to slosh onto his gut and soak the sheets. With surprising agility for a man his size, he vaulted from the bed, snatching a black robe from a nearby rack, which he hastily wrapped around his generous form. Golden dragons embroidered the fabric, the same as the one painted on the side of the jet.

"You really shouldn't sneak up on people like that!" he said, yanking off the headphones. "How the hell did you get in here?"

I dangled the set of keys I found in the office. "You didn't answer when I knocked."

Max snatched the keys from my hand, his eyes bulging. "Shouldn't you be peeing or pooping?" He hooked a thumb toward the exit. "Public restrooms' that way, kid. Now get out."

"Sorry. I've heard so much about you, I just wanted to meet you in person."

Max's expression softened, and he smoothed a stray strand of hair over his balding head. "Ah, you're a fan. I should have guessed. A bit young, but no worries." He dug through the covers and produced a remote. The screen blinked off. "Did you want an autograph or something?"

"Yes, sir."

"Call me Max. Now, let's see…" He ambled to a side table and clawed through a drawer, presumably looking for a pen and paper.

"My parents won't be happy to learn you were spying on us," I said. "What were you trying to find out?"

A flicker of unease crossed Max's features before he masked it with a forced smile. "You misunderstand. I was watching a movie. How about I have the steward bring you a little something? You like sweets? Bet you'd enjoy a crackle, a nice crispy treat with chocolate. Or maybe some pudding, a piece of cake, cookies, whatever you like. How does that sound?"

"Don't worry, I won't tell. But only if you answer a question."

Max shut the drawer and looked me over. "Are you threatening to blackmail me, boy? Have to say, I respect that. How old are you, anyway?"

"Older than you think."

"Uh huh, I'm guessing six or seven. An early start for a life of crime. What's your name?"

"Stevie."

"Oh, yeah. Megan told me about you. Named after your uncle, right? You know, he was like a brother to me. We were very close, and I miss him dearly. Now, what is it you want with me, kid?"

"I want to know who you met at the temple."

Max idly picked some lint from his belly button. "Why in the world would you care about that? Shouldn't you be more interested in playing with toys or learning how to read?"

"I'm reading you right now, Max."

"Aren't you a cheeky one. Maybe you should go back to calling me 'sir'."

I asked again, "Who did you meet? I'm just curious."

Max took an empty glass from the bed and refilled it from a bottle on the nightstand, studying me the whole while. "You're a strange kid."

"I know."

"You saw me watching a movie, right?"

I nodded.

"All righty, then. I accompanied my lady friend, and we spoke with a beautiful angel named Joybelle. Also, some uptight guard from the temple, along with Megan's bodyguard. Satisfied?"

"Did you meet with anybody else? Megan said you left her after a time."

"Has anyone ever told you you're nosy?" Max swilled the drink and smacked his lips. "Fine, if you must know, the master of ceremonies of that establishment showed me the truth of the world. Turns out, things aren't quite as I expected. Not that you would understand."

"Who is this master of…whatever you said?"

"Time for you to go, kid. Remember, keep your mouth shut and the crackles are yours. Come along, your parents are probably worried." Max grabbed my forearm, attempting to herd me from the room. But I slipped out of his grasp and dug my heels into the carpet.

"You didn't answer my question."

With a huff, Max leaned over me. "Look, despite my disagreement with your aunt, who's a wonderful lady, you have nothing to worry about. Trust me."

I wanted to believe him, but the metallic yellow rivulet twisting through his mind suggested otherwise. So, I considered doing something I hadn't dared in a long while. Not even Melody knew I was capable of this. But I had no choice, for I needed to understand what was going on. At least, that's what I told myself. In truth, a growing fear trumped any moral constraint.

Concentrating on the drunken swirl behind Max's bloodshot eyes, I brought forth the soundtrack of the conscious plane until the music echoed between my ears. When Max reached over to drag me from the bedroom, I slapped a hand onto his protruding belly.

Max slumped to his knees, his eyes rolling back as I wove the fingers of my will into the rippling currents of his mind. The deeper I probed, the richer the colors became and the more intricate the patterns grew. Max tried to resist, but crumbled under the weight of my intent. Now fully immersed in his thoughts, I sought out that strange eddy, determined to uncover its secrets.

A being brighter than any sun flickered onto the screen of my awareness. Tendrils of the past writhed through earthly flesh, thick as syrup from a bottle. Its shape shifted constantly, refusing to settle on a single form. The entity spoke, and though I couldn't discern the words, I felt Max's awe and desire pulsing through his consciousness.

"What did it tell you?" I whispered into Max's ear.

A surge of head-pounding rage was the reply. Fearing I delved too deeply, I pulled back from the precipice. Max's mind blurred, and his face came into sharper focus. In an instant, a meaty hand flung me away.

Max sprang to his feet, reeling backward until he collided with the bedside table. Fumbling blindly in the drawer behind him, he brandished a butter knife. "Leave me alone, demon!"

I took a step toward him. "Was that the Prophet you met? What did they offer you, Max?"

Just then, my father burst through the door. Assessing the scene in an instant, he snatched the butter knife from Max's grip. "What the hell are you doing, man?"

Max spluttered incoherently, jabbing an accusatory finger in my direction.

Keeping a close eye on Max, my dad knelt beside me. "You alright, Stevie? Did he hurt you?"

"Tell him what you are, boy," Max demanded, his voice quavering.

My father turned toward him, and whatever message was conveyed caused Max to visibly quail. Edging toward the door, he bolted from the room, his bathrobe flapping behind him like panic-stricken wings.

Dad's dark eyes pierced mine. "What happened here? I thought you needed to use the bathroom."

That wasn't his real question. Ever since my stay at the hospital, he had wondered about my origins. I intended to tell him eventually, but thought I had years to find the right time. Now, though, I needed help. Besides, Aunt Franny already knew. Still, I found it difficult. Though ancient in lives, I remained a kid.

I blurted out, "I'm a traveler, like Melody," then held my breath.

Dad slowly nodded, his gaze never wavering from mine. "I figured as much."

Tears welled up in my eyes. "You wonder if I'm really your son, don't you?"

Dad pulled me into a tight embrace, his voice fierce with emotion. "That never crossed my mind, Stevie. Not even for a second. I wish you could've met my brother. He was a good man, but struggled with who he was. Our father only made that worse—much worse. But not once did I ever consider him to be anything but my brother. And you remind me of him in so many ways—your quiet demeanor, your mature manner, and especially your smile. I won't make the same mistake as my father. You will always be my son, no matter where you're from. I love you, and nothing will ever change that."

Unable to speak, I nodded, my heart swelling with relief.

After a long moment, my dad gently pulled back, his hands on my shoulders as he looked into my eyes. "Now, tell me what this was all about with Max. Don't hold back anything."

I inhaled deeply, attempting to regain my composure. "Something's happening that I don't understand."

"Story of our lives," he said with a wry smile.

I nodded, feeling more centered. "Those people who followed us back home were travelers. Melody knows, and so does Aunt Franny." My dad lifted an eyebrow. "It must have something to do with the church Aunt Megan was talking about."

"Seems likely."

"I need to visit that temple."

His grip on my shoulders tightened. "That church is dangerous, Stevie, especially for members of this family. They have strange ideas about my brother and would love to get their hands on Melody. For what reason, I can't fathom. And even if I were willing to take you to that place—which I'm not—we're going in the wrong direction."

"Then we need to find another temple."

"Why in the world do you want to go there?"

Reluctant to voice my greatest fear, I hesitated to say it out loud. But Dad's steady gaze urged me on, patient but expectant.

Finally, I forced out the words: "I think this Prophet might be creating an army."

CHAPTER TWENTY

Megan settled into one of the sleek yet uncomfortable white leather chairs in the lounge where guests awaited their call to the set. The production assistant had dubbed it the "green room," though nothing about the space evoked nature or tranquility. Devoid of plants, the metallic coffee table reflected harsh fluorescent lights, while the transparent glass wall of the adjacent studio felt like a threat. Noise from the bustling newsroom seeped through the cracked door as filtered air hummed gently in the background. The clock's second hand ticked relentlessly, amplifying Megan's mounting anxiety. Armed only with her words, declaring war against the new administration seemed foolhardy, and she couldn't help but second-guess her intentions. The man scowling at her from across the coffee table didn't help matters.

"I wasn't told you would be here, Doctor McCullough," Senator Wigfall said. "What do you think you're doing?"

"At the moment, feeling extremely nervous," Megan admitted. "I admire your composure when speaking before a camera. Our public relations director says I could learn a thing or two from you."

The Senator leaned back in his chair, a self-satisfied smile playing at the corners of his mouth. "My wife can't get me to shut up, but I just can't help myself. Turns out, I have a lot to say and a constituency that can't get enough of me. But that's not what I meant, and you know it. What are you doing here?"

Megan kept her voice even. "The host of this show invited me to discuss the preliminary report concerning the second transmission. I'm doing my job."

"You should have sought my authorization."

"Forgive me, Senator. There's no established protocol for this type of situation. Besides, I didn't think it was necessary. As you said yourself, the world should bear witness to the unveiling of the alien message. Discussing our analysis is in that same spirit. That was your guidance, not mine—one I was initially against. But I've grown to appreciate your wisdom. As such, it seems appropriate that I comment publicly. Wouldn't you agree?"

Wigfall's tone became clipped, his displeasure evident. "You know I won't and knew I wouldn't. I believe your time would be better spent cleaning out your desk."

Megan refused to be cowed. "The decision to appoint the Director of ISBLIC is determined by a majority vote of the consortium. Your motion to replace me with Joybelle Leroux lost. By quite a few votes, if I recall."

He smiled thinly. "Better to resign of your own volition than be forced out. Despite your insubordinate attitude, I have nothing against you, Doctor McCullough. I really don't. ISBLIC accomplished a lot under your leadership. The job is done. Maybe it's time to tend to your roses. No reason for you to be humiliated... or worse."

"Is that a threat?"

"No, that's inevitable. U.S. taxpayers funded the construction of the Beacon, and, if I recall, the thing still sits on U.S. territory. It remains the prerogative of the new administration to allow the consortium access to the device. Rest assured, that privilege will be revoked if you remain director."

Megan had expected as much. She tapped the cheekbone below her left eye, drawing attention to his injury. "You've got a shiner. How did that happen?"

He shrugged, as if it were nothing. "I was riding my lawnmower and hit a gopher mound. Lost my seat. Nothing a little makeup can't fix. Thank you for your concern."

"You're welcome. But that sounds as unlikely as what really happened."

"Excuse me?"

"The pictures are all over social media, Horace. You must know that. While you and I don't agree on much, I don't think you're a bad guy. My advice: Part ways with this prophet and his Church before it's too late. They're completely nuts, as I'm sure you know."

Wigfall spat tobacco juice into a paper cup, regarding her for a long moment. "Megan, you don't realize who you're dealing with. If you insist on doing this show, I suggest you stick to the science and steer well clear of politics. For your own well-being, missy. That's not a threat. That's good advice."

"Pretty sure it's you, not me, who doesn't know *whom* they're dealing with," she said, not unkindly.

The production assistant entered the green room. "Doctor McCullough, the show's on a commercial break. You're on in a couple of minutes. If you'll come with me…"

"Gladly," Megan said, rising from her seat. "I appreciate the advice, Horace."

"My pleasure," he said, tipping his head.

Megan followed the PA out of the door, her heart pounding in her chest as she prepared to face the camera and the nation.

◆

"Good morning, and welcome back to *The Weekly Wrap*," said Timothy Farnsworth, the host of the show. "Today, we have a very special guest with us, Doctor Megan McCullough, Director of the International Space Based Laser Consortium. We've been trying to get you on for some time, Doctor. Glad you finally agreed."

Megan smoothed her pantsuit with a hand, a nervous habit. "A pleasure to be invited, Tim."

"This consortium was tasked with creating an observatory to detect what, until last week, was another suspected extraterrestrial message. After five years and billions of dollars, the Interstellar Gravitational Observatory Recorder, the IGOR, became operational and detected the transmission. In short order, ISBLIC deciphered the message and broadcast the results to the public. Congratulations, Doctor, an astonishing achievement."

Megan's chest lifted, her eyes brightening. "Thank you. We have an outstanding team of professionals working at the consortium, and they deserve all the credit."

"Of course. Let's dive right into it, shall we? The preliminary report raises more questions than answers. It also raises some concerns. But let's start with the most startling news. The analysis claims the message communicates the existence of more than one universe. A multiverse, once confined to the realm of science fiction, might be real. Do I have that right?"

"That was quite the surprise," Megan said, her nerves assuaged by the familiar topic. "The bubbles shown in the images produced by the program align with the theory that our universe is one among many that exist separately from one another, each a distinct region of space with different physical properties, such as the strength of gravity and speed of light. According to this theory, shortly after the Big Bang, small quantum fluctuations were magnified and stretched to cosmic scales. Apparently, it's happening all the time. To be clear, there's no observational evidence to support this hypothesis. It's well beyond our science, but maybe not theirs."

"And the images of the galaxy and planet that followed?"

"ISBLIC concluded it's not the Milky Way, nor any planet in our solar system. That's definite."

"Where is it then?"

Megan paused, thinking of Melody. When asked, she would point unerringly at the transmission's source, no matter the turn of the planet. Yet she couldn't tell Megan if her home world was in this galaxy or even in this universe. She would simply say, "Right there."

"Every astronomer is wondering the same thing," Megan said. "But there's a lot of ground to cover, and it may lie outside the observable universe. Like searching for a grain of sand on a beach where the grain may or may not exist."

"Your report suggested this star system may be the source of the transmission. Is that right?"

Megan clasped her hands together on the table. "We don't know for sure, but the possibility prompted ISBLIC to review the telemetry used to triangulate the first transmission. At first, it was believed the source was a trinary star system within the Draco constellation. Both the original AMIGO and IGOR are highly accurate instruments for detecting gravitational waves, but triangulating these waves is complicated and involves more uncertainty. It's like trying to pinpoint where lightning struck by timing the delay between the flash and the rumble of thunder—relying on the gap between what you see and hear to estimate the distance. Our signal engineers now strongly suspect the transmission originates much farther away than we originally believed."

Timothy cocked his head. "Another galaxy?"

"Possibly," Megan said.

"Fascinating, but how is that relevant to determining the function of the alien machine? The report was mostly silent on that question."

"Not entirely. What we just discussed may pertain to the range of function. The Beacon might operate on an inter-galactic scale, if not between universes."

"That still doesn't tell us what it does. Answering that question was the reason ISBLIC was formed. Surely, Stephen Fisher knew. He held the key to building the machine and claimed to be from the civilization that sent the transmission. You met him. Did you happen to ask?"

Megan fought down her irritation. This question came up in every interview. "As I've said many times, I don't know anything more than what he shared during his talk with Max Mystery. The same is true for his wife and daughter."

"Why would he keep it a secret?"

"Perhaps he intended to tell us but was murdered before he had the chance," Megan said, her tone sharper than she intended. Glancing at the clock, she noted the dwindling time. "My suggestion is not to overthink something that might be obvious. Keep in mind that simple arithmetic produced the alien program, basic chemistry assessed our technological sophistication, and two-dimensional pictures created the blueprint. Simplicity is a theme."

"What's obvious to you may not be to others, Doctor McCullough. What's your best guess?"

Inwardly, Megan wanted to groan. To her, the alien program's output was as clear as a message spray-painted on a barn door: the Beacon allows you to be reborn on another world. How could others not see it?

She leaned forward slightly, her tone measured. "The patterns inside the heads of those two anthropomorphic figures may represent information transfer. If true, there are various interpretations of the means."

"Such as?"

Megan chose her words carefully, having rehearsed them to avoid appearing speculative. "A transfer of consciousness might be a possibility. The Beacon could facilitate that transition. The alien message suggests multiple universes, so why not one encompassing them all? Recall that the message began by showing us a multitude of bubbles. But from what vantage point? It had to be outside those bubble universes. Space could be a common property of a master cosmos in which the multiverse expands." She paused, then added, "But that's purely theoretical. As you suggested, one answer often leads to another question. That's how science progresses."

Timothy's eyebrows shot up, his skepticism clear. "Are you suggesting reincarnation is real?"

"I suggest information may move through a common medium. That's consistent with the principle of conservation. In a closed system, information cannot be created or destroyed, but it can be transformed from one form to another. That's physics. The real question is whether thoughts, feelings, and our sense of being can be considered information."

"That seems far-fetched. Do you really believe that?"

"I believe in evidence-based conclusions. All I'm suggesting is that the concept merits further scientific investigation." She shifted in her seat, steeling herself for the potential backlash to her next words. "What I can state with certainty is that the Beacon is a technological construct, not a religious artifact. Claims about it being the seventh seal or a conduit for demonic possession are complete and utter hogwash. I urge extreme caution against accepting unsubstantiated claims from religious leaders or politicians who may leverage this situation for personal gain or influence."

Timothy nodded in what Megan hoped was agreement. "All right, let's explore that further. William Stoughton won the election in an electoral landslide. In his acceptance speech, he reiterated his intentions to withdraw from ISBLIC, transfer control of the Beacon to the Church of the Prophet, and establish a committee to investigate claims of children being under demonic influence. Just yesterday, he shared a post calling for every child to be tested in the Church's induction centers. While the idea seems outlandish, some might argue that the concept of consciousness transfer is equally far-fetched. And then we have this curious development…"

On the screen before them appeared the sigil of the Church, side by side with the symbol output by the program.

"The similarity between the two is striking," Timothy continued. "Since ISBLIC broadcast this symbol produced by the alien program, the Church's membership has skyrocketed. People seem to believe this prophet. What are your thoughts on that, Doctor McCullough?"

Blood rushed to Megan's head, thinking of her mother's fate at the hands of another pretender. She would do everything possible to ensure that didn't happen to another family. "The similarity between these symbols doesn't validate the Church's claims," she said, her voice taut. "On a personal note, and I want to be clear that I'm not speaking for ISBLIC here, I caution people not to believe the Prophet or any politician who compromises their integrity for support from what is essentially a cult. Their agenda has nothing to do with the Beacon or the transmission. What they truly crave is power over your actions and beliefs. For the sake of your children and your own safety, I implore you not to comply with this dangerous rhetoric."

Timothy tapped his pen against the table. "And that will have to be the last word. Thank you, Doctor McCullough. You're welcome back anytime."

Megan nodded, not trusting herself to speak.

"Next, we'll hear from Senator Wigfall, sponsor of the Protect Our Children bill."

CHAPTER TWENTY-ONE

The rental car crawled through the muddy parking lot, my father at the wheel, his eyes scanning the surroundings like wary prey. I pressed my face against the cool glass of the passenger window, taking in the sight of the enormous blue and white striped tent. Three canvas spires reached skyward, billowing in the breeze, while a stream of people wound between parked vehicles, all heading toward the entrance of what looked more like a circus than a place of worship. In the distance, cranes towered over the skeletal bones of the permanent temple being constructed by the Church of the Prophet. According to my father, it was the first to be built in this hemisphere.

Dad eased the rental into an open space and cut the engine. His hands remained on the wheel, knuckles white with tension. "You sure you know what you're doing, Stevie?"

"Not really," I said, knowing how inadequate that sounded.

"Can you at least tell me what we're looking for?"

I shrugged. "Something that's not right."

"Pretty sure we're going to find that."

A thick drizzle greeted us as we climbed out of the car, the gray sky matching my mood. Dad unfurled an umbrella, holding it over us both, his presence a comforting shield. "Any chance you can be more specific?"

"I'll know it when I see it, I guess."

"That's not particularly helpful," he said, then added in a lower voice, "By the way, best not to tell your mother about our little adventure today. She's not quite ready to hear about... um, any of this."

A lump formed in my throat. He meant Mom wasn't ready to hear about me. Last night, I'd overheard their conversation from the adjoining bedroom of our temporary home, one of Max's spare mansions. Dad had asked her if she thought I might be like Melody. Mom told him not to be ridiculous, though she said it too fast, her mind roiling viridescent with anxiety. Deep down, I think she suspected I was a traveler, but couldn't reconcile that with the son she imagined me to be. I longed to tell her, to explain that I remained her child, no matter where I came from. But would admitting my origin make things better or worse?

"She'll come around," Dad said, noting my silence. "Just give it time."

"I hope so."

He patted my shoulder, then looked up at the canvas spires, his lips pressed together. "Your safety is my first priority. Stay close. If I say we go, we go, no matter the situation. Agreed?"

"Okay," I said, having little idea what to expect.

We made our way across the parking lot, our shoes squelching in the mud. As we approached the canvas temple, the vibrations of music playing inside mixed with the excited chatter of the crowd. Despite the commotion, my attention was drawn to the badges everyone wore around their neck. I squinted at the lady next to us, noticing her picture accompanied by a strange maze of black and white squares. Discreetly, I tugged at Dad's sleeve and tilted my head toward the lady's badge.

"It'll be fine," he said, but I could sense the tension in his voice.

A gray-haired woman greeted us at the entrance, gripping a hand-held scanner. Above her head hung a banner: "The Kingdom of Heaven Is At Hand!" But whose version of heaven, and by whose hand? Those answers I hoped to find here.

"Badges please," the lady said.

Dad pulled out his wallet and flashed what looked to be a card from his old gym.

"New members," gushed the woman, beaming at me. "Children are especially welcome. You must have heard we're blessed with the presence of a cherub." She gestured toward a low-slung tent next to the spires. "Please make your way to the orientation center, where an acolyte will ask a few questions. The boy will take a routine test, but not to worry, it's harmless. After that, you say a pledge and collect your badge. Simple."

"We just came to check out the temple," Dad said. "No need to make a fuss."

The lady's smile faltered before brightening again. "Oh, you're Americans." She waved the family behind us forward and scanned their badges. "The Grand Temple in the States is glorious. More of a cathedral, really. I hope to visit one day. But I'm sorry. Holy ground, even under old canvas, can only be walked by the Chosen. Not to worry, though, induction takes minutes." She gestured again at the orientation center. "Better hurry if you want to attend the next service. A new disciple will be ordained today, our first."

Impatient congregants pushed their way forward, jostling us out of line. My dad immediately took my hand and tried to slip in with another family, only to come face to face with a barefoot, bearded man wearing a blue robe and a scowl. He slapped a metal shaft against his palm, the threat in his manner made all too real by the purple stain twisting through his mind.

Dad lifted his hands and backed away. "No problem, we're leaving," he said, then turned us around and marched toward the parking lot with me in tow. "Afraid that's a no-go, Stevie. I expect we're better off that way, as we don't want to draw undue attention to ourselves."

I glanced over my shoulder as we walked. The bearded man spoke into a headset with his eyes pinned to our backs, sparking an image of an assassin from my past life. By the time we reached our vehicle, the drizzle had built to light rain and my white shoes were now brown.

Dad opened the back door of the rental car. "Come along, Stevie. This place gives me the creeps."

I felt the same way, though I couldn't put my finger on why. Sure, the guard was menacing, but in a run-of-the-mill sort of way. Something else was happening here, something I had missed.

Unwilling to leave but unsure what else to do, I turned around and stared hard at the spires, trying in vain to pierce the veil of uncertainty. After a moment, I found my eyes drawn to the low-slung canvas tent adjacent to the main temple, recalling the lady saying something about a test.

Another is near, said the voice in my head, startling me.

Where have you been? I thought.

Keeping the ghosts at bay. Though dead, they're not without desire and their echoes can overwhelm you if not suppressed. Think of me as your guardian angel.

I'm glad you're here. I feel lost without your help.

There's not really a me, only you, said the voice. *And your subconscious already knows what you seek. Look deeper.*

Heeding the voice's advice, I closed my eyes and focused on the ever-present music playing in my head. The world around me transformed, becoming phosphorescent. Trees glowed a neon green, and even the mud beneath my feet shimmered with microscopic life.

Against this backdrop of radiant energy, I perceived an ocean of minds, each spinning in unique patterns and textures. But one stood out, rotating in opposition to those bound to this planet. Its distinctive pattern was unmistakable. Instinctively, I shielded my thoughts, wary of drawing attention.

Dad nudged me. "Stevie?"

I let the music recede, and the familiar outlines of reality snapped back into focus. Opening my eyes, I pointed at the square tent. "There."

"What's in there?"

Wiping the rain from my brow, I said, "Answers."

CHAPTER TWENTY-TWO

O badiah invited Megan to sit on the plush beige couch in the living room of his elegant Georgetown home. The soft fabric enveloped her as she sank into the seat, the room's warm ambiance a welcome change from the sterile hotel room where she'd been staying during her visit to Washington, D.C. She had come to meet with ISBLIC council members in a last-ditch effort to salvage her job, but so far, her attempts seemed futile.

Marcelo, Obadiah's husband, inspected bottles in the wine rack before selecting a red, the glass clinking gently as he removed it from the shelf. "I've been saving this for a special occasion," he said.

As Marcelo filled her glass, Megan's eye was drawn to his distinctive wedding band—a textured tungsten ring inlaid with gold, a testament to their commitment. Though happy for them, a pang of loneliness struck her. How long had it been since she'd even considered her own romantic life? The demands of her career had always come first, and now, with her professional future unraveling, she wondered if she'd missed out on something precious.

Megan brought the wine to her nose, the rich scent of black cherry and a subtle note of oak wafting up to greet her. She swirled the liquid, admiring the deep burgundy hue as it caught the light, before taking a generous sip. The wine tasted exquisite, its velvety texture gliding down her throat, leaving a pleasant warmth in her chest. She let out a contented sigh, savoring the moment, with Marcelo looking at her expectantly.

"Lovely," she judged, a smile playing on her lips. "A fitting end to a delicious meal for the about-to-be condemned."

"Don't worry about the job, *cara mia*," Marcelo said, his accent lilting. "Everything will work out in the end."

Megan didn't believe a word, though she was grateful for his and Obadiah's friendship. "That's the least of my worries," she said, her gaze drifting to the window. The weight of recent events pressed down on her, making even this pleasant evening feel bittersweet.

Over dinner, she had told them about the repercussions following the interview: the anonymous threats, the white powder sent to her office, and the ridicule from fellow scientists for even mentioning reincarnation as a possibility. There had also been demands for her to be fired or even imprisoned for daring to speak out against the new President-elect. Colleagues she had worked with for years averted their eyes as she walked the office hallways, their silence deafening. Then there were the crazies who believed she was part of a satanic group of alien cannibals that had been covertly running the world government for decades.

Predictably, Senator Wigfall called for an emergency session of the ISBLIC steering committee to censure her and appoint Joybelle Leroux as director. Megan held out little hope she would survive that vote, scheduled to occur in two weeks' time, as even the friendliest members of the committee had criticized her for turning ISBLIC into a political football. As if that hadn't already occurred. The truth was, the countries these members represented feared offending the Prophet's cult, which was gaining influence within their respective borders.

Obadiah tapped his glass against hers, the gentle clink drawing her back to the present. "You're a courageous and admirable woman."

Megan dismissed the compliment with a wave. Her mouth, the only tool she had left in her arsenal, had backfired spectacularly. "All I've done is harden people's opinions and scare others. Most are intent on twisting my words to fit their own agendas, the Church of the Prophet being the most prominent. If anything, I've only made things worse."

"Not so," Marcelo said. "Doing what's right isn't always popular, but that doesn't mean you're alone. You spoke out about what many others are afraid to say."

Obadiah's gaze softened. "You created ISBLIC, built IGOR, then detected and deciphered the second transmission. Those are not small feats."

She sighed, her shoulders slumping under the weight of her failures. That damned Church had turned the Beacon from a source of wonder into the spiritual foundation of a cult. For what reason, she could only guess, but that didn't mean she wouldn't do everything in her power to deny them their prize.

Realizing she'd been dwelling on her own troubles, Megan straightened and forced a smile. "Forgive me, O, I'm so obsessed with my own life that I haven't asked about yours. What are you planning to do next? Are you thinking of returning to the private sector? I'd imagine the soon-to-be-former National Security Advisor has options."

Obadiah leaned back, a thoughtful expression on his face. "To be honest, I haven't had time to think about it. Dealing with the transition to this new administration is consuming all my attention."

Marcelo topped off Megan's wine. "It's madness," he said, shaking his head. "This new president wants to turn the intelligence agencies into his private militia. People are resigning en masse."

"Including career professionals," Obadiah said, his usually calm demeanor showing signs of strain. "Those who remain are afraid to speak out, and the few who do are subject to threats. I'm trying to convince key people to stay on, but I'm not having much luck."

"Any chance you can be one of them?" Megan asked.

A rare chuckle escaped Obadiah's lips. "Not an option. I serve at the behest of whoever occupies the Oval Office."

"Stupidity is a feature of politics, not a bug," Marcelo quipped.

"Which is why I've learned to expect the worst," Megan said. "I'm never disappointed. Speaking of which, there's something I need to share with you, O."

"What's that?"

Megan glanced at Marcelo before dropping her eyes to the floor. No matter how pleasant the company, she wasn't willing to discuss Melody and the family in front of anyone but Obadiah.

"I can take a hint," Marcelo said, rising from his seat. "I'm not interested in your secrets, anyway." He squeezed Obadiah's shoulder and kissed Megan's cheek before leaving the room, the door clicking softly behind him.

For a time, Megan savored the wine, enjoying the silence and the illusion that all was well. Obadiah didn't press her on the news, seemingly content to do the same. Once Megan had drained the last drop from her glass, she sank into her seat. "Melody lied to us."

Obadiah didn't reply, only tilted his head.

"The Beacon works both ways, coming and going."

"You've always suspected that."

"Suspecting is different from knowing. And now that I do…" Megan expelled a weary breath, the implications still troubling her. Would these other travelers be like Melody, young and seemingly helpless? Or more like Stephen Fisher, who had rendered her unconscious, maimed an agent, and killed his assailant? Though she had never thought him particularly threatening, he was undoubtedly dangerous. "You remember those drops?"

"Of course."

"Well, every time one of those falls inside the chamber—"

"A traveler arrives," Obadiah finished for her, intuiting what she already knew. "Did Melody say why they're coming?"

"Only that they've come to 'help', whatever that means. I suspect their real mission is to judge whether this is a safe destination. Pretty sure I know the answer to that question."

Obadiah tapped his finger against the wineglass, his expression thoughtful. "The government suspects these travelers exist and has set up a task force to search for them."

"What? You never told me that. Did they find any?"

"So far, nothing, though they continue to surreptitiously monitor records from pediatricians and mental health experts—anyone who might have a lead on these kids. But I don't think the agents on this task force really believe these travelers exist."

"I'd certainly stay out of sight if I were them."

"I assume that's why Melody didn't volunteer that information."

Megan confirmed with a nod. "She also claims these travelers are like people. Of everything I've heard from her, that scares me the most."

"What did she mean by that?"

"Exactly what you'd expect—that some may be up to no good. I'm pretty sure this Prophet falls into that category."

Obadiah refilled Megan's glass, then topped off his own. "We don't

...ow for sure that he's a visitor."

"You forget I was at that temple. I saw the man, could feel his creepiness. Joybelle practically confirmed he's not from around here. But whether he is or isn't, we know what he wants—the Beacon."

"Also, a theocracy," Obadiah said. "That's not just my opinion; it's the conclusion of more than one foreign intelligence agency."

"Probably so, but that's still only a means to an end. The Beacon is all he cares about. Can you guess why? Bear in mind, these travelers are, for all intents and purposes, immortal. So, think big, in a timeframe measured in eons rather than years."

"You've obviously thought a lot about this."

"I have."

"And?"

"I think we're a staging ground. A place to consolidate power before moving on to the next target. That's why he wants control of the Beacon. And he's trying to find other travelers, either to recruit or eliminate as potential threats. Those he doesn't like, he calls beasts."

"Did Melody tell you this?"

Megan turned her palms up. "Nowadays, it's like pulling teeth to get information out of that child. Either she's scared or doesn't know. But it seems obvious to me."

"That's a touch overdramatic, don't you think?"

"You're suffering from a failure of imagination. They're bound together. I'm sure of it." Megan looked out the window into the backyard, where wicker chairs surrounded a blue and white checkered table shaded by an ancient elm. Tomato plants, parsley, and other herbs overflowed the banks of a raised planter set against a brick wall. The tranquil scene contrasted with the turmoil in her mind, reinforcing her resolve to act. She turned back to Obadiah, her expression grim. "Theoretically, how would one go about shutting down a power grid?"

Obadiah swirled the wine in his glass, studying her. "By preparing to spend five to ten years in prison. I know what you're thinking, Megan."

"The only way to stop this Church is to deny the Prophet what he most desires. Dolores tried to destroy that damn machine. Seems to me I should finish what she started. Should be simple: cut the power and, in a matter of hours, the machine decomposes into a lake of radioactive slag."

"Dolores failed."

"I won't."

Obadiah rubbed his eyes with a thumb and forefinger. "Since then, security at the site has been hardened. The airspace is patrolled, there's twenty-four seven surveillance of the perimeter, and two additional backup generators have been put in place to handle the load in the event of a failure. Not to mention an armed security force that responds to threats immediately. There have been several attempts to breach the perimeter, none of which came close to harming the machine. Some of those attempts," he gave her a hard stare, "were planned incursions funded by hostile nations. You, Megan, don't stand a chance. Forgive me for saying so, but you're a terrible criminal."

"That sounds like a compliment."

"It's advice."

Megan wrapped her arms around herself, thinking back to a time she felt similarly unmoored. "Before you came to my house those many years ago, I packed a suitcase for what I thought would be my first trip to prison. In all this time, I never unpacked that bag, leaving it as a reminder of the sacrifices I would make to do the right thing. Recent events have only reinforced that commitment."

"Getting arrested is certainly a commitment," Obadiah said. "But it won't achieve a thing. You have a powerful voice and should continue using it. That interview connected with millions of people. You're only hearing from the worst and the loudest. Choose to live so you can fight another day."

"An idiom told to the helpless whose day may never come," Megan said, her mind drifting to the fate of her mother. "I've never told you this, but I've experienced firsthand the power of a charlatan. My mother thought she could find salvation by transporting her soul to a spaceship traveling on the other side of a comet. All her life, she searched for some sort of meaning and ended up grasping at a lie. Now she's dead."

"I'm sorry, Meg."

"I don't talk about it much." Megan gulped down a healthy dose of wine without tasting it. "Point is, another pretender has appeared. But I think this one can back up his claims. There's an adage that any sufficiently advanced technology is indistinguishable from magic. I think the same goes for miracles, with the means not being technology but some sort of Jedi mind-trick. That's not theoretical; that describes what we've seen of Stephen Fisher. And I'm not eager to find out what happens when his evil twin gets control of a portal that enables fanatics to travel between worlds. I don't know about you, but I'd rather try and fail than stand by and watch another prophet ruin people's lives."

"Getting arrested isn't going to help anybody. The best thing you can do is stay clear of trouble. Please."

"No chance of that."

Obadiah absently twisted his wedding ring, frowning at her. "I'd rather not tell you this, but you're forcing my hand."

That got her attention. "Oh?"

"Ten days after the inauguration, the new President will sign an executive order placing the Beacon under control of the Department of Homeland Security. Senator Wigfall has been chosen to lead that agency and will be more than happy to execute that order. He'll evict civilians from town and send in the military to take over the site. President Stoughton then plans to hand operations of the machine to the Church in gratitude for their support. That's not theoretical, that's the plan."

"He'll offend every ally we have, and enemies to boot."

"He wants the confrontation, not the compromise."

"How do you know all this?"

Uncharacteristically, Obadiah drained his glass and leaned forward with his elbows on his knees. "I've been thinking about the repercussions of the new administration for a long while. Stand down, Megan, your efforts won't just fail, they're unnecessary."

Megan cocked an eyebrow, her pulse quickening. "Hold on, are you planning something ill-advised?"

Obadiah's eyes took on a distant, introspective look as he slowly traced the rim of his wineglass with his index finger. Megan held her tongue, noting the tension in his jaw and the way his shoulders seemed to carry an extra weight. She knew that look—it was the same one he'd worn before divulging Max's role as a government informant. Megan waited him out, fearing that if she said anything, Obadiah would reconsider whatever it was he was about to divulge.

The silence stretched, broken only by the clatter of dishes as Marcello cleaned up in the kitchen. Finally, he spoke.

"It'll happen on inauguration day. When you're asked about this visit to my home, tell whoever it is that I assured you our duly elected representatives are acting in the best interests of this country. I also urged you to comply with the wishes of the new president."

"This doesn't sound like you at all," Megan said. "To be honest, it frightens me a little."

"You can thank that little girl."

"Melody? How does she factor in?"

"She allowed me to see the world through her eyes," Obadiah said. "It was only for a moment, but the experience led me to question everything I thought I understood. That includes my oath of office. I swore to defend the Constitution against all enemies, foreign and domestic. You may have identified a foreign enemy, but I suspect we have a domestic one as well. And he's about to take office."

CHAPTER TWENTY-THREE

Dad and I joined the dozen people milling outside what the gray-haired lady had called the orientation center, a squat utilitarian structure dwarfed by the spires of the canvas temple next door. The lady mentioned a test would be performed here, but what that involved remained a mystery.

Two guards, barefoot and bearded, wordlessly pulled the tent flaps aside and gestured for our group to enter. As we filed inside, the stuffy atmosphere hit us like a wall. The air hung thick and warm, tinged with the acrid smell from flickering gas heaters. Beneath our feet, the ground was a damp, yellowing grassy lawn, slick from the rain seeping in from outside. Bare patches of dirt showed through in spots, squelching softly underfoot. Fake candles dotted the space, their artificial glow casting wavering shadows on the canvas walls. Three women in shimmering violet robes sat behind plastic folding tables, greeting us with serene and unwavering smiles.

At the back, another group of people faced a raised wooden platform where a girl about my age rummaged through a pink flowered backpack. She wore a dress patterned with white daisies, her dark complexion contrasting with the auburn ponytail that swayed as she moved. The girl pulled a tablet from her backpack and placed it on her lap, completely ignoring the people staring at her. Propping her elbows on her knees, she focused on the screen. Judging by her blank expression and the lavender current running through her mind, the girl was bored.

She was also a traveler.

One of the bearded guards stepped onto the platform and placed two fingers over his heart. "Repeat after me," he instructed the small crowd. "As a patriot of faith, I attest allegiance to the teachings of the Divine Prophet. I am a shepherd, ambassador, and sword given sacred power to be a watchman over this world and a steward to its children…"

The people mindlessly echoed back the words. Once finished, the guard handed each a badge and escorted them from the room.

One of the violet-robed women, her hair bound in a halo-like braid, rose from a table and approached us. There was an eagerness in her wide-set eyes that bordered on fervent as she extended her hand to my father. "Good day, my name is Glee. Welcome to the Church of the Prophet."

"Hello," Dad said. "I'm Eric and this is my boy, Stevie."

"Are you what they call a disciple?" I asked.

"Oh, heavens no," Glee said. "I'm an acolyte of the second triad, though I aspire to rise further in the celestial hierarchy." She gestured toward the table. "Please follow me."

After we were seated, Glee handed my dad a clipboard. "Information for the church directory," she explained.

Dad looked it over with a frown. "Why are you asking for a credit card?"

"That's for your monthly tithe. I recommend starting at twenty percent of your gross income, though you're welcome to commit more. Most of our congregation pledges at least twenty-five percent." Glee's smile widened. "Remember, the love of money is the root of all kinds of evil. Better to rid yourself of that now. Besides, salvation is priceless, and eternal life even more so. Wouldn't you agree?"

Dad pushed the clipboard back across the table. "I was hoping to attend a service first, then decide."

Glee's smile didn't waver. "Of course, you can have temporary badges, though you will have to view the service from our visitor gallery. I still need to ask a few questions before you access our sanctuary, if that's alright?"

"I guess so."

"Excellent. Let's get started, shall we? First question, does your son talk to himself or speak in tongues?"

Dad's eyebrows shot up, his jaw dropping slightly. "Are you serious?" He glanced at me before turning back to the questioner with an incredulous shake of his head.

"That's a no." Glee made a note on a pad of paper. "Next question, has your son ever experienced what you might perceive as a seizure?"

"What does a medical condition have to do with anything?"

"We care about the welfare of our young." Glee leaned over the table, meeting my eyes. "Stevie, have you ever dreamed of living in another place, speaking another language, or occupying a different body? It's okay to share, as many children have these same fantasies. You wouldn't be the first nor the last."

Dad eyed the exit. "This is ridiculous."

I wasn't so sure, as these questions seemed designed to flush out travelers. If I was right, what was their objective? I glanced at the next table, where another kid, obviously nervous, sat with this mother. "No, Ma'am," I said, returning my attention to the acolyte. "Why is that important?"

"The Beast is devious and takes many guises," Glee said. "I saw you hesitate. Don't you ever imagine having lived somewhere else? There's no reason to lie."

"Move on," Dad said, his voice taut.

Glee flippantly waved a hand. "Only following protocol. No worries, we'll skip to the last test, then you can be on your way." She pulled a metal rod from beneath the table, identical to the one I'd seen carried by the guard at the temple entrance. It was a couple of feet long, with a thick wooden handle and a shaft that ended in two blunt silver prongs. "This is a spiritual attunement rod," she said, tapping the prongs against her palm. "See? Perfectly harmless. At most, you'll feel a little tingle. Some kids say it tickles."

"Enough," Dad said too loudly, prompting the bearded man near the platform to move toward us. Glancing over my shoulder, I saw two other blue-robed guards closing in as well. I didn't have to look to feel the traveler's attention swivel our way. "Come on, Stevie, we're leaving."

Before I could react, the woman pinned one of my arms to the table and jabbed the shaft into my neck. My head exploded with fire and my back arched. Music, my constant companion, slipped out of reach as my vision faded to gray. I vaguely heard somebody yell, "We have a live one!"

In that infinitesimal space between ignorance and pain, I understood the purpose of this rod. Something similar had happened to my former incarnation, who was bound to a metal slab when he was about my age. He had lost all sense of who he was after that—a tragic mistake that had led to many problems that continued to this day. But that was an accident. This was purposeful. Instead of a doctor placing electrodes on my head, these were at the end of a club wielded by a soldier intent on flushing out travelers, severing their link to the conscious plane. The Church must consider travelers a threat, to be disarmed by forcing them to forget their origins.

Except this traveler could defend himself.

Through the hand gripping my arm, I redirected the pain coursing through me into Glee. Her eyes flew wide, mind blazing white. Still clutching the shaft, she toppled from the chair. I spun around, taking in three men wrestling with my father. As I watched, Dad elbowed one of them in the face.

Dropping from the chair to the ground, I turned my head and locked eyes with the girl, now standing on the wooden platform, gaping at me in astonishment. Then I slapped my palm onto the living earth.

Though soil wasn't as effective a conduit as human flesh, I could still feel them all: the puzzled traveler, the shock of the innocents who accompanied us into the orientation center, the anger of my father, and the rage of his assailants. Into those three bearded men, I plunged the fingers of my will...and squeezed.

The nearest assailant sank to the floor, curling into the fetal position. The next grabbed his head and reeled against the canvas wall, silently opening and closing his mouth like a fish. The third blinked before collapsing onto the ground, blood running from his ears. My dad whipped around, picking up a dropped club and holding it out like a sword. Cries of alarm rang out from the aspiring congregants at the other tables.

The girl yelled at the top of her lungs, "Everybody out! Out, out, out!"

People immediately converged on the exit, keeping well clear of the bodies on the ground. The bearded man against the wall rubbed his eyes until the girl ran over and kicked him in the shins, then pushed him toward the exit. Once everybody had left, save for the unconscious, the girl closed the tent flap and turned around.

I got to my feet and joined my father, who immediately placed a hand on my shoulder, his voice laced with concern. "Are you hurt?"

"No," I said, though my body still buzzed with adrenaline.

He nodded, then winced as he rubbed his elbow. "Did you take out those people?"

"No choice," I said, a twinge of guilt twisting my insides. That acolyte may never get up.

Dad raised his eyes to the girl, who stood silent and still, clenching and unclenching her fists. "Is that who I think it is?"

"A traveler," I confirmed.

A note of worry crossed my dad's face, his mind already churning. "I thought they were in hiding."

"They should be."

He tugged at my arm. "Maybe we should discuss this in the car."

"Not yet," I said, curiosity overriding caution. "She's what I was looking for: the something that's not right."

The girl finally spoke up: "My people won't detain you unless I order it. Now, who are you and why are you here?"

"I need to talk privately with this one," I said to my dad, then approached the girl, coming within an arm's length.

We stared at each other in silence, a pale-yellow rivulet of uncertainty flowing through her mind. She didn't recognize me. So, I dropped the veil obscuring my thoughts.

The girl stumbled back a step. "You," she breathed.

"Me," I said, just one child among billions. But to the denizens of planets bound to a beacon, I had many names—the Finder of Worlds, the First, the Last, the Undying One, and the Unbound. Yet I knew myself as a destroyer of civilizations, exactly what I feared somebody behind this church was trying to do here. That stain didn't come clean, no matter how many lives I strove to protect.

"You stranded me here," the traveler accused. "No way will these people let me into the Beacon."

"Activating it was a mistake," I said. "I'm sorry."

"No kidding."

"What are you doing here?"

"What you won't," she said, bitterness lacing every word. "Imagine my surprise when I woke to parents who believed I was crazy. Then I found myself ruled by a government that would hunt me down if they knew I existed. I hear you learned that lesson firsthand—murdered by a maniac."

"They're not all like that," I said, repeating what I had told the envoy from Lumina Minor. I wondered if I really believed it.

"Enough of them are. Too many."

"Then you understand why activating the machine was a mistake. But you put these people in jeopardy by leading them to believe somebody other than themselves will save them."

Crystalline shards hardened in the currents of the traveler's mind. "Not all are willing to give up everything for the sake of non-interference. Unlike you, I can't get off this rock without a beacon. If I die here, all my family, friends, and loved ones will be forever lost, never to be recalled again. But I expect that means nothing to one such as yourself."

"That's not true," I insisted.

"So you'll tell yourself when you leave me behind. But I choose to walk another path, a better path that will both take me home and offer hope to a people that would otherwise destroy themselves."

"Nothing is certain, especially that."

"Except your arrogance," she said.

"I call it experience. You don't have to like me, but you need to understand what you're doing carries great risk."

The girl scoffed.

"Are you who they call the Prophet?" I asked, getting to the question that mattered.

Tinkling laughter rang out. "I am a speck of dust compared to one far more ancient than yourself. He is more savior than prophet, promising to deliver everlasting life to his Chosen. True to his name, he knew you'd seek me out. And bid me to deliver a message."

She lifted her eyes and wrinkled her nose in thought before reciting: "I raise the fist of judgment against sacrilege. With great vengeance and furious rebuke, I will wipe you from existence and destroy all that you have built. Only then, when I have inflicted my revenge, will the Chosen recognize the return of the Lord of Light."

A cold dread settled in my stomach. I'd heard similar threats before, couched in different terms, from a foe I thought defeated long ago. "Does this prophet have a name?"

"You'll find out soon enough," the girl said.

"What does that mean?"

"It means the Prophet has known where to find you ever since you arrived on these shores."

CHAPTER TWENTY-FOUR

Megan watched the live broadcast of the presidential inauguration inside her office at ISBLIC headquarters with a mixture of revulsion and morbid fascination. Instead of the traditional swearing-in ceremony at the U.S. Capitol in Washington, D.C., President-elect William Stoughton stood beneath the arched entrance of the Grand Temple—a place she had vowed never to visit again.

Beside him stood the Prophet, dressed in cotton twill pants and an unbuttoned linen shirt. Stiff-necked political dignitaries, including Senator Wigfall, looked on, while white-robed disciples gazed adoringly at their cult leader. Joybelle wasn't in attendance, leaving Megan to wonder at her absence.

The Prophet turned toward the camera, his intense gaze seeming to bore straight into Megan. He clasped the President-elect's hands between his own, directing Stoughton to repeat after him.

"As a patriot of faith, I attest allegiance to the teachings of the Divine Prophet. I am a shepherd, ambassador, and sword given sacred power to be a watchman over this world and a steward to its children…"

Megan's gut twisted into a knot, for she knew the rest. She had seen it posted on the signboard at a kiosk in the temple courtyard. When the Prophet finished the dedication, the sycophantic new President mindlessly echoed back his words, concluding with, "In return for my sacrifice, I will be granted an eternal life."

The Prophet raised Stoughton's hand over his head, prompting a chorus of acclamations to pour from the audience. The camera panned out, capturing the tens of thousands of people lining the steps and filling the courtyard. A fitting event for a demagogic puppet of an aspiring theocrat, Megan thought. Disgusted, she turned off the broadcast.

For long minutes, she twirled a ballpoint pen through her fingers, more determined than ever to frustrate the aspirations of this church, though she had no idea how.

Since waking up this morning, she had braced herself for the obscure event Obadiah had hinted would occur on inauguration day. But so far, nothing. It was to be expected, she supposed, for the same reasons that made her feel so helpless. What could one do against the combined power of the federal government and a movement of pseudo-religious fanatics? Answer: not much.

A chime rang from her computer, piercing the newfound silence like the blade of an executioner's sword. Megan glanced at the screen, which identified the caller as Buzz, the head of security. Her heart skipped a beat, wondering if Obadiah had followed through. She answered, striving to keep the tremor in her hand out of her voice, "Everything okay, Buzz?"

"Yes, Ma'am," he said. "Except for the military squadron that just pulled up outside the main gate. The commanding officer would like a word."

Megan's throat constricted, then relaxed as she realized the military showing up had nothing to do with Obadiah and everything to do with the new President's campaign promise to renationalize the Beacon. She was just surprised he had acted so quickly. "It's been a pleasure working with you, Buzz. I'll do what I can to make sure you land on your feet."

"It's been an honor, Ma'am, and don't bother. I'm retiring."

Megan lowered her head. "I'm thinking of doing the same thing. All right, I expect our guest is getting impatient. Put them on."

A crop-haired woman appeared on the screen, introducing herself as Captain Emerson. She informed Megan that her unit was taking command of the site per the Executive Order. The Beacon was to be nationalized and operations transferred to the military. All civilians, except for essential personnel, were to evacuate immediately or face forcible removal.

"Does my company have permission to enter?" the captain asked.

Megan's gaze drifted from the screen to her barren office in the nearly deserted building, the eerie silence a stark reminder of recent events. Most of the staff had already departed, turning Mercury into a ghost town. Only a skeleton crew remained, essential for ongoing operations. Megan intended to go down with the ship.

As the reality of the situation sank in, the room seemed to close in around her. Her vision blurred, years of carefully laid plans dissolving before her eyes. Everything she'd worked for had slipped away, and there wasn't a damn thing she could do about it. She sighed heavily, then turned her attention back to the waiting captain. "You don't need my permission."

"This isn't personal, Doctor McCullough. As you surely know, I'm following orders from our new Commander-in-Chief. A smooth transition would be in everyone's best interest. I'd especially appreciate your assistance because, frankly, I have no idea what I'm about to inherit here."

Megan found it difficult to be rude to such a polite invader. "There won't be any trouble. There's hardly anyone left anyway. I understand you're just doing your job."

"Thank you, Doctor McCullough. I appreciate your coop—"

The screen went dark. The lights flickered off. And an alarm sounded.

Megan sprang from her chair, her stomach tightening. Peering out of the sixth-floor office window, she saw blinking traffic lights and only a couple of vehicles on the road. To the west, a spire of black smoke billowed directly above the primary electrical substation. To the north, flames engulfed the secondary substation, which also housed the backup generators. An attack! And it had to be due to Obadiah. There was no joy in that thought, only a profound sense of dread.

With trembling fingers, she set a timer on her mobile device for two hours and seventeen minutes—the critical window before the Beacon, without power, would deteriorate into a pool of radioactive slurry.

Adrenaline surging, she bolted from her office and raced down the hallway. Taking the stairs two at a time, she descended toward the Emergency Operations Center in the basement. The eerie crimson glow of emergency lights illuminated her path, casting long shadows that chased after her. Her phone chimed repeatedly, but she ignored it, focused solely on not stumbling down the stairwell.

As Megan burst into the EOC, she was met with a flurry of activity. The room was already abuzz with staff trained to handle such crises. Her eyes darted from screen to screen, taking in the situation.

The main display blinked red along the electric transmission corridor leading into town, while another showed a live feed of the primary substation engulfed in flames. Several screens were ominously blank—a sign that cameras were down, including those monitoring the Beacon itself. Smaller displays cycled through weather and news stations, none of which had caught wind of the emergency.

The arc-shaped room was sparsely populated, with only essential personnel manning the stations for command, communication, logistics, and operations. All were engaged in urgent phone conversations, including Tom, the Director in charge. Until now, his job had been to document procedures and oversee drills based on simulated scenarios. But this was no drill. They faced the worst-case scenario: a power failure that, if not restored, would cause the draconium of the Beacon to become unstable and release radioactive isotopes into the atmosphere.

Tom rushed toward Megan, his hand covering the mouthpiece of his phone. In a staccato burst, he rattled off the status.

"Power's out across southeast Nevada, including Vegas. The utility is dispatching troubleshooters. We've had explosions at both the primary and secondary on-site substations—they're completely out of commission. The solar array remains functional, but without the substations, we can't feed power to the Beacon."

He paused, his breaths shallow and rapid. Megan didn't need to feign alarm, it was genuine.

"I saw the smoke," she said. "Do we know what caused the explosions?"

Tom nodded grimly. "The rapid response team was pre-positioned in the area. They expected trouble, but got more than they bargained for. They're on the line now." He thrust the phone into her hand.

"Megan here. What's happening?"

A breathless voice replied, each word punctuated with anger: "A swarm of kamikaze drones took out every transformer, including the spares. Another swarm destroyed the batteries. Two transmission towers leading to the substations are down as well. We haven't assessed those yet. This had to be an inside job."

Megan's heart pounded. "Is anybody hurt?"

"No, Ma'am."

She pressed her palm to her chest, taking a deep breath. Though the attack wasn't her doing, she felt responsible nonetheless. "Contact Buzz," she said, her voice steadier than she felt. "Have him secure the base. Nobody in or out until he receives orders from the EOC Director. And be advised, there's a military column inside the perimeter. They could help."

"Copy that."

Megan handed the phone back to Tom. "What's the direction of the prevailing winds?"

Tom tapped a keyboard and pointed at the leftmost screen at the front of the room. Small arrows overlaid a satellite map of the territory. "Northeast, eleven knots."

"And the forecast?"

Tom opened the weather app, dragging the timeline out three days. "Winds will remain northeast, lessening to four knots…away from population centers."

Megan breathed a sigh of relief, echoed by Tom. Obadiah had chosen the moment well: minimize casualties while depriving the Prophet of his toy.

The hand of the communication station operator shot into the air, fingers splayed. "The Governor is on line one."

"I'll handle it," Megan told Tom, striding over to take the call. "Governor, this is Megan McCullough, Director of ISBLIC."

"Your people contacted my Chief of Staff," the Governor said curtly. "Be quick, I'm at my kid's ballgame."

Megan summarized the situation, concluding, "The radiation release is equivalent to a fifteen-kiloton nuclear blast. There's no explosion, so the radioactivity will be contained. But isotopes spread with the wind. Our models predict fallout will dissipate to safe levels within seventy-two hours. As a precaution, all residents in surrounding areas should shelter in place, especially northeast of the site. You need to activate the state's Emergency Operations Center."

A pause, then a string of expletives. "My office will be in touch," the Governor said, then hung up.

Before Megan could catch her breath, Captain Emerson swept into the room. "Can someone tell me what just happened?" she asked, her voice clipped.

Megan gave a rapid-fire account of recent events, concluding with the Governor's call. She yanked a hefty manual from the shelf, its cover screaming 'Emergency Operating Procedures' in bold red. "As of this moment, you're the officer in charge." She dropped the manual onto the table with a reverberating thump and pointed at Tom. "I suggest you follow the guidance from the Director of Emergency Operations. He's ex-military, so you have something in common."

Tom only stared at the woman. The Captain stared back, then turned to Megan, backing up a pace. "Like I said, I need your assistance, Doctor McCullough. I have no intention of taking over. Just let me know how my people can help."

"An excellent decision," Megan said. "First off, reinstate Buzz as head of security, and follow his orders to secure the site. Once that's done, escort non-essential personnel off the premises. Shouldn't be more than a couple dozen at this point, mostly laggards." She eyed the countdown on the screen, mirroring the one on her phone. "You have one hundred and twenty-two minutes before things go to hell."

Tom chimed in, "You need to get your people in protective gear."

"Will do," said Captain Emerson. "One question: why attack the substations and not the machine? I presume that's the target."

Megan explained, "Once the Beacon activated, the alien material hardened. A diamond-tipped drill doesn't even scratch it. We tried. That's not a secret, and the attackers will know this. Bottom line, no chance an explosive would do any damage."

"Understood."

As the Captain barked orders to secure the site, Megan sank into a chair to handle the barrage of calls from local law enforcement, federal officials, the press, and every politician imaginable. And those were just the calls escalated from the Communication Station. No matter the jurisdiction or the person on the line, the questions boiled down to "What happened?", "How the hell could you let this happen?", and "What do we do now?" The answer to the last question was simple—people needed to stay indoors. To that effect, the Governor's office issued an emergency alert for residents and travelers to remain inside their homes or hotel rooms. The result was clogged traffic on every highway leading south. Fortunately, the winds remained favorable and there were no further attacks.

Amidst the hubbub, Megan fielded a call from the CEO of the utility, reporting that the transmission towers brought down by explosives had been repaired by stringing conduit between temporary structures. Power had been restored. But it didn't matter. The substations feeding electricity to the machine were down for the count. The die had been cast: the Beacon would be destroyed.

Megan should have been happy about that, but found herself conflicted. The alien machine could have opened minds and changed history, but instead, would become a casualty of a movement that amplified people's worst instincts.

At thirty minutes until doomsday, Joybelle Leroux glided into the command center, her flowing white robes a stark contrast to the protective gear worn by everyone else. Megan shot her a scathing glance before returning her attention to the videoconference with the state's EOC.

Joybelle's voice cut through the room. "The fifth angel poured out his bowl on the throne of the Beast, and his kingdom became full of darkness."

Tom's conversation with his counterpart at the state stuttered to a stop. Captain Emerson, having returned from securing the site, tilted her head, trying to decipher Joybelle's meaning.

With a serene smile, Joybelle continued, "The President has authorized the Church of the Prophet to take possession of the Beacon and this base. I am its caretaker, and you, Captain, are the means to make that happen."

"Yes, Ma'am," said Captain Emerson, shifting uncomfortably. "But I'm afraid your charge is about—"

Joybelle raised a hand, silencing her. "Fear not, for what can man do against the throne of heaven?"

"I'm sorry, what?"

Megan stepped forward, noticing with some satisfaction the flesh-colored bandage affixed over Joybelle's button nose. "She means there's nothing to worry about."

The Director at the state EOC intervened, his voice crackling through the speaker, "Can we deal with whatever this is later, please?"

Tom waved Joybelle off to the side. With a slight bow, Joybelle took Captain Emerson by the elbow and guided her out of the room. Megan, sensing trouble, followed close behind, catching the tail end of their conversation.

"… your orders were to assist me in any way possible," Joybelle said, her tone sharp. "I expect you to do that, starting right now."

Unable to resist, Megan interjected, "This isn't the best time, Priestess. Besides, don't you have a goat to sacrifice?"

Joybelle briefly closed her eyes, breathing through her nose. "I believe civilians were to be escorted from the area, Captain Emerson, especially this one."

"Given the emergency—" the Captain started, but was silenced by Joybelle's open palm.

"Your fears are misguided. What I require of you now is an aircraft and pilot to execute the order you failed to accomplish."

Captain Emerson's jaw tightened. "I won't put the men and women under my command at risk. Or civilians, for that matter."

"With one call, I can have you relieved of command. But I'm not unreasonable and will leave it to the civilian to decide." Joybelle turned to Megan. "Before you're banished to the wilderness, Doctor McCullough, I invite you to join me on the aircraft. Together, we shall see the Prophet's will be done."

Megan bit back the harsh words on the tip of her tongue, her confidence wavering. Did Joybelle know something? Either way, Megan wanted to be there when the object of Joybelle's desire turned to slag.

"Captain, I suggest you give her the pilot," Megan said. "Given the cameras are out, I'll provide real-time status to the EOC of what's happening on the ground. Should be perfectly safe if we stay downwind."

Begrudgingly, Captain Emerson agreed.

◆

From the vantage point of a helicopter hovering 1,500 feet in the air and downwind of the inevitable fallout, Megan looked out over the sea of solar panels laid out in neat rows on a bare plain pockmarked with craters from past nuclear weapon tests. In the middle of this glass sea, earthen walls surrounded the black dome of the Beacon. Beside her, Joybelle murmured, "Heaven's Gate," her eyes fixed on the structure below.

Megan spoke into the open line to the EOC. "Once the Beacon decomposes into the heavy elements and rare earths that created the alloy, gamma rays used in the forging process will be released. All that should remain is the titanium superstructure of the outer dome along with a lake of toxic material." She paused, pondering whether the machine would collapse or slowly melt away like a scoop of ice cream in the sun. Either way, the result would be the same. "What's the time, Tom?"

"Sixty seconds," he said, his voice tense. The chatter within the EOC subsided, leaving only the muffled sound of the helicopter's rotors to fill the space. Megan fit the rebreather over her mouth and checked the seals of the hazmat suit. Joybelle dismissively waved away another suit offered by the co-pilot, her confidence unwavering.

"Ten seconds," Tom reported over the headset.

Megan strained her eyes against the midday sun to keep the Beacon in sight. She waited, waited some more, and then some more. "Was the power somehow restored?" she asked into the headset.

"No, Ma'am," Tom replied. "What's happening there?"

"Standby." Megan tore off the mask and raised the binoculars to her eyes. The structure remained standing. There was no collapse, no dripping material, no exposed superstructure. Nothing.

Slowly, Megan turned to face Joybelle, who stared back at her with folded hands and a knowing smile on her ruby-red lips. After muting the microphone on the headset, she asked, "How did you know?"

Joybelle bowed her head toward the Beacon, her voice calm and assured. "No craft of man can close Heaven's Gate once it's been opened. Not nuclear fire and certainly not a power switch, so says the Prophet."

That possibility had never crossed Megan's mind, and there had been no way to test it until this very moment. "The draconium stabilized when the Beacon activated," she thought aloud, realization hitting like a thunderbolt.

Joybelle gave a curt nod, then raised her voice to speak to the pilot. "We've seen enough. Please drop us outside the main gate. I'll guide you to an appropriate spot."

The helicopter touched down on a barren stretch of desert, far from any signs of civilization. The only landmark was a lonely highway cutting through the scrub-dotted landscape. As Joybelle slid open the hatch, she handed Megan a water bottle. Megan stepped out onto the asphalt, the heat rising in shimmering waves, and turned to face Joybelle.

Over the roar of the rotors, Joybelle called out, "May the Prophet deliver you from the wilderness."

Megan locked eyes with her. "The leader of your church is a villain, Joybelle," she said, and repeated the verse she had once told her mother about another false prophet: "When he lies, he speaks his native language."

Joybelle reached into the folds of her robe and retrieved a small object, tossing it onto the road at Megan's feet. "Nothing is covered that will not be revealed or hidden that will not be known. Farewell, Megan, though this won't be the last time we meet, for the Prophet has foreseen your fate as being intertwined with another."

"And who might that be?"

A cryptic smile played on Joybelle's lips. "A demon in the guise of a child." She slammed shut the hatch and in a rush of blades and a flurry of sand, the aircraft rose into the air, leaving Megan to shield her eyes from the flying debris.

As the sound of the rotors faded into the desert silence, Megan's gaze fell on the item lying on the sun-baked asphalt: a textured tungsten ring inlaid with gold. Her breath caught in her throat.

Obadiah's wedding band.

CHAPTER TWENTY-FIVE

L ight rain pattered against the canvas walls of the church's orientation center, which to me seemed more like an indoctrination camp. My father and I stood together, looking at the traveler—a little girl wearing a dress patterned with white daisies. She stood astride the sole exit, defiantly staring into my eyes.

"We're leaving," I told the girl. "Try to stop us, and I'll do to you what I did to your people."

The girl cast a fleeting glance at the bodies of the two men and the woman sprawled on the ground, her mind betraying cool indifference. "You'll get no interference from me," she said, stepping aside and parting the tent flap.

Dad led the way, armed with a metal prod seized from one of the attackers. Immediately, six figures cloaked in blue robes emerged from the shadows, forming a barrier to block our retreat. My dad swung the prod, but they continued to close. Before I resorted to my own form of violence, I glanced over my shoulder.

The traveler emerged from the tent, appearing only as a silhouette against the amber glow spilling from inside. With an impatient gesture, she commanded the men to stand down, which they did, fading back into the shadows from which they came.

My dad grasped my hand, and we broke into a trot toward our vehicle. People who had evacuated the orientation center pointed at us as we fled. The gray-haired lady who'd greeted us on arrival cried out for someone to apprehend the "demons". When I looked behind us, the girl had vanished, and the blue-robed men were nowhere to be seen.

Mud flew as my father sped the car out of the dirt lot. Once on the open highway, he kept looking in the rear-view mirror. But nobody followed, nor did I sense anyone near. Though the ease of our escape caused me some disquiet, I dared to breathe easier as we put distance between ourselves and the temple.

"Are you hurt?" Dad asked, his voice heavy with concern.

I rubbed my temples, trying to soothe the throbbing in my head caused by that acolyte's prod. "I just need to rest. Are we going back to the house?"

"That's where we're heading," he said, then paused. "Stevie, what did you do to that lady and those men?"

The image of the woman falling from the chair flashed through my mind, and I wondered if she'd ever wake up. Part of me—the eternal side—knew I had no choice. But the other part—the scared boy—felt crushed by guilt. Whether by mistake or on purpose, I kept hurting people. It seemed everything I did here turned to ash, making me feel like both a curse and a plague. Tears welled in my eyes. "I didn't mean to hurt anybody."

Dad reached over and ran his fingers through my hair. "It's not your fault. You defended us. Who knows what would've happened otherwise?"

I did, but that knowledge didn't make me feel any better.

"You said that girl was a traveler," he continued. "But Melody claims they're here to help."

"That one's more interested in helping herself."

"What did she say to you?"

"That she's stuck and wants to go home. That's why she was so mad."

"Seemed to be more than that." Keeping one hand on the wheel, Dad raised the metal prod from his lap. "What did this thing do to you?"

"Can I see it?"

He handed me the prod. It was lighter than I expected, with a dime-sized button set flush against the wooden handle. I pressed the button, and a snap of electricity crackled from the prongs at the end of the shaft. Steeling myself, I tapped my palm against the metal conductors. A jolt surged through me, far stronger than any shock I'd ever felt. Gasping, I jerked my hand away, my headache intensifying.

As I suspected, the device had been calibrated to deliver a burst of energy to disrupt a traveler's link to the conscious plane. Any doubts I had about the Church's intent were now erased.

Dad snatched the prod from my hands. "Why did you do that?"

"A test. That prod makes a traveler forget who they are and where they come from. The same thing happened to your brother when he was a kid, lying on that cold metal table."

Dad almost swerved off the road. "How did you know about that?"

"I listen when you and Mom talk," I said, which wasn't exactly a lie—they discussed Stephen Fisher a lot. "Your brother lost all memory of who he was because of what happened on that table. This prod does the same thing."

"Does that church believe travelers are a threat?"

"Probably. We're not supposed to interfere, but sometimes travelers get involved and make things worse—much worse. We call them the Fallen. The Church is trying to find us because they know we'll try to stop them. But since we're just kids, we can't do much of anything."

"The prime directive. Makes sense."

"The prime what?"

"Never mind." He tossed the prod into the back seat. "Isn't that machine interfering? I mean, that's the root cause of all our problems."

"The Beacon never should have been turned on."

Dad gripped the steering wheel, his knuckles white. Silence stretched between us as he drove, until he finally spoke, his voice thick. "I should have been there for him at the end. My brother... I always looked out for him, you know? Kept him safe, especially when we were kids. But when it mattered most..." He trailed off, unspoken regret hanging in the air.

"He was trying to keep you safe," I said, knowing it was true.

"Stevie," Dad said, collecting himself. "Did you... did you ever meet my brother? Before he came here, I mean."

I stared into the distance at a dark smudge marring the horizon, unsure of what to say. Existence flowed as an unbroken chain of birth, death, and rebirth—a stream of consciousness that each person perceives as their own. In this current, the things we do, think, and experience shape who we are, much like a flame passing from one candle to another. Yes, I knew his brother, but I wasn't him, even though that life helped shape who I am. For a moment, I thought about telling him this, but feared I didn't have the right words.

"I knew *of* him," I finally said. "All travelers do, for there are few beings who can bind a world to a beacon. If he were here, he would tell you that everyone, including you, will move on to a new life. That's where he is now."

My dad slowly nodded, his expression thoughtful. Eventually, he cleared his throat. "What about this Prophet? Is he one of the Fallen?"

A good question, and one I hadn't stopped thinking about. If the Prophet was one of the Fallen, he must have arrived at the same time as my first incarnation on this world—which meant he didn't need a beacon to travel. A trick few could pull off, leading me to wonder yet again about his identity. "Maybe."

"You told me he's building an army."

"We just met some of his soldiers."

"How do we stop him?"

I chewed on my thumbnail, having pondered this dilemma since hearing Megan's story. Even if this Prophet died, he would only return. Like gum stuck to my shoe. "I don't know."

The rain faded, and a sliver of sunlight slipped from behind heavy clouds. My father leaned forward, narrowing his eyes at the growing smudge in the distance. As the minutes rolled by, the smudge transformed into a roiling cauldron that spread across the sky like a colossal umbrella.

Dad fumbled for his phone, his fingers shaking as he dialed Mom's number. My heart sank when the call went unanswered. He tried Aunt Franny next, but got the same result. I could see the panic in his eyes as he jammed the accelerator. The car lurched forward, making my stomach flip.

As we sped down the road, my eyes widened in horror. Flames danced on the rooftop of Max's mansion—our temporary refuge, where we'd left Mom, Melody, and Aunt Franny.

An officer on the roadside waved for us to pull over, but Dad didn't slow down. He swerved around the patrol car, tires screeching. We skidded to a stop next to a fire truck, and before I could even unbuckle my seatbelt, Dad was out of the car.

He sprinted toward the burning house, arms waving wildly at the flames, as if he could somehow beat them back. A firefighter caught him before he could get too close, but Dad struggled against the man's grip. I'd never seen him look so desperate.

Feeling a surge of dread, I stepped out of the car, only to be slapped in the face by a gust of heat that stole my breath away. With a sudden crack and resounding boom, the roof collapsed within the stone walls of the mansion, sending embers hurtling into the air. I heard my father howl. But despite the tragedy, I felt an unusual sense of calm.

Extending my awareness into the dimension that coexisted with our own, I followed an agitated vibration along a familiar thread until I sensed Melody's presence. She was alive. And the moment I realized this, the spectral manifestation of her face emerged amidst the flames raging above the ruins. Fear radiated from the turmoil in her mind, not for herself, but for Aunt Franny and Mom. But where were they?

Before I could delve deeper, the thread abruptly snapped, and the apparition disappeared, as though someone dangled bait only to snatch it away. That's when I realized they'd been kidnapped because of me. And I knew exactly where they would be taken: the place where I'm most vulnerable.

I jogged up to my father, who was on his knees, gazing at the flames with tears leaving tracks on his ash-stained cheeks. Despair filled his downcast eyes as he whispered, "I never should have left them."

"They're not dead," I said.

Dad didn't react, just dropped his head into his hands.

I shook his shoulder until he lifted his eyes to mine. "They're alive. Melody, Mom, and Aunt Franny."

"They're alive," he repeated, voice shaking.

"Somebody took them from the house and set the fire to cover their tracks."

"How do you know that?"

"The same way I knew that girl was a traveler. The Prophet knows we're here, and whoever took them waited for us to leave. You saw why they wouldn't want me around."

Dad sat back and licked his dry lips. I could see the change in his face and feel it in his mind–determination replacing despair, like a light switch being flipped. "Where are they?"

"I'm not sure, but I know where they'll be taken," I said.

PART III – THE BEAST

And the great dragon was thrown down, that ancient serpent, who is called the devil and Satan, the deceiver of the whole world—he was thrown down to the earth, and his angels were thrown down with him.

— Revelation 12:9

CHAPTER TWENTY-SIX

Megan waited at the side of the road outside her office at the University of California, Santa Barbara, her heart heavy as she watched the hired car approach, carrying Eric and Stevie on the final leg of their journey from Melbourne. Around her, students raced along bike paths and hurried down walkways, their carefree chatter a stark contrast to the grief that shadowed her every breath. Off the beach, paddle boarders navigated the sparkling water, framed by picturesque islands set against an azure sky. The cries of gulls mingled with the faint scent of seaweed carried on the breeze. A beautiful day that belied her reality.

As the car passed beneath Henley Gate and rolled to a stop, Megan rushed forward. The moment Eric and Stevie emerged, she enveloped them in a fierce embrace, her voice breaking, "I'm so sorry for your loss."

Though the local news reported the fire as a tragic accident, Megan suspected otherwise. But it didn't matter how the fire started, only that Tara, Fran, and Melody had suffered the most horrific deaths imaginable. And she had put them in harm's way. Her insistence that they leave the country, combined with her misguided attempt to clear her conscience by speaking out, had led a fanatic to make good on threats that had stalked this family for years. Everything Megan loved had now been taken from her—her work at ISBLIC, Dolores, Obadiah, and now members of a family she considered her own. If not for her actions, they would still be alive today.

"Thank you, Meg," Eric said, patting her on the back. Stevie squeezed her hand, as if she was the one who needed reassurance. "And thanks for getting us out of Melbourne. My credit cards didn't work, and my account had been drained. We had nowhere else to turn."

Megan pulled back, wiping away tears that weren't rightfully her own. "Of course, it's the least I could do. You'll be safe once we get to my house. Stay for as long as you need."

Stevie gently extricated himself from her arms, his haunted gaze far too old for his youthful face. "No place is safe, Aunt Megan."

The quiet conviction in the boy's voice settled like a leaden weight in her gut. He was right, of course. Stevie had spent his short life fleeing shadows, and now one had finally stolen his mother. Nothing she could do would ever bring Tara back. Swallowing past the lump in her throat, Megan reached out to cup Stevie's face. "I loved your mom like a daughter."

"She feels the same about you."

Megan pressed a hand to her chest, stifling the sob that threatened to escape from the bunker of her soul. He spoke as if his mother still lived. "That's very kind of you to say."

"It's true," he said, his gaze drifting across the bustling campus.

Eric collected their bags from the trunk and rejoined them as the hired car drove off. "I'm afraid we need another favor, Meg," he said.

Megan tried to collect herself. "Anything, anything at all."

"Don't agree until you hear me out. This one's a whopper."

Megan spread her hands. "Whatever you want, whatever you need. But keep in mind I don't have much pull these days. I've been exiled, vilified, and targeted. The crazies are crazier, politicians are calling for my arrest, and Obadiah can't help either of us anymore. My own colleagues avoid me like the plague. I'm lucky I had tenure at the university, or I wouldn't have a job at all."

Consternation clouded Eric's features. "What happened to Obadiah?"

Megan briefly closed her eyes against a wave of despair. She hadn't been able to reach him, and his husband was frantic. "I'm afraid O is… well, I'm not sure. What's the favor?"

"That will take some explaining."

A passing grad student waved to Megan, reinforcing her belief that the younger generation seemed immune to the Prophet's charms. Mustering a smile in return, Megan gestured for Eric and Stevie to follow. "Let's get out of the public eye, shall we? I'm sure you're hungry, and I've got a well-stocked fridge upstairs. This way."

◆

In the quietude of Megan's second-floor office, Eric sipped mango-flavored water while gazing out the window. Stevie absently munched on a green apple while examining the scale model of IGOR perched on her desk. They both seemed eerily calm, as if today were just another day.

Setting the water aside, Eric asked, "What do you know about this Prophet?"

"That he's a deluded demagogue bent on destroying the country," she said, an edge to her words.

"Besides that."

"All right, well, Joybelle, the disciple I told you about, claims he's not of this world. I believed her for a time. But it doesn't make sense; he's too old to have come through the Beacon." Megan paused, a sharp pang of grief hitting her as she added, "Melody agreed. Besides, we have plenty of bad actors already here, no need to import another."

Eric turned from the view to face her. "What if he's exactly what he appears to be?"

"Nothing changes. He's a threat, regardless of where he's from."

"It may change how we deal with him."

"Deal with him? You can't be serious. There's nothing we can do, Eric. Believe me, I've tried. Call the authorities. Tell them your suspicions. That fire was no accident."

Eric placed his hands on her shoulders, his grip almost painfully tight. "The Prophet took them—my wife, Fran, and Melody. They're still alive and we have to get them back."

Megan stared at him, stunned. Despite human remains having been pulled from the ashes, Eric still insisted his family was alive. Upon reflection, she understood. For weeks after her own mother had passed, she had walked around in a daze. Even after all these years, Megan still wondered if she could've done more to save her mom. "I want to believe you, I really do."

"The remains were planted," Eric said, his eyes intense with conviction. "Think about it, it's the perfect cover. If I report them missing, the authorities will just point to the ashes. No way to confirm their identity and no messy kidnapping charges. The Prophet's far too clever to have done the dirty work himself. He probably got one of his blue-robed goons to do it."

Megan frowned, trying to make sense of it all. "But what would the Prophet stand to gain by that?"

"Me," Stevie said softly. "He wants me."

Her heart clenched at the boy's words. She knelt and took his small hand in hers, unsure of what to say. Stevie didn't elaborate, only looked at her in that unsettling way of his.

Eric began to pace. "You already know about the travelers, right Meg? The ones that came through the Beacon?"

Rising to her feet, Megan wondered where he was going with this. "They're never far from my thoughts."

He stopped, fixing her with an intent look. "My son is one of them."

A mixture of disbelief and sorrow washed over Megan, reminding her of countless arguments with her own mother about outlandish beliefs. She swallowed hard, searching for the right words. "Oh, Eric…"

"I know you don't believe me. My wife doesn't either, but her doubts come from a different place. I think, deep down, she's afraid that Stevie wouldn't be her child anymore."

The boy moved to Eric's side. "She's wrong about that."

Eric dropped a protective hand on his son's shoulder. "She'll come around. But you, Megan, we don't have time to wrestle with your doubts. You're a scientist to the core and need tangible proof. I get it. Fortunately, you don't have to take my word for it." With that cryptic statement, he retreated to lean against the windowsill, leaving Megan face to face with the boy.

Stevie extended his hand. "This might feel weird."

More than a little nonplussed, Megan glanced at Eric. "What's going on?"

"Evidence," he said.

Again, Stevie proffered his small hand. "It won't hurt."

Megan stared at him, wondering if it could be true. At most, only a couple thousand drops had fallen inside the chamber. Assuming those drops equated to a traveler, the chances were vanishingly small Stevie could be one of them. Then again, the same was true for Melody. With nothing to lose, she grasped the boy's cool hand. And the world changed.

From within Stevie's guileless brown eyes came swirling currents that enlarged and combined into a vortex that filled the boy's head. Shimmering tendrils erupted from his skin, moving in time to the same melody she heard inside the chamber. Heart hammering, Megan risked a glance at Eric. Luminous filaments wreathed his form as well, his eyes twin maelstroms of light and color. Beyond the window, the trees shone with a lime-green radiance. And the ocean was awash with an array of brilliant hues.

"The past moves within us all," Stevie said. "In you, in me, and in every living thing."

"Beautiful," she murmured.

Stevie released his grip, and as suddenly as it began, the visions vanished. Megan staggered back, collapsing into an upholstered chair. "You're one of them."

"Now you understand," said Eric.

Megan took an unsteady breath, her mind reeling. Then a thought struck her. "You said they're alive!"

"That's right."

"The Prophet took my family to get to me," Stevie said, quiet but sure. "He thinks of himself as the Lord of Light, the guardian of all existence. But it's a lie, just like his promise that only he can grant his followers eternal life. I once stopped him from doing what he's trying to do here. He hasn't forgotten. Or forgiven."

Megan studied Stevie with fresh eyes, struck by the uncanny resemblance to Melody in his preternaturally mature manner of speaking. Struggling to reconcile the child before her with the traveler he claimed to be, she asked, "What does the Prophet hope to achieve by taking you?"

"Revenge. He's also afraid that I'll try to stop him. And he's right, because when the Prophet is done with this world, he'll lead his followers to another. That's why he wants the Beacon, and that's where we'll find him."

Megan clenched her jaw, squared her shoulders, and rose from the seat, shoving down her doubts and fears. Fate had placed her in the eye of this storm, and she'd be damned if she stood by and let it consume everything she held dear. Not again. Never again. "What can I do to help?"

Stevie turned to the window, his narrow shoulders rigid as he watched pelicans glide effortlessly along the cliffs outside the office. "I need you to take me to him."

CHAPTER TWENTY-SEVEN

Megan brought the car to a stop behind a line of vehicles stretching down the highway leading to the town of Mercury. In all her years traveling to ISBLIC headquarters, she'd never seen more than a handful of cars on this desolate stretch of road. But today, the traffic rivaled the congestion in the heart of Los Angeles.

The van in front of them pulled onto the dirt shoulder to park amidst a cluster of other vehicles. Well-dressed passengers filed out and joined the procession trekking toward the main gate. Megan parked behind the van and twisted in her seat to face Eric and Stevie in the back. "Not too late to change your mind."

Stevie's gaze wandered to the northeast, where she knew the Beacon lay hidden beyond the horizon. "It's the only way to save the people we love," he said.

"And you're okay with this, Eric?" Megan asked.

A fleeting grimace crossed his face. "Absolutely not. This smells like a trap, but I don't have a better idea."

"More a trade than a trap," Stevie said. "Them for me."

"That sounds a thousand times worse," Megan said. "But all right, putting aside what the Prophet wants with you, how do you know he'll let your family go?"

"Because he made me a promise."

Megan shifted uneasily in her seat. What lay behind that boy's unfocused gaze? And why did she find it so familiar? She didn't bother asking how the promise was made or why he believed it; she just accepted it. Melody had given her plenty of practice with that over the years, but that didn't mean she had to like it. "We could still call the police, Eric."

"And tell them what? That the President's biggest supporter kidnapped my family? With no evidence? Even if they believed me, which they wouldn't, the local cops would never raid a military base. Besides, I tried going to the authorities back in Melbourne. The police treated me like a suspect. Take my word for it: I like this situation less than you do."

Eric climbed out of the car with Stevie. Megan followed, only to have the heat slap her in the face. Even this late in the day, the temperature hovered around a hellish hundred and five degrees. She grabbed her floppy hat and an umbrella from beneath the seat.

While Eric took Stevie's hand, Megan did her best to angle the umbrella to protect them from the sun. Anxiety churned in her gut as they trudged through the sand toward the gate. Megan couldn't help but stare at the people plodding alongside them—everyone from young children to stooped octogenarians leaning on canes or towing portable oxygen tanks. Most wore beatific smiles, as if this grueling hike through the desert was no more taxing than a Sunday stroll. A profound sense of unease prickled along Megan's scalp. How could these people seem so normal, so benign, when in truth they served the cult of a megalomaniac?

Her spirits sank further as they passed a trio of handwritten posters thrust into the sand:

Out of the mouth of the beast come three unclean spirits. They assemble at the place called Armageddon. Where they will wage war on the Lord of Light.

He is clothed in a robe dipped in blood, and he is known as the Prophet. His eyes are like fire, and he has another name that no one knows but himself. From his mouth comes a sword with which to strike down the Beast.

Come, the Chosen of the Prophet, arrayed in fine linen, white and pure. Gather for the great battle, where the Beast will be thrown into the lake of fire, where you will be granted an everlasting life, and the Prophet will rule with a rod of iron.

Eric strode past the signs without sparing them a glance. Perched on his father's shoulders, Stevie kept his gaze fixed firmly on the ground. Megan swallowed past the tightness in her throat, trying to convince herself that the "unclean spirits" couldn't possibly be referring to their little group.

They joined a queue before the gate and as the line inched forward, Megan watched armed soldiers meticulously search every bag. Just inside the perimeter, women clad in flowing violet robes—acolytes of the church—moved among the crowd, sheltering beneath a sprawling canvas canopy. A fleet of converted school buses waited nearby. One trundled up the road as another pulled away. But it was the sleek black charter bus parked a short distance from the canopy that captured her attention, its darkened windows throwing back the harsh glare of the sun.

"Think they'll try to stop us?" Eric asked, keeping his voice low.

"No telling," Megan said. "But if they recognize me, just go about your business. I'll catch up."

"They're looking for us right now," Stevie said.

Fighting the urge to whip her head around, Megan instead covertly glanced to the side and up front. No one seemed to pay them any attention, but she didn't doubt Stevie's intuition. "Where?" she asked, her lips barely moving.

Stevie extended his pinky finger toward the black charter bus. "There. Five people inside."

Megan squinted against the glare, but the bus's tinted windows revealed nothing. Beside her, Eric's lips compressed into a bloodless line. They kept walking.

Once they arrived at the checkpoint, Megan raised her arms, submitting to an efficient but thorough pat-down. Eric lifted Stevie from his shoulders, then received the same treatment. The guards didn't bother to search the boy, only impatiently waved them through with no awkward questions or untoward glances. Megan breathed easier.

They joined another line that snaked toward the canopy. As they waited, Megan watched a beaming acolyte dip her finger into a stone bowl and trace the ankh-like symbol onto the brows of a family ahead of them—a middle-aged mother, her teenage son, and an elderly man she took to be the grandfather.

"May you live an undying life," the acolyte intoned before pressing a white robe into the grandfather's hands and motioning for the trio to board the waiting bus. The acolyte pulled out a cell phone and studied the screen while absently waving Megan and her companions forward.

Eric stepped up to the table. "I'll pass on the forehead art, thank you very much."

The acolyte didn't lift her head. "The seal is mandatory for all who enter the temple. No exceptions."

"Are you talking about the Beacon?" Megan asked, pasting on a brittle smile.

At that, the young woman looked up. Her jaw went slack, and her eyes darted between Stevie and Eric before the phone slipped from her fingers. She stumbled back a step, colliding with another acolyte at the next station. Megan didn't need to hear their frantic whispers or see the other woman wave at the black bus to know their cover was blown. People backed away, muttering among themselves, leaving them alone in a growing bubble of empty space.

"Well, they know we're here now," Eric said.

Megan opened her mouth to reply, but before she could get a word out, Stevie slipped from his father's grasp and started toward the black bus with single-minded focus. With a strangled cry, Eric launched himself after his son, shoving his way through the murmuring throng.

"Shit," Megan breathed, taking off after them both. She'd thought she understood what it meant to feel powerless in the past, but that was nothing compared to the dread now flooding her veins. She barely made it halfway to the bus when the doors hissed open, disgorging four barefoot, wild-haired men gripping prods. Megan recognized them at once—the Sword of the Lord.

Eric and Stevie stopped ten yards short of the men, and Megan skidded to a stop beside them, her heart jackhammering against her ribs. The Swords surrounded them, then looked toward the black bus, where Joybelle Leroux appeared in the doorway. Wearing a jeweled tiara and a loose-fitting robe that flowed around her like a silk pond, her crimson lips smiled upon them. Megan could smell her lavender perfume from where she stood.

"Where's my family?" Eric demanded of the disciple.

"Safe, I assure you," Joybelle said, gingerly lifting her robe, and gliding onto the dirt. "They are the Prophet's honored guests."

A flicker of relief passed through Megan. Despite assurances the family remained alive, she had no confirmation until this very moment. Judging by Eric's bowed head, he felt much the same. If Stevie shared that feeling, he gave no sign, only stared up at Joybelle with that disturbing gaze of his.

"Hostages, you mean," Eric said, his tone flat.

Joybelle's eyes swept past the boy before landing back on the father. "Unfortunately, that was the only invitation your son would understand. Did he tell you of the demon that lies within?"

Eric gripped Stevie's shoulder. "You know nothing about him."

Joybelle raised a hand to the sky, her gold bracelets jangling like shackles. "He is the Destroyer of Worlds, the Angel of the Abyss, and the King of Plagues. Only the Prophet can stop the Beast that intends to enslave this world. But not to fear. Once the evil has been expunged, your son will be returned to you—purified and whole. As will the rest of your family. Even the little princess who wandered so far from her flock, the traveler you call Melody."

"Don't you dare hurt that child," Megan said, seeing red.

A tinkling laugh, sharp as broken glass. "Ah, the Herald speaks!"

"Herald? Seems like you've demoted me to an unclean spirit."

"All but the Chosen are unclean. But worry not, you have played your part to perfection. With the Prophet's blessing, you may depart in peace, secure in knowing that your work has brought New Jerusalem that much closer."

Megan planted her feet. "I'm not going anywhere."

"As you will. You are of no further use to us. Come, Eric—if I may call you Eric—and bring the one you call a son."

"Don't trust a word she says," Megan warned.

Eric glanced past the Swords to the gate from which they had arrived. Megan could guess his thoughts—the guards were military, not part of the church. They might still get out of here. But the question occurred to her just as it surely occurred to him: What would become of his wife, Franny, and Melody? For that, she had no answer.

"I understand your suspicion," Joybelle said, "but I assure you, there is no need for deception. The truth is more than enough."

"Then I want proof they're alive," Eric said.

Megan couldn't agree more. Joybelle gestured to one of the Swords, who raised a cell phone. A moment later, an achingly familiar voice crackled through the speaker. "Eric? Is that really you?"

"I'm here, sweetheart," Eric said, his voice thick. "With Stevie and Meg. Are you alright? Are Franny and Melody with you?"

"Yes, but they took—" The Sword cut off the call while Joybelle looked on, smiling placidly.

Eric took a slow, measured breath, despite the anguish Megan saw in his eyes. "What happens next?"

Joybelle spread her hands in a parody of benevolence. "The Prophet will open the gates of heaven, where the veil will be lifted from your eyes. There, you will see the truth of all I have told you."

"What gate? What the hell are you talking about?"

"The Beacon," Megan translated. "Gaining control of the machine has been their objective from the very beginning."

Joybelle inclined her head. "The Herald speaks truth."

Eric stepped forward, prompting a Sword to lift his prod. But Joybelle dissuaded him with a flash of her eyes. "Let him speak," she commanded.

"I don't give a shit about your church, your prophet, or your delusions," Eric said. "Give me my family back."

"You care deeply for them," she said, her voice devoid of emotion. "But it is your son who controls their fate."

A vein pulsed in Eric's temple, causing Megan to place a restraining hand on his elbow. Violence would only make a bad situation worse. Besides, they were outnumbered a thousand to one. Eric shook her hand off.

Before he could do something foolish, Stevie strode forward to stand directly before Joybelle. He looked up at her in that disconcerting manner of his. "Your prophet is expecting me."

Tilting her head, Joybelle regarded Stevie for a long moment. "I admit, you don't look like much of a beast."

"The real beast stares back at you from the mirror."

Joybelle recoiled as if struck. "How dare you!"

"We are more alike than you know," Stevie said.

"The wicked whet their tongues like swords and aim bitter words like arrows."

"But you have the wrong target," Stevie said. "The Prophet isn't who you think he is."

"He is the Lord of Light that will open the gates of heaven so the Chosen may ascend."

"You know little about the Beacon, nothing about your prophet, and less about me."

"I know—" she began.

"That I'm the Beast, yes," Stevie interrupted. "Almost like you're trying to convince yourself."

Joybelle's lips thinned to a slash of crimson. "You make war on the Lamb, and the Lamb will conquer you, for he is the Lord of Light and the King of Kings—"

"Hold on," Megan cut in. "You told me that Stephen Fisher was the Lamb. Make up your mind."

"My brother was no lamb," Eric muttered.

With a flurry of her hand, Joybelle made the ankh-like sign over her bosom. "The blood of the Covenant runs through them both."

"That makes absolutely no sense," Megan said.

"Because the Prophet's wisdom is beyond your ability to comprehend."

"Or maybe it's you who don't understand," Stevie said. "The best lie is the one you want to believe."

Color bloomed on Joybelle's cheeks. "You are the Beast, the Destroyer, the Great Dragon of old, and you will be hurled into the Abyss where you belong!"

Megan was stunned by the naked vitriol in the woman's voice. In all their previous dealings, even when she'd abandoned her in the desert, Joybelle had been a creature of eerie calm, every word honeyed poison, every gesture calculated to disarm. To see her composure crack so utterly, so violently...

"It was you," Megan realized, the pieces realigning in her mind. "You ordered the family followed, then kidnapped, set the fire, everything."

Visibly struggling to master her emotions, Joybelle closed her eyes briefly. When she opened them again, her gaze was steel. "I alone see the truth of things, and I alone have the strength to do what must be done. As the Prophet's most faithful servant, I am the sword he wields without mercy."

Eric spat out some choice words concerning Joybelle's heritage, causing the Swords to edge closer to him.

Joybelle tossed her head, snapped "Enough," and gestured to the Swords. One grabbed Eric's wrist while another pulled his arm behind his back. Megan didn't think—she whirled around and jabbed the point of the umbrella into the privates of the nearest assailant. He gasped, dropping the prod.

"Stop," Stevie barked, or more like squeaked in that prepubescent voice of his. He pointed at Joybelle. "You know what happened to your acolyte in Melbourne. I don't want to do that again. I really don't. But I will."

Joybelle lifted her chin. "You think you can stop me?" she said, though Megan heard the manic edge beneath her contempt. "You can't stand against the might of the Prophet. He has shown me his secrets, taught me to wield power beyond your wildest imaginings."

"You can try these secrets on me if you want. But I'm warning you, those are empty words."

Megan shivered at the boy's implacable tone, the maturity in his manner, the eerie flicker in his eyes.

"I'll make this easy for you," Stevie continued. "Tell your guards to back off, and we'll come quietly."

For a long, stretching moment, no one moved. No one breathed. Megan noted the rapid flutter in Joybelle's throat, the tremor in her hands.

"You don't have to do this," Eric said to his son.

Stevie replied without taking his eyes off Joybelle. "There's no other way."

With a deep, shuddering breath, Joybelle brusquely nodded at the guards. Eric sloughed off his assailants with another curse. Megan scrambled to his side.

Straightening her back, Joybelle fixed Stevie with a look that was equal parts triumphant and unsettled. "The Prophet has commanded I escort you to the Holy Temple, which has been prepared as a bride adorned for her blessed husband."

CHAPTER TWENTY-EIGHT

The black bus cut through shimmering waves of heat as we journeyed toward the Beacon. Inside, I sat between my father and Megan on a white leather couch, the AC's frigid air raising goosebumps along my arms. Recessed lights bathed the polished wood floor in a warm glow, creating an uncomfortable contrast with the tense atmosphere. At the front, one blue-robed guard drove while another occupied the passenger seat, periodically turning around to ensure we behaved.

Across the aisle, Joybelle perched on the edge of a high-backed armchair, her spine as rigid as a steel rod. She openly stared at me. Only the low hum of the engine and occasional creak of leather dared to break the suffocating silence.

Curious about the mind behind those calculating eyes, I pushed aside the distractions of the physical world, allowing my perception to encompass the conscious realm. As my vision narrowed, a symphony of colors and sensations swirled around me, the edges blurring as I looked beyond Joybelle's penetrating gaze to confront a shielded mind. Another trick she must've learned from her prophet. But with a gentle push, I pierced through the veil, the patterns and hues becoming as familiar to me as my own heartbeat. Though her innermost thoughts remained hidden, her emotions lay bare.

Symmetrical currents moved within her mind, a sign of a determined yet inflexible will. Ripples of turquoise pulsed through those streams, suggesting elation—likely due to her success in capturing me. A thin finger of lime-green roiled through the center, indicating anxiety or excitement. She either feared what I'd do to her beloved prophet or looked forward to what he'd do to me. There was also curiosity, contempt, and a surprising streak of jealousy. But what I found most interesting was her attempt to shield her mind. In my experience, that meant one thing—she had a secret, one she desperately wanted to keep hidden. Sensing the intrusion, Joybelle averted her gaze to look out the window. Having seen enough, I did the same.

As we traveled along the two-lane highway, the Beacon appeared in the distance. Rather than the smooth black dome I had expected, this structure glowed white and was topped with spires that reached for the sky. Birds circled overhead, drawn to the thinning membrane between the conscious and physical planes.

The music in my head grew louder as we neared, causing reality to slip away like sand through an hourglass. My vision swam, and I once again found myself on a long-dead planet.

Peering through a blood haze overlooking a field of battle, I exulted in victory, believing the sacrifice of countless lives taken over generations a small price to pay to free my people from bondage. I then issued my final command: to round up every heretic on the planet. Further, to track down their mates, spawn, relations, and acquaintances. I ordered my forces to recycle them all and erase all records of their existence. Nothing would remain of the unbelievers.

Lost in these dark memories, I barely noticed the concerned glances Dad was casting my way. It wasn't until he squeezed my arm that I snapped back to the present.

"You okay, buddy?" he asked, his voice laced with worry.

I only nodded, fearing words would betray my anxiety. All I had really done on that forgotten world was replace one oppressor with another. Over time, I came to realize I served a lie and organized a revolt. But it took a hundred generations and untold suffering to overthrow the one who believed they were a god. Now, as we approached another beacon, I feared a repeat of that same tragedy.

Seeking an escape from Dad's scrutiny, I looked out the window.

A massive crowd had gathered around a stage at the base of the earthen mound surrounding the Beacon. Two giant screens showed a rock band performing, the singer's voice piercing the windows of the bus. People danced and sang to lyrics scrolling at the bottom of the screens. Lasers cut through the smoky air, flashing in time with the beat and painting the sky in a kaleidoscope of colors. The scene reminded me of a carnival, despite the sullen, blue-robed men patrolling the grounds. Food trucks and a forest of porta-potties waited on the outskirts of the party.

We passed a dirt lot where other buses dropped off passengers. Most people eagerly walked toward the event, while a smaller group of elderly individuals, clad in white, boarded a nearby tram. One of those trams cut in front of our vehicle, forcing our driver to slam on the brakes and honk the horn.

Joybelle's voice rang out, "Behold, the City of Heaven that has no need of the sun or moon to shine, for the glory of the Prophet gives it light."

Megan let out a contemptuous laugh. "You covered the dome with phosphorescent paint. You people are beyond ridiculous."

Dad stood up, causing the guard in the passenger seat to put a hand on the prod at his belt. "Where are they?"

"Rejoice in hope, be patient in tribulation, and constant in prayer," Joybelle said. "As prophesied, the blind will see, the deaf will hear, and the dead will rise again. Only then will your family be set free."

Fearing what he might do, I pulled on Dad's sleeve. "Melody is in there. Mom and Aunt Franny are somewhere else, scared but fine." Another waited for us as well, oppressive as a physical weight.

Dad sat back down, glaring at the guard. "All right, Stevie. I'm going to follow your lead here."

The crowd thickened as we neared the stage, the beat of music rattling my teeth. People jogged alongside the tram we followed, handing bouquets of flowers to the white-clad passengers, their faces alight with misplaced devotion. Some threw confetti onto the passengers, the colorful bits of paper fluttering in the desert wind. Others looked up at the darkened windows of our bus, wondering what lay within. If only they knew it was the Beast.

We came to a full stop before a jewel-encrusted arch. White smoke poured from the sides, creating the illusion of clouds. At the top, a neon sign flashed: "Welcome to New Jerusalem."

Two women wearing long purple robes opened the metal gate, revealing a golden path that wound its way up the earthen mound. Guards held back the crowd as we drove through, their expressions stern and unyielding.

"At the twelve gates were twelve pearls," Joybelle intoned, "and the street was pure gold, like transparent glass."

Megan leaned close to my father. "I'd be laughing if these people weren't so dangerous."

The bus climbed the hill, passing under a series of arches with numbers blinking above them—twelve in all. Statues of religious figures flanked each gate, their faces serene, hands outstretched in welcome. I presumed the intent was to make followers believe their prophet was a greater deity among lesser ones.

Megan offered snide comments all the way up. "Very subtle," "Those jewels can't be real," "What kind of paint did you use on the road?" and "Where's your statue, Joybelle?"

Joybelle bore the comments in silence, her eyes hardening with each gibe. But the lady was no fraud. Her devotion was as genuine as it was misguided. Generations ago, the being that called himself the Prophet took me under their wing as well. Like Joybelle, my gullibility had led me to take part in a plan of subjugation all too familiar.

The strategy was as methodical as it was insidious. First, amass a following by harnessing the conscious plane to enthrall believers, convincing them of your divinity. Then, use that influence to co-opt and corrupt those controlling the levers of power, securing their loyalty with promises of unending life. Finally, lead an uprising to subjugate the outliers who refused to comply, wielding the fervor of the Chosen as a weapon more powerful than any gun or bomb. The leader of this country had already bowed to the Prophet. Other nations would eventually fall in line, their resistance crumbling under demands from their own populace. Though it may take generations, the outcome was inevitable.

The road leveled out near the summit, and our bus parked in a clearing alongside an identical vehicle. The tram, however, continued its journey, disappearing into a tunnel carved through the heart of the mound. Beyond the tunnel lay an elevator leading to the Beacon's inner chamber. It was there the Prophet would fulfill his promise to his Chosen, granting them the gift of rebirth and cementing their loyalty forever more.

"What's going on?" Dad asked, or more like, demanded.

Joybelle placed her hands in her lap and pursed her lips, the contraction of her mind mirroring the language of her body. She hadn't expected the bus to stop here, nor did she approve.

Despite knowing what awaited me, an icy knot settled in the pit of my stomach. The bus doors folded open, letting in the sounds of the concert below along with the lingering heat of the day. I wriggled off the couch, my attention locked on the mind burning like a flare just a short distance away.

"This is my stop," I said.

Dad's hand flew to my shoulder. "Slow down, buddy. You're not going anywhere."

"You can't help me with this, Dad. Not this time."

"Is there another traveler over there, like the kid in Melbourne?"

"It's the Prophet," Megan said, certainty adding weight to her voice.

I nodded.

"What does he want?" Dad asked me.

"To talk," I said.

"I'm going with you."

"That's not a good idea."

"Where you go, I go."

A sense of dread settled in my chest as I met his determined gaze. His coming wasn't wise, but I knew he wouldn't change his mind. With a slight incline of my head, I reluctantly agreed.

Joybelle let us pass without a word or glance, her silence a palpable presence. The two guards watched us warily, their hands resting on the prods at their hips. As we stepped outside, the gravel crunched beneath our feet, the sound mingling with the distant pulse of music. The few steps felt like an eternity until we stood before the closed doors of the second bus. Above us, the Beacon loomed, its dome glowing with borrowed light from the setting sun.

"You need to stay here," I said.

"I won't do that. No way, no how."

"If you go in there, you might not come back."

"Even more reason for me to go," Dad said. "Who is this prophet, anyway? Sounds like you've met him before."

The question triggered another memory from the before-time:

looking upon an unmoving form asleep in a cryo-pod. I had abducted Dalkhu—that's what the Prophet had called themself back then—and transported their body to a waiting vessel. For long years, we traveled through the dark until I put us in orbit around a singularity. I had ended my life on that ship, entering the conscious plane to be reborn. But not Dalkhu, for I had intended they would never wake until the end of time. A forever prison, or so I had thought.

Pushing the memory aside, I said, "Someone I never expected to see again. Trust me. I need to do this. If there's any hope of stopping this being, I need to understand how they got here."

Dad's expression softened, the lines around his eyes easing. "I do trust you, Stevie. You know that."

"Then you need to let me go."

My dad inhaled forcefully through his nose, then ran a hand down his cheek. "If I hear any trouble, any trouble at all, I'm coming in there."

If he heard trouble, it would be too late. "It'll be fine."

Dad's arms wrapped around me like a shield. I clung to him, taking comfort from the steady rhythm of his heartbeat. For a moment, I was a child again, safe in my father's arms. But the illusion couldn't last.

With a deep breath, I stepped back and turned around. Like a serpent waiting to strike, the doors of the bus folded inward with a pneumatic hiss.

CHAPTER TWENTY-NINE

A foul stench assaulted my senses as the bus doors shut behind me—a noxious blend of body odor, spoiled milk, and skunk.

Pausing at the top of the short stairwell, I let my eyes adjust to the dim light. The driver's seat was empty, and the galley behind it and across the aisle was a mess. A grease-stained pizza box perched atop a small refrigerator, and dirty dishes filled the sink, flies buzzing above. When I looked down the length of the corridor, my gaze fell upon a lanky man sprawled on a U-shaped couch.

Tattoos snaked down his face, across his bare chest, and along his legs. A mane of long, twisted hair cascaded over his shoulders, and a loincloth barely covered his privates. From one hand dangled a smoldering joint, while the other clutched a bottle of beer. On the armrest of the sofa balanced a slice of pizza and a half-empty bag of chips. Empty bottles littered the stained carpet. The man's eyes were glued to a television screen affixed to the side of the bus, where another singer gesticulated wildly on the stage we had passed below.

I looked beyond the flesh to the swirling patterns coursing through the man's body, a tapestry of experiences from past lives. They were so dense that distinguishing one from another was nearly impossible. I had not seen that in any other being. Even more peculiar was the chaos in his head, billowing and swirling in a tempest of multi-hued lights and textures. At the center of the maelstrom, a single eye, calm and serene, stared unwaveringly back at me.

An ancient memory bubbled to the surface of my awareness, confirming the pattern belonged to the same being I had once imprisoned. Yet that didn't explain the strange eddies that appeared out of nowhere and vanished just as quickly. Like a mind at war with itself. This was new. After ages trapped in a cryo-pod, had he lost his sanity? Those eddies might be a sign that he had. Or had his desire for vengeance warped his mind?

Steeling myself for whatever was to come, I walked down the hall and settled on the opposite side of the couch. After observing him for a couple of minutes, I extended the ritual greeting: "May you live an undying life."

A tremor rippled across the Prophet's face, accompanied by another flurry of blooming eddies. He tossed the empty bottle onto the floor and slowly rose to his feet with a yawn, stretching his limbs and arching his back. Turning, his lanky frame towered over me in a purposefully menacing posture. He extended an arm and wrapped a hand around my neck, pressing his thumb against my windpipe. I didn't dare move, even when the fingers of his mind stabbed into my own.

He squeezed until I gasped for breath. "We can snap you like a twig. Nobody's here to save you, certainly not the one you call a father. You were wise to leave him behind. Tell me, why shouldn't we recycle this latest body of yours right here and right now?"

"Because I'll come back and find you," I croaked. "No matter how many times you kill me."

He tossed the joint aside and put both hands around my neck. My head swam, and panic rose from a place of despair. The world darkened, and all I could think of was the fate that would befall my family in my absence. But there was no doubt I would return. I made sure the Prophet knew this with a burst of anger that cut deeply into his own mind.

Surprise caused his eyes to widen. Releasing his hold on my neck, he struck me on the side of the head so hard that my ears rang. "Correct," he said.

I curled into a ball and sucked in air, bracing myself for worse to come. Instead, he retrieved the joint from the floor and walked to the kitchenette, grabbing another beer from the refrigerator. He returned to the couch, sank into the cushions, and tossed a leg over the armrest. After draining half the bottle, he said, "You wonder how we escaped your treachery."

Lifting myself back into a sitting position, I rasped, "I do," seeing no point in denying it.

"Though we choose not to volunteer that information, we will allow you a guess."

I rubbed my neck. "I don't know. You found a cheat code?"

"We missed many things in our imprisonment, but not your sense of humor. Try again. The penalty for sarcasm is ignorance."

I pondered for a moment, recalling how I had left his inert body orbiting a collapsed star. That should have been his fate until the very fabric of space was torn asunder or the singularity dissipated into the void.

"The ship's orbit must have decayed," I said.

"A simple answer from a simple mind. Do better."

"One of your Chosen found the ship."

"No. Your plan worked. Surprisingly clever to trap us in a body that refused to die. Once again."

"The cryo-pod failed, and you woke up."

"Close, but no prize."

I grew tired of his game. "This isn't why you brought me here."

"True, but we feel generous and will answer before killing you. The solution, my once-loyal vassal, is that we learned to extend our consciousness outside the physical plane. Eventually, we escaped the shell in which you imprisoned us by willing ourselves to die. It seemed but an instant, though ages have passed for you. Never would we have learned how to do this without your help. We thank you for gifting us with this power."

His words defied my understanding. Separated consciousness? Willing themselves to die? It seemed impossible, yet here he sat. Brushing blood from my split lip, I held it out to him. "Did you do the same thing to my family?"

He tapped the joint against the edge of the couch, causing an ember to fall onto the carpet, where it smoldered. "Your real question is, will we let them live?"

"Will you?"

"We treat them as honored guests, especially the precocious one, Melody." Hearing she remained safe, my shoulders relaxed, which the Prophet noted with a wry smile. "You never told her about your past, did you? Don't worry, we let her know about your treachery—how you betrayed us, then destroyed those who once loved you. Over the generations, how many billions have you recycled in pursuit of personal ambition? Hundreds? More? At least we gave them hope rather than despair."

The attack hit home. Whether out of shame or fear that Melody would think less of me, I hadn't told her what I had done on that long-dead planet. But what the Prophet didn't seem to know was that I hadn't supplanted him. I never even returned to that world. Before I left, I destroyed every beacon, denying the Chosen their source of power and legitimacy. Though I didn't know what happened afterward, I was confident the Bound Worlds had been set free.

But the Prophet wasn't interested in the past, only in the satisfaction of hurting me. So, I hit back where I knew it would hurt him the most: his ego. "I didn't tell her because I forgot all about you."

A crimson flare spouted from the void in his mind, then just as quickly melted away. Chuckling to himself, the Prophet took another puff from the joint and sniffed the air. "This place smells different, tastes different, feels... wrong. Not only this world, but the space it occupies." He wiggled his fingers before his eyes. "We're still trying to get used to this place and this form. We don't like it. It's why we numb ourselves with psychoactive substances. Not sure it helps. Tell me, is this the same universe as the prison in which you bound us?"

I shrugged, uncertain.

"We expect it is not." He popped open another beer, paused, then held it out to me.

"I'm a kid."

"If you insist." He drained the bottle in three swallows. After wiping his mouth with a forearm, he tossed the empty onto the floor, where it shattered against another bottle. "We have been looking for you for a long time. But no matter where you flee, no matter where you go, we will always find you."

"I wasn't hiding."

"We recognize the lie, but appreciate your defiance. Beings can diminish over time, and most disappear entirely. After traveling for so long and to so many places, we had wondered if that happened to you. But here you are, our old friend. Anger is the fuel that sustains us, wraps us in its embrace, and carries us forward. We are much the same in that regard."

"We are nothing alike," I said. "And it's not anger you perceive, but fear at what you will do here."

"Anger and love are different facets of the same gem. That's the reason you come back. You need to scratch that itch."

"You forget pride and greed."

He snuffed the joint out on his thigh and flicked away the remnant. "We embrace who we are. You, however, are loath to look within. So be it. Bathe in ignorance until the stars wink out. The people here suit you. Is it true one of these savages murdered your previous form?"

"They're not all like that."

The Prophet curled his lip. "You know what will happen here. We've seen it time and again. When technology outstrips wisdom, the creators are consumed by their creations. Like a leopard waiting in the grass."

"Nothing is certain," I said, hoping that was true.

"That's the difference between us. We would save them, while you would watch as the leopards eat their faces. The Beast is a fitting name."

"Leave them alone."

"At the risk of their extinction? Let me remind you of the survival equation: a factor of technological advancement, environmental decline, population pressure, and, most importantly, the ability to discern truth from fiction. I've estimated their chances. Would you like to know the result?"

"You'll take control, regardless."

"And why not? Sentience is vanishingly rare. Even the slightest chance of destruction is unacceptable. Can you not see that?"

"What I see is ambition dressed up as virtue," I said, growing heated. "You care nothing for this world or these people."

Studying me, he took the slice of pizza from the armrest and bit into it. "Then join us, advise us, and I'll let you try to save what can't be saved. We won't interfere. But when indifference fails, we will rebuild what was lost. You know the process: depopulate the planet, hobble the technology, and provide the living with a purpose greater than themselves. We will give them the greatest gift of all—survival."

"Your only desire is control. When you've taken this world, what comes next? Do you take another, then another? You've done that before, on a far greater scale. How much is enough?"

"When every world is pulled back from the abyss, not just in this universe but in all that harbor life. That will be enough, for that is our purpose—to save them all."

I couldn't help but laugh aloud. His was a mind searching for meaning and grasping at anything to fill the void. Stimulation, the sense of relevance, and power were existential to his existence. And the lack was worse than death. "You fool yourself as you try to fool others. I think you're bored and need something to do."

He finished the pizza slice and smacked his lips. "That's the crucible of creation, is it not? A painter paints, a sculptor sculpts, a writer writes. In the end, every artist does what they do for the same reason—to escape the meaninglessness of existence. There's a word for it here. They call it hell."

"You're an artist now?"

A laugh, genuine, I thought. "We sculpt the future and give meaning to those who have none. So, yes, an artist. We like that."

"There's a reason for our existence, and it's not you."

"The biggest lie of them all." Another tremor rippled across the Prophet's face, spawning more eddies in his mind. I had no idea of the cause. Was it a medical disorder, or was it the drugs and drink? Either seemed as likely as the other. "You've always clung to the adorable notion that there's a greater purpose to existence. There is not. Life is merely the result of the random interaction of matter and energy. Cause and effect, nothing more. We, however, provide purpose to the purposeless. That's why people flock to our church. We are the light in a dark room."

"Do you really believe you're a god, or is that a lie you tell others for your own amusement?"

"Is there a difference? Not to us. You once aspired to greatness. What happened? Why bother planting a beacon here or anywhere? Truly, I'm curious. Where's the meaning? What's your purpose?"

I told him the truth. "To make up for the evils I've done. For now, that means stopping you."

He kicked an empty bottle against the side of the bus. "Then you leave us no choice. But we wanted to try. After all, compassion is our greatest weakness. It's a shame, really, but there is another to keep us company."

"Joybelle," I said.

"An excellent student with ambition to match our own. But as you noted, we easily grow bored. We grant you two more questions. Though I know what you will ask, we do you the courtesy of not answering before you speak."

It was true; I had two questions, which made me wonder if he had learned how to read more than emotions. "How did you get here? You're too old to have come through the Beacon, and I would've known if you were here before it was built. It's like you popped out of nowhere."

He shook his head. "Disappointing that you can't figure that out. Joybelle will be a more worthy student. Last question and we're done. You've become tedious."

What I really wanted to know was how to rid the world of him. But the Prophet seemed as strong as ever, with a following that numbered in the millions. I was just a little kid.

I can help, said the voice.

I startled, surprised at the intrusion, and immediately regretted it because the Prophet's eyes narrowed. He recognized my past had come forward but wouldn't know the purpose. Neither did I.

How? I thought, keeping my outward expression neutral.

By showing you that you don't need me.

I couldn't stop myself from frowning. *That's the opposite of help.*

You'll understand when the time comes. Tell your father and Megan to be ready. Now let's get the hell out of here. You have a family to save.

Returning my attention to the Prophet, I asked my last question. "Are you going to keep your promise?"

Steely eyes bore into mine, trying to discern what I had really been thinking. With a shrug, the Prophet said, "We have no further use for what you call a family. Because you have amused us, we will not harm them in any way."

"Thank you."

The Prophet swung his legs off the couch and placed his elbows on his knees. "We will miss our talks, but that doesn't mean you will be spared. You have become an irritant, like a burr in our shoe. For that reason, you no longer require a past, present, or future." Another tremor rippled across his face, puzzling me as it had before. "We will not speak or meet like this again. But little Stevie *will* meet the power of the Prophet."

CHAPTER THIRTY

Stevie and Eric reentered the bus and settled onto the white leather couch beside Megan. She glanced inquisitively at Eric, who said, "You were right, we never should have come here," before shaking his head to discourage further questions. Stevie stared blankly out the window, lost in thought. Joybelle, having retreated to the front seat to escape Megan's constant gibes, signaled for the driver to depart. The motor hummed to life, and the doors hissed closed.

Darkness enveloped them as the bus entered a narrow tunnel carved through the earthen embankment. Megan's chest tightened with the onset of claustrophobia, a familiar sensation in confined spaces. Her apprehension grew when they emerged beneath a forest of metal lattice struts, flanked on one side by reinforced concrete and on the other by the dome of the Beacon. The driver slowed to a crawl, carefully navigating the winding path toward the elevator at the end of the road.

Averting her eyes from the window, Megan noticed a bead of blood forming on Stevie's lips and the welt on his cheek. She pulled a tissue from her purse and gently dabbed the blood away while clucking her tongue.

"He claims to have tripped," Eric said.

"You weren't in there with him?" Megan asked.

"I asked Dad to wait outside," Stevie said.

Eric turned to his son. "Tell her what you told me."

"You're going to see a ghost of somebody you once knew. When you see it, be ready."

"Ready for what?" Megan asked.

Stevie fixed his unsettling gaze on her. "To get my mom, Melody, and Aunt Franny out of there."

"And you," Eric said. "We're not leaving you behind."

"Of course," Stevie said, though Megan found his tone unconvincing. She pulled him close.

"Listen up. I know these types of people; my mother used to be one of them. A true believer who traded common sense for the ravings of a lunatic. Let this prophet wave his arms and do his voodoo. Agree with everything he says, no matter how absurd. Pretend the demon was exorcised, if that's what he wants. Thank him when it's over. Remember, he's performing for an audience and you're just a prop. Once the show's done, we leave. Understand?"

Stevie nodded, though Megan sensed he was only placating her.

The road leveled off, and the bus came to a halt in a clearing bordered on three sides by cement walls. The tram, now empty of passengers, maneuvered around them to ascend the winding path. Up ahead, a flickering lamp cast a yellow glow over a cinderblock building that housed the elevator leading to the injection chamber deep underground. Acolytes and blue-robed men milled around the structure, with piles of equipment stripped from the control center stacked against the walls. Bile rose in Megan's throat at the stark reminder that a movement led by a madman had cast aside her life's work.

Joybelle exited the bus without a backward glance, joining the group of acolytes waiting by the cinderblock building. Together, they entered the structure and disappeared from view. The driver gestured for Megan, Stevie, and Eric to stay put, while the other Sword loitered by the exit to ensure their compliance.

"Live to fight another day," Megan said to Stevie, well aware that she hadn't taken that same advice from Obadiah. But regardless of Stevie's origin, he was still a child. "And don't provoke him."

"Too late for that," the boy said.

"We stay together," Eric told them both.

After several minutes, the elevator returned to the surface, and the guard signaled for them to depart. Heart pounding, Megan joined Stevie and Eric as they walked toward the solitary building. She couldn't help but glance up at the enormity of the Beacon's outer sphere, feeling goosebumps rise on her arms despite the desert heat.

Even after many visits, she still felt insubstantial in its shadow, as if she were about to be sacrificed to a jealous god. Eric held Stevie's hand, and the boy stared at his toes.

They entered the cinderblock building, where the elevator awaited. Four blue-robed Swords joined them inside the cabin, pressing their backs against the walls as far from Stevie as possible. Megan moved closer to the boy, finding a strange comfort in his presence.

The elevator shuddered as it came to a stop. The Swords positioned themselves in front and back as they escorted Megan, Eric, and Stevie along a golden carpet that stretched down the corridor toward the soft glow at the end of the passageway.

Stepping into the familiar half-moon-shaped control center, Megan found the walls painted emerald green and littered with pictures of the wild-eyed prophet and his disciples. The cylindrical glass lift was now adorned with a neon sign reading, "The Gate to Heaven." Exposed wires dangled from the walls, remnants of the equipment that once filled this space. But what really drew Megan's interest was the red marble tub set in the center of the room, the same one she had seen at the Temple. Two tables stood on either side of the container, one empty and the other holding goblets arranged in a broken pyramid.

After a glance at the blue-robed men, whose amused expressions suggested they wouldn't interfere, Megan approached the tub and filled a goblet with the ladle. She sniffed the liquid. "Wine, a merlot, I think."

One Sword nudged his comrade. "Go on, have a taste."

Stevie stood on his toes to peer inside. "It's poison."

Megan shuddered as the realization dawned on her. The people in the trams hadn't come to attend a service; they'd come to end their lives, fulfilling the Prophet's promise of granting his followers an eternal life.

Stevie nodded, as if reading her thoughts. "That's right."

Eric took the glass and dumped it back into the tub. "What did you expect, Meg? You know how this works."

Stunned, Megan shook her head. Melody had told her repeatedly that to be reborn with memories intact, one had to die inside the Beacon. That was the kernel of truth around which the church spun its web of deceit, and the Prophet wielded the lie that he controlled rebirth as a reward for his most loyal followers. For the first time, she glimpsed a grand plan that spanned generations. Diabolical. "We have to stop him."

"That's why we're here," said Stevie.

Megan studied the boy. Even after hearing what Stevie had done in Melbourne, she still found it hard to believe this slight, unassuming child could stand against the church's machinations. He seemed as harmless as a butterfly. Before she could express her doubts, one of the blue-robed men pointed his prod at the lift. "Time to go. The Prophet is eager to see you."

Eric and Stevie entered the lift hand in hand, the boy's small fingers gripping his father's in a white-knuckled hold. Megan hesitated for a heartbeat before stepping into the cramped cabin. As the doors slid shut, one guard peeled away to take a seat at the main console, while the others remained motionless, their eyes fixed on Megan and her companions. The aperture in the ceiling dilated, and the lift ascended.

When the cabin door opened onto the central dais inside the chamber, it revealed more Swords standing in a semicircle, their backs to the railing. The one closest to Megan acknowledged her with a narrowed gaze, but otherwise remained expressionless. She peered further into the space, her eyes widening at the scene before her.

Hundreds of people sat in plastic chairs facing a raised stage at the south end of the chamber, reminiscent of the setup at the Grand Temple. A tall wooden scaffold lay beside the stage. Above, seven short angels hovered, sporting tiny wings, white wigs, glowing halos, and trumpets—cherubs, Megan realized. She squinted at the nearest one, a child she had seen at the Temple. As she watched, a cable snapped, causing the child to spin helplessly in place. Someone below frantically tugged on the line, making the child spin around even faster. Megan would have found it comical if fear hadn't driven all humor from her mind.

A tower of speakers topped by spotlights stood on the north side, casting harsh light across the cavernous space. The congregants, clad in white robes provided at the gate, were elderly, some infirm, accompanied by wheelchairs, canes, and oxygen tanks. They held goblets on their laps, presumably filled with the toxic wine. Most of the crowd stared at their small group, whispering or pointing at Eric.

"They're wondering if you're the Beast," she said.

"Let them wonder," Eric said, edging closer to Stevie, whose eyes were fixed on the stage.

Megan followed his gaze. Joybelle Leroux, outfitted in wings and a halo, stood poised between a wooden chair and a throne encrusted with shimmering gemstones and religious iconography. Four young kids, whom she was sure had been at the Temple, stood in a line behind the woman. A velvet curtain concealed whatever lay beyond the stage, with a walkway stretching from the dais to the throne, flanked by blue-robed men.

Eric scanned the chamber. "Where's Melody?"

"Behind the curtain," Stevie said.

Before Megan could ask how he knew that, a blinding light focused on the dais, forcing her to shield her eyes with her hand. Then, the introduction from a familiar show boomed throughout the room:

"You are tuned in to another dimension, a dimension not only of space and time, but of mind. Streaming live on your favorite platforms, this is your portal to the paranormal, esoteric, and all things strange and unexplained. Find the answers to questions that others are afraid to ask. Pry the truth from rumor and uncover the face hiding behind the mask. Introducing your host, cynic, truth-seeker, and radiant beacon of light: the one and only...Max Mystery!"

A large screen above the stage flickered to life, showing a pear-shaped man with a jet-black goatee and a thin handlebar mustache. Megan silently cursed, wondering what the hell he was doing here. She searched for and found the body attached to the mustache.

Max stood atop the wooden scaffold, facing a camera, leading Megan to believe this event was being live-streamed to his millions of deluded followers. If she cared, which she didn't, she might have thought Max glanced her way with a hint of self-consciousness.

"Is that who I think it is?" Eric asked.

"Afraid so," Megan said, her mind racing. What was Max doing here? Could he have disclosed the family's whereabouts to Joybelle? If he did—and she wasn't convinced of that—he was worse than a scoundrel. Then again, hosting the livestream would surely boost his show's ratings. Whatever the reason, she hoped his presence would make it more likely they would get out of here in one piece.

Max clanged a cowbell over his head, causing her and everyone in the audience to cover their ears. "Greetings, Mysteryites! I'm coming at you live from inside the alien machine. You heard that right, I've brought you into the mystery of mysteries, the Beacon itself, where the Prophet will preside over the Ceremony of Ascension. I don't know exactly what that means, but we're about to find out. Exclusive access, brought to you by yours truly. For more content and insights you won't find anywhere else, head over to my website and sign up to be a platinum member. Payment plans are available."

Angry shouts from the audience demanded he get off the stage, but Max only raised his voice. "Only the most devout have been selected to take part in the ceremony, those who've run down their clock and are about to die a most painful death. These are the winners in the cosmic lottery, holders of the golden ticket. In exchange for a pledge of undying dedication, they have been promised a new life. The Prophet calls them his Chosen, privileged to see what lies behind the silver curtain."

Max inhaled a lungful of air, his complexion transforming into a constellation of pink splotches. "The dead will rise this very night, Mysteryites, and you have a front-row seat! It's what we all want, isn't it, to come back with a full head of hair?" He chortled at his own wit, though it fell flat among the unsmiling crowd.

Max leaned over the platform's edge to speak to a gray-haired woman in the third row. "What ailment brought you here, good lady?"

"None of your business!" the woman snapped back.

Max mournfully shook his head while looking at the camera. "Stricken with cancer and only days to live." He pointed at a man a few rows back. "And you, good sir? What's taken you down?"

"Bring on the Prophet," the man said, repeating himself until others joined him. Soon, the entire congregation was chanting and stomping, "Bring on the Prophet! Bring on the Prophet!"

Max clanged the bell to drown them out, then outstretched his arms to the congregation. "Time for the main event! I present to you the miracle man, the holy spirit bound in flesh, the promised one, the legend, the one and only Prrrooophhhet!"

Spotlights zigzagged across the chamber as trumpets sounded from the cherubs, except for the one still spinning in place. Then, abruptly, darkness fell. Silence blanketed the chamber, made more pronounced by the absence of Max's bellowing. A minute passed, then three.

Eric whispered, "Maybe we should take the lift back down."

"He's here," Stevie said.

A blinding flash caused Megan to see stars, followed by a collective gasp. When her eyes adjusted, the Prophet was seated on the ornate throne. And in the chair beside him sat Melody, clothed in a disciple's robe and wearing a frown.

Megan thought she knew anger, but it was nothing compared to the rage building inside her now. "What does he want with that poor girl?" she asked, her fists clenched.

"Once he's done here, he'll use Melody to create more beacons leading to other worlds," Stevie said.

Eric went rigid. "I'm going to rip his tonsils out."

"He'll only come back. People need to reject him. That's the only way."

It was far too late for that, Megan knew. The Prophet's followers were too deep in the rabbit hole, and his enablers had deluded themselves into thinking they could escape unscathed. Senator Wigfall was proof of that. But none of this explained why Max was here. If she could get to him, maybe he would try talking sense into these people.

The children filed behind the curtain, emerging with baskets of bread, flowers, and fish that they placed at the Prophet's feet. Offerings, Megan supposed. She tried to catch Melody's eye, but the girl had her attention locked on Stevie. Then Joybelle's voice rose in song: "And the angels rejoiced, for the marriage of the Prophet has come. His Bride has made herself ready, clothed in fine linen, bright and pure, for the righteous deeds of a saint."

Two Swords yanked Megan off the dais. She tried to kick one of them until the other twisted her arm behind her back, forcing her to gasp in pain. He leaned in and whispered, "Calm down, or you'll get the same treatment as your friend."

"Leave the boy alone," Megan said. "He's done nothing."

"I'm not talking about the kid."

They shoved her toward the chamber's western edge, the crowd hurling insults along the way, branding her a demon and a beast. She caught sight of Eric receiving the same rough treatment, leaving Stevie alone on the empty dais. After throwing her against the wall, a Sword said, "The First Disciple sends her regards."

Megan whipped around in time to see Joybelle fold her wings behind her back and shake her fist at the sky. "A coward tried to desecrate our sacred temple!"

To Megan's horror, three burly Swords dragged a struggling Obadiah onto the stage. Even from this distance, she could see the bruise on his cheek and his swollen eye. One man forced Obadiah to his knees, another yanked his head back by his hair. A third raised a knife into the air.

The crowd shouted, "Defiler!" "Sacrilege!" and "Throw him into the lake of fire!" A woman tossed a goblet, striking Obadiah on the cheek. But he didn't flinch, only stared back at her with a defiant eye.

"This nation's great leader has granted the church the authority to dispense justice to those who do us harm," Joybelle proclaimed, then looked to the Prophet lounging on his throne. He raised a fist, held it for a beat, then turned his thumb down. Joybelle turned back to the congregation. "The Lord of Light has passed judgment."

In one swift motion, the blue-robed Sword slit Obadiah's throat.

Megan screamed, watching in glassy-eyed terror as a pool of blood spread around Obadiah's body. Melody leaped up, only to be restrained by Joybelle, who bound her arms to the chair with plastic ties. The crowd, initially stunned into silence, broke into ragged cheers. Megan slumped to the ground, utterly defeated. Everything she'd done—building IGOR, deciphering the transmission, protecting the family, fighting the church—had only made the Prophet stronger.

Joybelle pressed her hands together and lifted her eyes. "The Chosen have gathered for the great battle. Woe to the earth and the sea, for the Beast has come with great wrath, knowing his time is short. As it once began, so it will end."

Trumpets blared from above as a metallic voice resonated through the chamber, counting down—"Thirty seconds, twenty-nine, twenty-eight..."—each number marking the moments until the shield disengaged, allowing gravitational energy to flood into the chamber.

Through grief and tears, Megan saw the Prophet leap atop the throne. Wearing only a rag, he took a drag from a joint while pumping a fist in the air. Music boomed from the speakers, battering her already frayed nerves. Then he began to rap,

> *From ancient scrolls, my visions unfold,*
> *Prophetic tales of the future, so bold.*
> *Seven seals break, and the trumpets sound,*
> *The world's fate uncertain, chaos unbound.*

Megan's eyes darted to Eric, who was shielding his head as the Swords pummeled him. Stevie stood frozen on the dais, staring at the Prophet.

> *Four horsemen ride, a harrowing sight,*
> *A beacon is built, breaking the endless night.*
> *A scroll is opened, the secrets are revealed,*
> *The end of days approach, humanity's fate is sealed.*

A buzz of power prickled Megan's skin as mechanical gears parted the shield. The countdown continued: "Ten, nine, eight…"

> *Angels and demons, clash in the skies,*
> *As the heavens and earth, make their final goodbyes.*
> *The dragon's wrath, the mark of the beast,*
> *In this apocalyptic dance, all shall feast.*

The instant the countdown ended, sapphire medallions embedded in the dome high above emitted a dull yellow sheen.

> *The Lord of Light, orders the righteous to rise,*
> *Battles of Armageddon, paint crimson skies.*
> *A new city rises, a haven of peace,*
> *From the ashes of destruction, they shall be released.*

Blue luminescence poured from the medallions, coating the ceiling, while the same blue fog rose from the chamber floor. Awed congregants waved their hands through the mist, creating ripples that darkened into violet hues. The Prophet's voice intensified, continuing his apoplectic rap,

Only the Chosen, are reborn in this quest,
Rising from the ashes, among the blessed.
In the end, the final battle takes its toll,
Good versus evil, consuming every soul.

A multi-hued drop, shimmering with unearthly light, formed above Obadiah's body and stretched toward the ceiling. Megan intuited that his essence lay within, and though it should have inspired hope, it only filled her with dread.

As the world quakes, beneath the relentless beat,
Revelation's climax…bring forth the Beast!

The music ceased, the Prophet bowed, and the lights blinked out, leaving only the blue luminescence to reflect off people's faces. The chamber erupted in noise—people clapping, stomping, dancing, and shouting adulations at the top of their lungs.

Amid the frenzy, Megan saw little Stevie step onto the walkway and move toward the Prophet. She wanted to scream for him to stop, but the words lodged in her throat. Paralysis gripped her—the same that had struck when her mother had left home, claiming she would soon ascend to the next level. Even as a young child, Megan had known she'd never see her mother alive again. Then, as now, she'd said nothing, only cried uncontrollably.

As sobs wracked her body, the cacophony inside the chamber gradually subsided. Gasps and whispers rippled through the room, prompting Megan to raise her tear-stained eyes.

At first, she thought the wispy form pouring from the Prophet's head was a shock-induced hallucination. But it solidified, ballooning in size until it loomed over the audience—a nightmarish fusion of a blimp and a jellyfish, with four bulbous eyes and a curtain of arms hanging from its bloated body. Two long appendages trailed beneath it, twisting together to form the symbol of the church.

Whispers turned to murmurs of awe and cries of fear. Some people knelt while others clutched their companions. A few fled toward the back of the chamber. Megan could only stare in mute panic, her worst fears amplified a thousandfold. Whatever this was, it wasn't of this world, and it wasn't her friend.

A single spotlight fell on little Stevie, now standing alone in the middle of the walkway. He looked not at the Prophet, not at the apparition, not at Melody, but at the drop that had just parted from the body of her dear friend, slowly spiraling up toward the mist-covered ceiling.

CHAPTER THIRTY-ONE

I strode toward the Prophet, resolved to sacrifice myself to save the ones I loved. To my right, Aunt Megan remained paralyzed, her gaze locked on the ethereal essence rising from Obadiah's lifeless body. On my left, Dad defended himself from the guards' relentless blows. On the stage, Melody remained bound to the chair, desperation etched into her every feature. Four of the fallen stood at the back, one of them the girl I had encountered in Melbourne. For a brief instant, our eyes met, before she averted her gaze. And before me, an apparition from a long-dead world billowed from the Prophet's mind.

Luminescent arms dangled from a gelatinous mantle, while siphons along its edges expanded and contracted, mimicking breathing in a non-existent atmosphere. Four bulbous eyes beneath its carapace focused on me as two whip-like neurolashes unfurled from its underside, twisting into the symbol of eternal life—an especially offensive gesture given the countless lives those appendages had ended.

The apparition took the shape of the Prophet's former incarnation, the same entity I had imprisoned in the before-time. Back then, it had called itself Dalkhu, a being that considered itself a god. Anguish twisted my insides, not from the sight, but from my utter helplessness. What could one do against such power?

Defeat it, said the voice within.

Easy for you to say. You're already dead.

But not gone, said the voice. *Nor are you. Time to call forth the past.*

I responded with a solemn nod, my attention shifting to the drop containing a man's immortal essence. Though the Prophet intended to erase me from existence, I could at least spare Megan's friend from suffering that same fate.

When one dies inside a beacon, memories of the past are retained by linking one life to the next. This continuity manifests as a sphere rising from the haze to be reborn. But the process momentarily exposes one's soul, making it vulnerable to beings who can reach into the plane of consciousness to bring forth an entity of its past—like the one looming before me now. What the Prophet didn't know was that I had learned that trick as well.

A spotlight blazed down on me from above, and trumpets blared from the fallen travelers suspended from the ceiling. From the stage, Joybelle's voice rang out, "The Prophet is the way and the truth, and the Chosen who believe shall not perish but have eternal life." The congregation tried echoing back those words, though most faltered or trailed off. Joybelle jabbed a finger at the sphere. "Except for this one, for the price of sacrilege is everlasting destruction!"

I knew what was to come. The Prophet intended to demonstrate the fate of those who dared challenge his will. But I would show them something else: defiance.

Reaching deep into the conscious plane, far deeper than I'd ever dared, I summoned the one being who had defeated Dalkhu. I had been called Shurruppak back then, one of the Chosen—and the source of my current nightmares. But rather than suppress these memories, I set them free, allowing Shurruppak's shadowy form to billow over me, neurolashes raised to confront its old master.

Quick as lightning, the apparition of Dalkhu lashed out at the sphere, intent on destroying the ethereal essence that had once animated the man.

I willed my specter to deflect the blow, which it did, but at the cost of that past life disintegrating into a shower of ash-like tendrils, taking with it all memory of my previous existence. Pain, sharp as an ice pick driven into my skull, dropped me to my knees, but I kept my eyes locked on the sphere encasing Obadiah's life force. I harbored no illusions—the Prophet could overwhelm any resistance. But I could at least delay the inevitable. And so I did, summoning another ghost from another life to battle the apparition.

Panicked congregants cried out in fear, scrambling away and knocking over chairs to distance themselves from the twin monstrosities. Trumpets squealed, Joybelle screeched, and an inhuman cry erupted from the all-too-human Prophet. I had surprised him, both with my defiance and my willingness to sacrifice my own essence for what he perceived to be a lowly human.

In any other place and time, the Prophet's wrath would have turned on me. But not after making a show of punishing one who had committed sacrilege. Like a god's judgment, once declared, the Prophet couldn't show weakness in front of his followers.

Again and again, the apparition of Dalkhu tried to destroy the sphere. Each time, I deflected the blow, sacrificing one incarnation after another until the remnants of the before-time swirled around me like a dark cloud. Slowly, inch by inch, the essence of the man spiraled toward the blue haze above. Finally, with a flash of violet, the sphere vanished into the haze.

Obadiah was safe.

Still on my knees, I glanced at my father, relieved to find the guards had stopped their assault to watch the spectacle unfold. Our eyes met, and I hoped he could hear my silent goodbye. I then turned to face the Prophet, his mind a tempest of rage. Pulsing above him, the apparition of Dalkhu swelled even larger.

"Your lives belong to you and no other," I shouted to the crowd. "The one you call a prophet is a liar, a fraud—"

A neurolash tore across the floor, ripping through innocents before slamming into me. Agony beyond anything flesh could experience tore at the very fabric of my being. I raised my hands over my head in futile defense, but there was no stopping the pummeling. Worlds dissolved, experiences vanished, and loved ones faded into oblivion, leaving only a yawning void where memories once resided. As the Prophet shredded every specter from my past, time itself became nothing more than a growing chasm of emptiness. Perhaps I deserved this fate for all the suffering I had once caused. Redemption, it seemed, would close on me as a curtain of ignorance.

When nearly every apparition and memory from the before-time had been stripped from my consciousness, the manifestation of my last incarnation billowed over me, wearing the same bloodied shirt from his final moments in this very chamber.

Help me, I pleaded.

You don't need my help, said the voice.

That's not true.

What you see and hear of me is an illusory construct, a mirror reflecting what you already know but fear to face.

Tell me what to do.

Let go, the voice said. *Not just of me, but of evils long past. You are not defined by those sins, just as you are no longer the being who made those choices.*

You're telling me to die.

In a way, yes.

Don't leave! Stay, protect me, protect my family.

Goodbye, Stevie.

The manifestation of Stephen Fisher looked up at the apparition poised over the Prophet. With a final act of defiance, he raised a fist, then extended his middle finger. The neurolash struck, and my last link to the before-time exploded in a shower of ash.

Nothing remained of me now but a waning flame, kept alive by the fading glow of this one life's experiences. I recalled the bedtime stories my mom used to tell, the feel of sand between my fingers as I built castles with my dad, the weightless joy of Melody pushing me on a swing, and the sound of Aunt Franny's infectious laughter. Those cherished moments, along with everything else I had ever known, teetered at the edge of oblivion.

The apparition paused. The crowd stilled. And the Prophet smiled. "My precious Chosen," he said, "you are blessed to witness the final destruction of the Beast!"

More strikes from the lash cut into the essence of what remained of my being, each swing holding a promise to end the pain. I wanted to surrender, to dip my head beneath the waves, until a warm presence brushed against my consciousness. With great effort, I lifted my head. My gaze fell on Melody, bound to the chair, her mind ablaze with fiery streaks of color. Though no words were spoken, her message resonated as clearly as if she had shouted: "Don't you dare leave me!"

Her silent plea reignited a spark of life…. and resistance. The lash of Dalkhu fell once more, but this time, to my great surprise, it passed through without effect. If anything, I felt lighter than before. Rising to my knees, I turned my eyes to the man who had terrorized my family.

The Prophet's gaze bored into mine as visions of horror flooded into my awareness—my mother executed, my father's head rolling down the aisle, Megan's decaying corpse, and unspeakable torture inflicted on Melody. All threats of what would happen if I failed to succumb to his will. Another strike of the lash passed through me, feeling like a gentle breeze on my skin.

"You can't kill me," I realized, a thought as shocking to me as it would be to him.

More visions came—mushroom clouds rising from the horizon, firestorms spanning continents, and charred bodies covering the ground. A risk to this world, for sure, but the Prophet's remedy would prove far worse. I shook my head, rejecting these latest threats. Then came the image of pretty women and handsome men pleasuring me on a bed. Did he forget I was a kid?

"You can't tempt me either," I said.

The apparition of Dalkhu shrank in size, and the chest of the man from which it emerged heaved. "Slay the Beast!" the Prophet raged.

The guards warily approached from either side of the walkway, their minds betraying fear of their Prophet—and of me. Eyeing the metal prods they held before them, I had a thought: if those devices worked on me, surely they would work on another traveler, no matter how ancient. And in that short space between pain and peace, I found clarity.

In Melbourne, I had disabled the guards by extending my will through the microorganisms in the soil. That would work even better here, as the draconium lining the chamber floor served as a far better conduit than dirt.

I slapped my palm onto the floor, searching for and invading the minds of every blue-robed assailant in the chamber.

CHAPTER THIRTY-TWO

Megan's pulse pounded in her ears as she watched a stream of incorporeal creatures pour from Stevie's slight frame to confront the towering specter looming over the Prophet. Each time the specter's lash struck, the apparitions emerging from the boy disintegrated into ash-like threads, only to be replaced by another, then another. First came a figure mimicking the monstrous shape above the Prophet, followed by a dizzying array of otherworldly forms: a winged torpedo, a gilled balloon, finned insects, and stranger beings with tentacles, antennae, and features beyond description.

Time stretched, with seconds feeling like minutes as the flurry of lashes blurred together, reducing the shapes above the cowering boy to sporadic flashes of ghostly light. On the dais, Stevie fell to his knees, his small hands raised in a futile attempt to shield himself from the onslaught.

Sweat dripped onto Megan's brow. Once again, she was that helpless little girl watching a stranger pull a purple shroud over her mother's lifeless body. Now, another innocent suffered at the hands of another cult. As before, she observed silently, trapped in the depths of a long, dark tunnel. Even in this suspended state, a corner of her mind struggled to comprehend the surreal horror unfolding before her eyes.

A human shape materialized beside the child, far more substantial than the translucent creatures that had appeared before. Megan could have sworn the figure looked like the late Stephen Fisher—except that wasn't possible. Then again, none of this should be happening. Yet when the figure raised a defiant middle finger, she knew without a doubt it had to be him.

The specter's lash fell once again, and the ghost of Stephen Fisher winked out of existence.

"Slay the Beast!" the Prophet roared, his face a mask of rage.

The Swords exchanged uncertain glances before stepping forward, closing ranks around the boy.

Then Stevie's palm struck the floor with a sharp, resounding crack.

In that instant, Megan heard a voice as if whispered directly into her ear: *"I could use some help."*

It was the boy. And the figures rising above him weren't monsters—they were Stevie, echoes of his past lives, the last of which belonged to his uncle. It all fell into place with startling clarity. Rebirth wasn't a theory; it was real, which was why the child's distant gaze had felt so familiar. As that realization washed over her, every one of Megan's senses snapped to high alert.

The world rushed back in.

Congregants babbled, trumpets blared, and bodies littered the floor—most of them Swords who had fallen where they stood. The Prophet's face contorted as his eyes darted between his downed goons and little Stevie. Across the way, Eric was on his hands and knees, surrounded by downed blue-robed men. A quick scan revealed her own attackers sprawled on the ground, one drooling from his mouth, the other bleeding from his ears. What had happened to them?

Eric's voice rang in her mind: *He did something at the orientation center. Disabled the guards and the woman. I have no idea how.*

But Megan did, for Stephen Fisher had done the same to her.

Her attention snapped back to the walkway.

Stevie was on the move, his small hands gripping a metal prod he'd stripped from a fallen Sword. He strode toward the stage with a determination that made her stomach lurch.

She knew what he intended, for Eric had told her what that acolyte had done in Melbourne. Now Stevie intended to stop the Prophet in the same way. But the boy was half the size of the man and didn't stand a chance.

Megan leaped to her feet and dashed toward Stevie, weaving around chairs and prone bodies. Her eyes flicked to the stage, where the Prophet casually leaned over one of the fallen Swords. Her heart froze when she saw what he was reaching for—the knife used to kill

Obadiah, gleaming in the ethereal light of the blue haze.

"Get to Stevie!" she yelled at Eric, who had just managed to get to his feet.

A sudden blow struck Megan in the ribs, sending her crashing into a row of chairs. Pain exploded in her side, and she gasped for air as she hit the floor. Through the blur of adrenaline, she saw Joybelle advancing—cheeks flushed, halo askew, feathery wings sagging, and a metal prod gripped tightly in her hand.

"And the great dragon was thrown down," Joybelle said, her voice trembling with righteous fervor. "That ancient serpent, the deceiver of the whole world."

Gritting her teeth, Megan pushed herself upright just in time to evade a vicious thrust from the prod. Breath ragged, she said, "And the woman was given the wings of an eagle so she might fly from the serpent. Except your wings don't work, Joybelle. They're a fraud—just like you."

"The Herald mouths blasphemous words," Joybelle spat, then lunged forward, wielding the prod as if it were a rapier.

Megan shifted her weight onto her back foot, slipping just out of the weapon's reach. Years of training kicked in as she circled her opponent cautiously, hands up in a defensive posture, her focus locked on Joybelle. To counter the woman's greater reach, strength, and height, she needed to close the distance. Hoping to provoke the priestess, she said, "And the dwellers marvel to see the Beast. Pretty sure that's you."

"Into the lake of fire!" Joybelle shrieked, swinging the prod in a wide arc.

Megan ducked low and sprang forward, grabbing the harness connecting the wings to Joybelle's back. She yanked hard, forcing the priestess off-balance. The taller woman hit the floor with a heavy thud, and Megan pounced, driving a knee into her spine.

Joybelle thrashed wildly, trying to buck Megan off with sheer strength. With a sudden twist, the priestess managed to wrench herself free, the prod flailing wildly. Megan dodged in time to avoid a strike to the head, but the blow glanced off her shoulder, sending a jolt through her body. Pushing past the pain, she caught the offending arm and twisted it behind Joybelle's back, causing the woman to cry out. With her other hand, she slammed Joybelle's head onto the edge of an overturned chair, yelling, "You… are… not… an… angel," until only a moan escaped the woman's lips.

Megan snatched up the prod and struggled to her feet, wincing all the while. But it was too late; the Prophet had the knife poised at Stevie's neck.

◆ ◆ ◆

I stepped onto the stage, gripping the prod I hoped would send the Prophet back to where he came from. Seeing me approach, the fallen fled toward the lift, except for the girl from Melbourne, who rested a hand on Melody's shoulder as she struggled to free her wrists from the chair. Rage twisted the Prophet's features as he leaned over the body of the man who murdered Obadiah. I ran toward him, hoping to catch him unaware.

With effortless disdain, the Prophet kicked the shaft from my hand. Before I could react, he snaked an arm around my chest and twisted me toward the crowd. A blade pressed against my neck, cold as death.

"The Beast!" he shouted.

Few paid any attention. Terrified congregants swarmed the central dais, clawing and shoving each other to enter the lift. Others stood motionless, staring at the bodies scattered across the floor or transfixed by the apparition still pulsing above their false savior. I saw Aunt Megan dodging toppled chairs to reach the stage. On the opposite side of the chamber, Dad hauled himself to his feet and hobbled in my direction. Neither would reach me in time.

A strange calm settled over me. "You can destroy this body, but I'll always come back."

The Prophet's breath seared my ear. "You want to test that theory?" He nicked my chin with the knife. "Look at these fools. Fear so blinds them they trample over one another to escape what they don't understand. A guiding hand is what they need; it's what they deserve. Save them by joining me. It's not too late. Your friend Melody already has."

"I'll join you, but as your shadow. No matter where you go, I'll be there to stop you."

The Prophet's arm tightened against my chest, crushing the breath from my lungs. "Then you leave us no alternative. A pity, given your potential. But we are curious. When your bubble rises from your corpse, we shall see if you can truly defy our will. Even if you can return, it'll be too late. These people will have been bound to the Lord of Light."

"Once they get to know you, they'll reject you."

"Fear silences dissent. Since you seem to have forgotten that lesson, we will give you another demonstration." The Prophet raised his voice, which thundered through the chamber,

> *The Beast, that serpent of old,*
> *We now do boldly hold!*
> *Into the pit he'll be thrown,*
> *So freedom for the Chosen will be known!*

A sinister grin curled on the Prophet's lips as he raised the dagger. I closed my eyes as the blade fell—only to hear a familiar cry and feel his grip slacken. I wriggled loose and turned to see Melody, now freed from her bindings, clutching his arm with fierce determination. My gaze darted to the chair, where the girl from Melbourne stood clutching the severed plastic ties that had bound Melody to the chair.

With a furious twist, the Prophet flung Melody aside and spat at the girl's feet before turning back to me. Suddenly, firm hands yanked me backward just as the Prophet's knife sliced through the air where I'd been a moment before. Megan, bloodied and bruised, stepped in front of me, holding a prod.

"Pick on somebody your own size," she said, then feinted left before jabbing the weapon into his thigh.

I heard an electric snap, and for an instant, the apparition above us blinked before the Prophet batted the prod away with a pained smile. But I learned he was vulnerable, just as I was. He could also disable people with a touch, as I could, which raised the question: why hadn't he done it already?

"You think you can hurt—" the Prophet began.

Then my father slammed into the man, sending them both to the floor. They grappled for the knife, the Prophet cackling with manic laughter. A wave of dread surged through me—once the Prophet had his fun, he'd kill us all.

Desperation flared as I scanned the stage for the prod I'd dropped, but it was nowhere in sight. Then I spotted the girl from Melbourne holding it out. Meeting my eyes, she said, "You remember this," before rushing into the fray and driving the shaft into the Prophet's neck with a swift, forceful jab.

Megan charged forward, slamming her prod into his ribs as Dad straddled the Prophet's chest, pinning his knife hand to the floor with both hands. The Prophet convulsed violently, his limbs jerking against the hands that restrained him.

Above us, the apparition of Dalkhu flickered like a failing neon sign. A piercing shriek tore from the Prophet's throat as his back arched, every muscle straining, while Megan and the girl from Melbourne pressed their prods deeper into his flesh. Then, all at once, his body went limp, and the ghostly image of Dalkhu winked out of existence.

I staggered to my feet, hands trembling, the air thick with the stench of sweat and ozone. Against all odds, the Prophet's link to the conscious plane had been severed. Dalkhu could still return, but not in this lifetime. For now, that was the most I could hope for.

But my past was gone forever. The manifestation of that long-dead being had reached into the immaterial realm and shredded every memory of every life I'd ever lived.

An eerie silence fell over the chamber, broken only by the low groans of blue-robed men regaining consciousness. The congregation, which moments ago had been in a state of panic, now fixed their eyes on us.

Aunt Megan, breathing heavily, took the knife from the Prophet's limp hand and tossed it off the stage. She then kicked him in the side. Melody clambered to her feet and stood next to the girl from Melbourne, both of them looking down at the Prophet, who curled in on himself with a pitiful moan.

Limping over to me, Dad pulled me into a fierce embrace, his voice thick with emotion. "I thought I lost you." I clung to him just as tightly, adrenaline coursing through my veins. After a long moment, he held me at arm's length, scanning for injuries.

"I'm fine," I said, ignoring my bruised ribs, bone-deep exhaustion, and the stinging cut on my chin. My gaze dropped to the red stains on his shirt. "But you're not."

Dad wiped his bloodied nose. "I'll manage."

Megan asked Melody, "Are you okay, dearie?" and pulled her into a tight hug. "Did that awful man hurt you?"

Melody rubbed her chafed wrists, her eyes hard. "He just bored me to death trying to convert me. Wanted me to become a cherub, like her," she said, gesturing to Melbourne, who winced at the comment.

"Thank you," I said to the girl.

She nodded in response.

"Where are Franny and Tara?" Dad asked, his voice tight with fear.

"At the temple," Melody said. "Mom was furious when that lady, Joybelle, dragged me here." She walked over and kissed the top of my head. "That lady threatened to hurt them if I didn't play the Prophet's game."

I looked down at the being who had tried to destroy everything I held dear. Without the force of his personality, he seemed smaller, diminished. "Now, he's just a sad, broken man."

"He's not who you think," Melbourne said.

Before I could ask what she meant, Megan's head jerked up, her gaze darting around. "Where are those...things? Are they coming back?"

"Ghosts from the past," I said. "You made sure they won't come back by breaking the Prophet's connection with the conscious plane."

"And yours?" Dad asked.

Focusing inward, I searched within myself for any trace of the voice. But there was nothing, leaving only a hollow ache where eons of experiences had once resided. "Mine are gone too."

"But you're still here," Melody said. "I knew you could do it."

"I didn't."

"That last figure that appeared next to you..." Dad began, but didn't finish.

"Yes, that was your brother," I said, unsure how he would react. "He was my guardian angel, always looking out for me. But the Prophet took him away, along with every memory of every life I've ever led."

"Guardian angel," Dad repeated, his tone free of surprise or judgment. "That sounds exactly like him."

"You knew?"

"I wondered. You're a lot like my brother, Stevie."

"It's only me now," I said, my throat swelling.

Dad's eyes softened. "That's all I've ever wanted. I can only hope my brother forgave me for not being there when he passed."

"There's nothing to forgive," I told him, knowing it was true. "Stephen Fisher made a choice and didn't want to put you and Mom in danger."

Dad pulled me close once again, and I nestled into his embrace, my vision blurring. Though I'd lost the past, I still had people who loved me for who I was, not who I had been.

"This isn't over people," Megan said, angling her chin off the stage.

I squinted into the depths of the chamber, dimly illuminated by the blue haze. Amidst the debris of fallen chairs and scattered chalices, the blue-robed men shook off their daze and groggily pushed themselves up from the floor. The panic that had gripped the congregation was fading. Some sobbed, others stared in shock at their fallen leader, while most huddled in small groups. But a few began creeping our way, their minds betraying an intent to inflict violence.

Joybelle was among them, limping onto the stage with her nose bent and her face a bloody mess. She fell to her knees beside the Prophet. "Get up, Hosea. Reclaim your throne!"

Hosea? I studied the Prophet more closely, peering past the physical shell to the essence within. Tendrils still churned beneath his flesh, but not nearly as thick as before. The frenzied eddies that once radiated from his mind had vanished, leaving only currents that flowed in a singular direction with the texture of wind-rippled water—like any other earthbound being.

I examined the tattoos etched into the man's skin—claws enveloping his face and teeth inked onto his upper lip and lower jaw, like a man being devoured from within. Recalling the tremors in his face, a creeping suspicion took hold: the consciousness that had once moved with untamed fury wasn't at war with itself but was fighting to be free.

On the bus, the Prophet had told me he could leave the bounds of flesh; that was how he'd escaped the cryo-pod. It seemed he had also learned to control the mind of another—a new and terrifying trick. And those prods, by severing the connection to the conscious plane, had also broken the link to whoever controlled this man.

"This isn't the Prophet," I realized.

Joybelle whirled on me. "Leave him alone, Beast!"

Melbourne moved within the protective shield of my father, who eyed her warily. "Are you going to tell him or shall I?" she asked Joybelle.

A crimson storm raged behind Joybelle's hardened eyes. "You are a false witness who breathes lies."

The girl turned to me, hugging herself. "She and Hosea have a son, about our age, staying at a house near the Grand Temple." She dropped her head. "He promised to get me back home."

I nodded slowly, the pieces falling into place. Hosea was no prophet; he was a father. And Joybelle the mother—the secret she wanted to keep hidden. Her child was the power behind the throne.

Joybelle abruptly stood and ran to the edge of the stage, her arms spread wide. "Protect the Lord of Light!"

Dad's hand clamped around my forearm. "Time to get out of here."

"Good idea," Melody said, grabbing the girl's arm and moving toward the walkway. But as I looked out over the expanse of desperate souls gathered near the lift, their emotions teetering between confusion and anger, I feared our escape wouldn't be so simple. We were badly outnumbered, and if the crowd turned on us…

"Where's Meg?" Dad asked.

I looked around, unable to find her. Closing my eyes, I used my inner compass to scan the chamber for her familiar presence. Then I found it—a bright spark of determination amidst the turmoil of other minds. My eyes flew open, and I pointed to the wooden platform beside the stage. "There, climbing the ladder."

CHAPTER THIRTY-THREE

Megan scanned the chamber from the stage, her gaze sweeping over the crowd as clusters of congregants whispered and pointed at their fallen leader, now a crumpled heap at little Stevie's feet. Cherubs dropped from the ceiling, shedding their wings as they sprinted for the exit. Among the crowd, disciples aided the downed faithful—collateral damage from the nightmarish creature that had emerged from within the Prophet. Tear-shaped drops rose from some of the bodies, a grim sign they wouldn't be getting back up. Blue-robed Swords lifted themselves out of the haze, murder gleaming in their collective eyes. And Joybelle limped toward the stage, blood trickling from her forehead.

"This isn't over, people," she said, knowing the momentary reprieve wouldn't last. They needed to get out of here, and fast. But then what? Even if by some miracle they fought their way through the crowd, they'd have to hijack a bus and get past the military personnel stationed at the main gate—not to mention the small army of Swords at the base of the mound. Even if they somehow managed all that, a bigger issue loomed—the Prophet may have lost this battle, but his army of goons backed by a congregation that numbered in the millions would continue waging their holy war. A no-win situation all around.

Then Megan got an idea. An outrageous, impossible idea.

Her gaze flicked to the raised platform beside the stage. Max perched on the ledge, glassy-eyed, his stout legs dangling. The camera was still pointed at the crowd, its "ON AIR" light glowing red. Megan glanced at her companions, who remained fixated on the Prophet, huddled into a ball. They wouldn't like what she had in mind, not one bit, but there was no time for a debate.

Vaulting off the stage, Megan waded through the shimmering blue haze and climbed the platform's wooden rungs. Her late mother's devotion to another demagogue had taught her a harsh truth—some beliefs ran so deep, people would rather die than abandon them. No amount of reason could pierce those convictions, not even the prospect of orphaning a child.

But this situation differed in one key aspect—the church's doctrine contained a kernel of truth: rebirth was real, as was retaining memories of the past. The crux of the issue lay with the messenger, who had built a following based on fear and the false promise of an afterlife only he controlled. Had her mother survived, she would've been the Prophet's biggest fan.

"Max," she barked, reaching the top.

Basset-hound eyes rolled toward her. "It's not my fault."

"Cut the crap. You led Joybelle right to them, didn't you? Taking the family out of the country was just a ploy to get an exclusive for your stupid show."

"That's not true. I was compelled."

"What else did that monster promise you, huh? An interview? Eternal life? You're an idiot."

Max laid a hand over his heart. "I confess, the prospect of an exclusive intrigued me. But I swear, I never breathed a word about the boy or the family's location. Joybelle kept pressing me for that information, but I didn't tell her a thing. She figured it out all on her own. I don't know how. It's not my fault."

The memory of her own encounter with Joybelle resurfaced, and Megan bit back a retort. Maybe Max was telling the truth—or at least his version of it. "Then why are you here? Ratings, am I right?"

"To save you."

"Excuse me?"

Max angled his head toward the stage, where Joybelle was now screaming at the crowd. "Unless I cooperated, she threatened to give you the same treatment as your mate."

Megan's jaw clenched. "Obadiah."

"I swear, I had no idea they'd murder the man." He pinched his lips and lowered his gaze. "And to go after the kid like that...inexcusable."

"How do I know you're not lying?"

Max shook his head emphatically. "I've been known to bend the truth a time or two, but never with you."

Megan almost scoffed, then reconsidered. Strictly speaking, Max had never lied to her face. Anger cooling, she noted his sickly pallor, bloodshot eyes, and trembling hands. "All right. If you want my forgiveness, you need to do exactly what I say. No questions, no delays."

Max's eyes brightened, and he perked up. "Anything, my dearest. Did you know you have blood on your shirt?"

"That's not mine. The camera's been live streaming this whole time, yes?"

"Since the moment you set foot in this god-forsaken place."

"How many are watching?"

"North of a hundred and twenty million. All hanging on our every word. See, I've nothing to hide."

Megan's heart seized at the thought of so many people listening to their conversation, but it suited her purpose. Swallowing hard, she refocused. "Did you see who appeared over the boy?"

"I did indeed," he said, nodding solemnly. "That explains quite a lot."

"And the camera captured that, along with the…thing over the Prophet?"

"Got it all in high definition, my dear. Once I convinced myself I wasn't hallucinating, I double-checked the monitor. What was it, do you know? It looked like a demented jellyfish."

Mindful of the millions watching, Megan chose her words carefully. "The prevailing theory at ISBLIC is that the Beacon weakens the barrier between overlapping dimensions. That could explain the mist, those drops, and that creature…" She paused, wanting to give weight to her next statement. "This is pure speculation, mind you, but I believe we witnessed the past incarnations of both the Prophet and little Stevie."

"My thinking exactly, dearest. What can I do to help?"

Megan looked at the crowd converging on the stage, their eyes darting between the Prophet, Joybelle, and little Stevie. For the moment, indecision gripped them, but that wouldn't last. These people were true believers, ready to sacrifice themselves and others in service to their faith. Her own mother was proof of that.

A man shook his fist and shouted something about "The Beast." Someone else hurled a shoe at Eric, narrowly missing his head. The tension was stretched as thin as a piano wire, ready to snap at the barest spark. Megan intended to strike the match herself.

"Hand me the mic," she said. "Then crank up the speakers and point the camera at me."

"Really?"

"Really."

The big man practically glowed. "Excellent! Will you permit me to introduce you?"

Megan glanced down at herself—ripped slacks, bloody shirt, and her hair a tangled mess. To think she'd once fussed endlessly before an interview. But her current look fit the occasion. "Fine. Just make it quick."

Max hefted his considerable bulk off the wooden planks, smoothed his mustache, and ambled to the front of the camera.

"G'day, Mysteryites," he began in a low, somber tone. "I have to confess: I haven't the foggiest clue what's happening here. We've witnessed a brutal murder, an eldritch horror, and a stampede toward the exit. Somehow, the guards dropped where they stood. Pure pandemonium."

He gestured toward the stage. "I'm glad to report the boy is unharmed. Some call him a Beast, but I'm not one of them. Surely, you all saw it—Stephen Fisher's ghost. I don't know why or how he appeared, but he was a good friend of mine and I miss him dearly. The lad's father, Eric, is here too—another mate of mine. And you all remember Melody. For what it's worth, I don't believe she willingly... um, married the Prophet." He cleared his throat, then continued. "Anyway, a dear friend is here to help untangle this mess. None other than the Executive Director of ISBLIC, Doctor Megan McCullough." He handed her the microphone and stepped out of camera range.

Megan glanced briefly at the camera—she only needed it as a witness—before turning to the real audience, where puzzled yet hostile gazes stared up at her. "Hello, everyone," she began, just as a sharp squeal of feedback burst from the speakers. Max quickly adjusted a dial and flashed her a thumbs-up. Swallowing, Megan pressed on, feeling tightness grip her throat. "The Prophet isn't who you think he is. You all saw it—his people murdered my good friend, and then he tried to kill a young child. That boy's name is Stevie, and I think we can all agree he's no monster."

Jeers erupted from the crowd, and a woman shook her fist. Megan flinched as a goblet shattered against the rail, then ducked too late as another grazed her head. Her eyes snapped to the walkway where Eric, Stevie, Melody, and the other child inched toward the elevator, the crowd shadowing their every step. Up ahead, a line of Swords blocked any chance of escape. Eric motioned for her to come down, but what was the point? They were all trapped.

From the stage, Joybelle pointed at little Stevie and shrieked, "They must pay sevenfold for their sins! Unsheathe your swords and strike down the Beast!"

The crowd's anger swelled, and Megan knew she had to act fast—and change tactics. Drawing on childhood memories etched into her mind by years of forced recitation, she spoke the language of Joybelle. "Satan masquerades as an angel of light and as a servant of righteousness. He performs signs and wonders that serve the lie and all the ways wickedness deceives. Like this false prophet, who peddles empty promises of an afterlife you've already earned. You saw his true nature—a serpent spawned from the depths of hell!"

"Lies! Poison!" Joybelle spat, her voice cracking.

Megan jabbed a finger at the Prophet, still curled up on the stage. "If you don't believe me, believe the sigil he carved into his own flesh—a dragon, born from the likeness of what lies beneath the earth!"

One by one, the faithful turned from Joybelle to focus on Megan. Some nodded in agreement, while others traced the ankh-like symbol over their chests. Even the Swords lowered their weapons, exchanging uncertain glances.

Megan pressed her hands together, softening her tone. "And we saw the divine light appear over the child in the form of the Lamb, an innocent traveler who activated the Beacon in hopes of bringing salvation to our world." She spread her arms wide, encompassing the entire congregation. "The serpent takes many guises, and one of them is the man who calls himself a prophet!"

Joybelle howled from the stage, "Do not listen to the devil's handmaid!"

But most of the crowd ignored her, glancing at little Stevie. From the corner of her eye, Megan caught the boy's silent plea, his young face a portrait of despair. He knew what she intended and silently begged her not to do it. Turning to him, she mouthed, "I'm sorry," certain there was no other choice. A movement of this magnitude couldn't be stopped, it had to be redirected.

Megan flung her arm toward Stevie, her voice piercing the air like an arrow. "Behold! The true Prophet rises! Stephen Fisher reborn, our deliverance made flesh! You saw him for yourself, the walker between worlds, come to vanquish the true Beast and unshackle us from the bounds of Earth!"

On the stage, the self-styled prophet struggled to his elbows. "She's right," he said, then repeated it more forcefully to ensure his voice carried. Megan was astonished.

Murmurs rolled through the congregation, swelling into a wordless roar. All eyes shifted to little Stevie, who shook his head in mute horror at the mantle she had thrust upon him. Eric stiffened, while Melody squeezed Stevie's hand, a faint, almost sad smile on her lips.

Chaos broke out on the chamber floor as Swords began battling one another. In moments, six lay crumpled on the ground and the rest threw down their weapons, bowing their heads toward the boy.

Max sidled up beside Megan, leaning close and gripping her hand. "My clever girl. Bravo."

"Thanks for your help, Max," she said, not pulling away. Once you got to know him, he wasn't so bad.

Slowly, like a synchronized wave, the congregation sank to their knees, the rustle of fabric and popping of aged joints filling the vast chamber. Megan followed suit, as did Max. After a brief hesitation, the disciples and acolytes knelt as well, followed by the remaining Swords.

All except Joybelle, whose anguished wail spiraled into the uncaring air: "Nooooo!"

CHAPTER THIRTY-FOUR

From within the home of the self-proclaimed prophet, my gaze swept across the estate's vast grounds. Waterfalls cascaded over rock ledges into an immense pool that could have been mistaken for a lake. At its center, a tiki-style swim-up bar perched on a small island, flanked by docked paddle boats. On the far shore, an undulating wave machine sent gentle swells lapping against a pristine white sand beach. A lazy river wound around the perimeter, weaving past a towering corkscrew waterslide that plunged into a lush, jungle-like grotto feeding the pool. Tennis courts and a manicured golf course bordered the waterfront, while in the distance, a herd of giraffes grazed peacefully. The estate was as ostentatious as its owner.

I shifted my attention to the kid seated at a poolside table, focusing on the mind that spun in the same way as the possessed Hosea's, though without the chaos. Probably because the boy no longer had to battle for control over his father's mind. That instability had been a blessing, as it hindered his ability to harm Megan and my dad.

"So, this is him," Dad said, standing beside me. "Doesn't look like much."

"Hosea told me his real name is Jezreel," I said. "This world knew him as the Prophet, but to me, he was Dalkhu."

Melody shielded her eyes against the late morning sun. "I've heard that name before, but thought it was just a story parents told kids to make them behave."

"I never expected to see him again," I said quietly.

"Do you really have to talk to that boy?" she asked.

"I'd rather not, but I need to make sure he doesn't cause any more trouble."

Dad glanced at his watch. "We're supposed to be at the Temple of the Prophet by noon. Should I make a call?"

"This won't take long," I said.

Mom and Aunt Franny were already at the temple, working with the newly appointed acolytes to prepare for my appearance. I had no desire to be there, just as I had no desire to be here. All I wanted was to go home.

"I'm going with you this time," Dad said, his tone leaving no room for argument.

"That's fine. Melody, you can come too. We're going to be dealing with this boy for a long while."

Melody wrinkled her nose in distaste. "No thanks. I just wanted to see him. He looks mean."

Dad sniffed. "That's putting it mildly."

"Be careful," Melody said.

"I will," I assured them both.

With Dad at my side, I walked down the path from the house to the beach. As we approached, I watched the boy idly picking at the lavish breakfast spread before him. Letting the music wash through me, I peered into the maelstrom of his mind, the eye in the center studying me as intensely as I studied it. Hard to believe this being, eons beyond me in experience, remained frozen in time—unchanging and unchanged. I settled into a chair at the opposite end of the table, while my father stood behind me, arms crossed.

After a charged silence, the boy abruptly swept his arm across the table in a violent arc. Dishes, glasses, and food crashed to the sand in a noisy avalanche. Leaping to his feet, he let loose a primal scream, grabbed a stack of plates, and hurled them one by one against a rocky outcropping where they shattered in sprays of porcelain.

Dad moved to intervene, but I stopped him with a raised hand and a slight shake of my head. I knew the fit would pass, for this was his way. Sure enough, Jezreel returned to his seat and calmly scooped scrambled eggs onto a fresh plate as if nothing out of the ordinary had occurred.

"Come to gloat, have you?" he finally said, mouth full.

"A little bit," I admitted. "Also, to give you fair warning."

He chuckled dryly, piling the plate with potatoes and vanilla pudding. "No need to sit way over there. Come, eat, drink. I won't bite. Well, not this time anyway."

"You tried to kill me."

"Only because you interfered. We lost our temper."

"Then you murdered my friend and tried to destroy his soul."

"Don't be so dramatic. We were making a point."

"And you ordered your people to abduct my family and hurt my Aunt Megan."

Jezreel swirled the food on his plate into a stomach-churning concoction, made worse when he spooned ketchup on top. "You grow too attached. That's always been your problem."

"I won't let you harm the people I love, or anyone else."

He jabbed the spoon at me. "They are but pieces in the great game. Like you."

"You're the only one playing, Jezreel."

"You know that's not our name."

"That's the name your mother gave you. Did you know the police arrested Joybelle as an accessory to murder, along with your blue-robed soldiers? You should care more about what happens to your mom."

He waved a dismissive hand. "We've been born so many times by so many mothers that the concept has lost all meaning. When and where we choose to return is entirely up to us. She was nothing more than the vessel. The sow, if you will."

"Charming," Dad muttered.

The boy ignored him.

"Everything has a beginning," I said. "Here, that beginning has a name…" Pausing for effect, I enunciated clearly, "Jez-reel."

He inhaled deeply through his nose, as if trying to regain the composure I intended to upset. "Annoyance is a gift of yours. This may be a surprise, but the closest thing we have to a family is you."

"Who you tried to kill."

"Don't be so sensitive. It was just a spat between an older and younger sibling, that's all." Jezreel shoveled a spoonful of the revolting pudding-potato-egg mixture into his mouth and smacked his lips, a deliberate act to unsettle me.

"I'm not your brother, but you're going to have a little sister soon, which I'm sure you know." I paused. "That's gross—not the food, but getting your mother pregnant while controlling your father."

"Pfft. Your petty concepts of morality are nothing more than tools to control the masses. We are above such trivial concerns—as you should be." Jezreel licked the plate clean with an obscene slurp. "Come along now. You mentioned a warning. I'm eager to hear about your next move."

"This isn't a game, but I had a long talk with your dad—"

"I have no father," he said sharply.

"Hosea doesn't agree. Despite what you did, he still considers you his son. You can have a real dad, Jezreel, and not just a puppet."

The boy twirled his spoon with a smirk. "The man is a vessel, nothing more. One I can control any time I please."

"Listen to me. If you dare possess him again, I'll know." Rising from my seat, I leaned across the table and poked him in the chest. "And I'll make sure those metal rods get used on this body. This time, your link to the physical plane will be severed, and you'll forget who you are and where you came from."

"Why not do it then?"

I sank back into the chair, growing tired of the back and forth. "I might. Everybody here would be better off if I did. But your dad asked me to give you another chance. I'm not sure that's wise."

"That's your warning? I expected more from the newly appointed prophet."

"A part of me hopes you don't listen."

Jezreel ladled more pudding onto his plate. "Enough posturing. We so rarely have these little chats. Tell me, what exactly are you planning? Besides having Hosea hound me."

"My plans are no secret. The Beast was slain—that's you—and Hosea freed. That's what people believe, and it happens to be true. Your dad will remain the head of the church, and he promised to keep an eye on you."

The boy nodded approvingly. "With you pulling the strings from the shadows. That's good, that's very good, Shurruppak. You remember that name, don't you? A worthy strategy from my best pupil."

"My name is Stevie, and the only strings I'll be pulling are yours."

"Call yourself whatever you like, but you are still my favorite and have much to learn."

"You have nothing to teach."

He tsked. "So young. So arrogant. Without me, you'd be an infinitesimal speck in the blackness of eternity. Consider this our final lesson, and this world your teacher."

"I won't allow you to interfere, Jezreel. No matter where you go or what you try, in this life or the next, I'll be there to stop you."

"No need. I'm content to watch these people annihilate themselves through their own stupidity. As their new prophet, you could put a stop to it. I would have."

"Their fate is in their hands," I said. "Not mine, and not yours."

"Easy to say until you watch those you hold dear suffer. I won't stop the inevitable, though I will enjoy the moment you beg for my assistance. As this world sickens and dies, may you finally find wisdom. Only then will I deign to help."

My father extended his arm and tapped his watch.

I locked eyes with Jezreel one last time. "You're dying now, though you don't realize it. A fading memory of the being you once were. To be truly reborn is to let go of the past. That's the lesson I've learned, and one you should consider."

Jezreel smiled serenely and clasped his hands together. "You will make an excellent prophet."

"Goodbye, Jezreel. I hope we don't meet again." I pushed my chair back and stood, feeling my dad's supportive arm encircle my shoulders as we walked away.

Jezreel called out to our retreating backs, "Don't be so sure I didn't plan to make you the prophet all along."

I didn't turn around.

CHAPTER THIRTY-FIVE

Inside the sanctuary of the Temple of the Prophet's vestry, Mom guided my arms into the voluminous sleeves of a flowing blue robe. Trimmed in gold and emblazoned with the ankh-like symbol of life, the garment settled heavily on my shoulders, weighted with expectations I couldn't meet and wasn't ready to carry.

Our arrival prompted a whirlwind of activity and emotion. Mom had nearly knocked Dad over in her rush to reach me, rocking me as she whispered, "My boy, my boy," over and over. Neither of us mentioned the ghost that she and millions of others had seen next to me inside the inner chamber of the Beacon. In that moment, held in my mother's arms, the past seemed far less important than the present—and the uncertain future that lay ahead.

Now, as Mom stepped back to admire her handiwork, a hesitant smile softened her features. "You look the part, sweetie," she said, her voice tinged with worry.

I turned to the full-length mirror and grimaced. "I hate this."

Dad, hovering over my shoulder, rubbed the back of his neck, his expression weary. "We'll burn the costume once this absurdity is over with."

"No, we won't," Mom said firmly. "I hate this too, but Stevie will have to make an appearance every so often to make sure *that man* stays on script."

That man was Hosea, whom my parents didn't fully trust. Neither did I, though I was confident that self-preservation would keep him in line. With a single word, I could have him replaced as head of the Church. He also feared his son, and with good reason. Hosea now waited for me at the top of the grand stairwell, accompanied by an honor guard of freshly minted acolytes. Although my mom struggled to accept that I had once lived as Stephen Fisher, she had no qualms embracing this scheme to establish me as the Prophet. She and Megan argued it was the only way to stop the madness. I reluctantly agreed, unable to come up with a better alternative.

Megan popped her head through the door, took one look at me, and said, "Better than a loincloth."

"This is your fault," I said.

"You'd prefer to be trapped in that chamber?"

"Maybe."

"Too bad. Act the part and buy us some peace. It's not easy saving the world." Megan shot Dad a wry look. "More like your brother every day."

"Stubbornness runs in the family," Dad said.

Mom's stricken expression made Megan roll her eyes. "Oh, get over it, Tara." She refocused on me. "The delegation's here. Are you ready to see them? If you need more time, that's not a problem. I can tell them to wait."

Dad answered for me. "Let's get this over with."

Megan signaled to the group waiting just outside, then stepped back to join my parents against the far wall. As she passed, she murmured, "Don't forget what we talked about. I'm going to need their help."

"Me too," I told her.

Aunt Franny entered first, resplendent in the flowing white robes of a high-ranking disciple. She'd fully committed to her role in Megan's scheme, even going so far as to install herself as head of the Temple in Joybelle's place. "I'm done running" had been her fierce declaration. No one dared argue, least of all Hosea, who promptly made the appointment official.

Filing in behind her came a somber procession of fifteen travelers, including the girl from Melbourne. At the tail end of the group, hand-in-hand with the traveler I'd met at school, was Melody. They silently fanned out to encircle me, with the notable exception of Melbourne, who lingered near the door, conspicuously avoiding my gaze.

In a clipped, formal tone, Aunt Franny made the introductions. "Stevie, these are travelers from the First Cohort who've risked exposing their identities to come here today. Others remain in hiding, but I've been assured these few can help spread the word about our discussion. First Cohort, may I present my nephew, Stevie Fisher, who, along with my daughter, activated the Beacon."

Taking my cue from Aunt Franny, I replied in an equally formal tone. "Thank you for coming for what I hope is a new beginning."

A few inclined their heads, but the rest just studied me.

Melody extended the arm of the girl whose hand she clutched. "Stevie, you remember Tina, from school?"

"The envoy from Lumina Minor," I said, offering her a kind smile. "Welcome. It took courage for you to come here today."

Tina's inner eye focused on mine. "Is that really you? You seem…different."

She was right. After my memories had been stripped away, the currents of my mind flowed more smoothly than before. At least, according to Melody. "You're not wrong. Everything that came before is gone."

"You chose to intervene," Tina said, making the sign of eternal life. "Thank you."

"You're welcome, though it wasn't my choice." I swept my gaze over the Cohort. "All memory of every traveler, every place, and everything I've done over uncounted lives is gone. A parting gift from the one who called himself a prophet."

The travelers stirred uneasily, then formed a circle, consulting one another without words, looking within themselves as they looked within me. All except the girl from Melbourne. After a time, Tina raised her head and locked eyes with me. "We recognize you as the Unbound and grieve your loss."

I didn't. I had allowed the sins of my past to define who I was and constrain the futures I created. No longer. Losing that burden opened my eyes to new possibilities, including what I would do to protect this world from further interference. The past wasn't fixed, and neither was I. For the first time, I felt truly human. But I didn't say any of those things.

"A small price to pay to ensure the Prophet can no longer threaten this world."

Another traveler, his eyes flashing, stepped forward. "The Prophet knew you, and you knew him. Why didn't you warn us about this threat before we came here?"

I met the boy's accusing glare head-on. "Because I thought he was gone. I can't tell you more because those memories are no longer mine. The good news is you can return home. When you do, warn your people this being is on the loose. While this world might be more vulnerable, none are immune. I'm afraid Dalkhu—that's what he calls himself—will forever be a threat. The only way to stand against him is to stand together. That starts now."

The boy thrust an angry finger at Melbourne, standing still as a statue by the door. "What about her?"

"As far as I'm concerned, it's never too late to do the right thing. She saved my life. Besides, her people need to be warned, just as yours do."

"The Fallen betrayed us! None of them should be allowed near a beacon again. They knew the risks of being part of the First Cohort."

I turned to the girl. "Anything to add?"

Eyes downcast, Melbourne hugged herself and mumbled just loud enough for everybody to hear, "I made a mistake."

The room burst into a clamor of outraged voices as the travelers took turns airing grievances—people hurt, taken against their will, the rods cruelly used on their own kind. All valid points, as far as I was concerned.

"Nobody will be left behind," I said, pitching my voice to cut across their grumbling. "The Fallen should be the last to leave this world, and their fate decided by their own leaders."

Reluctant nods followed, even from the girl, no doubt fearing being stuck here otherwise.

The boy then gave voice to what I expected they all were thinking: "I'm ready to leave now."

Megan stepped out from behind me. "What about your families and the people who love you? Who worked so hard to keep you safe? Are you going to put them through the agony of losing a child? Would you really do that to them? Would you do that to yourself? You came here for a purpose. Just because it's not what you expected doesn't mean you should flee. Don't abandon us as the Fallen abandoned you. You have a life here. Live it."

Sniffles broke out. Tears welled in a few eyes. But the boy stood firm. "That's not your choice to make."

"Everyone," I said, placing a hand on Megan's elbow. "This is Doctor Megan McCullough, the Director of ISBLIC."

"Former Director," the boy said.

I shook my head. At my request, Hosea had contacted President Stoughton to demand the Beacon be returned to ISBLIC's jurisdiction and Megan reinstated as head of the organization. The President tried to brush him off until Hosea threatened to publicly denounce the Administration. That worked like a charm.

"No longer," I said. "She's not only in charge but has taken back control of the Beacon. Consider her the spokesperson for the people of this world."

Surprised, Megan said, "What? No, no, that's not me."

"I say it is, and that's what I've told everyone who's contacted me since you appointed me as the Prophet."

"You shouldn't have done that, Stevie. That's not how it works."

The corner of my mouth ticked up. "Somebody told me it's not easy to save the world. I suggest you act the part."

Megan huffed, glancing at my mom and dad, who only smiled.

"Anyway," I continued. "I know you're all eager to go home. To that end, I want you to hear about this new, um…"

"Charter," Megan supplied.

"Right, and the Director is going to need your help."

I stepped back to allow Megan to directly address the gathered travelers.

◆ ◆ ◆

Megan swept her gaze over the children, their youthful faces belying the fact that each hailed from a distant world far more technologically advanced than Earth. But beneath the veneer of maturity, they were still kids, no matter their origin.

She cleared her throat, drawing their attention. "ISBLIC has a new charter and a new purpose. We're shifting our focus from pure scientific inquiry to establishing guidelines for the Beacon's use. Our priority is to set clear rules for when a person can choose to end their life within the machine. Terminal illness confirmed by a physician's assessment, for starters. Some states already have laws in place, which we'll respect. But where there are gaps, ISBLIC will provide a framework. As it stands, none of you come close to meeting that basic criterion. And that's as it should be. I fully expect you all to live long, fulfilling lives."

She paused to let the words sink in.

The boy crossed his arms, his brows knitting together in a defiant scowl. "You don't get it. The Prophet may be gone, but that doesn't mean we're safe. Crazies are hunting us down, thinking we're devils or something. And nations want to steal imagined secrets to better fight their wars. We need to leave now."

Megan met his defiance with a steady gaze. "I understand your concerns, I do. But the fact remains, you're a minor and need to respect our laws and customs. That's non-negotiable."

The boy exchanged meaningful looks with his fellow travelers. "If we die outside the Beacon—by accident or otherwise—we'll be reborn here with no memory of who we are and where we came from. Stranded."

Stevie walked up to the boy and placed a reassuring hand on his shoulder. Though the boy flinched at the contact, he didn't pull away. "If that happens, I'll find you. I promise not to leave until every traveler is safely off the planet."

"And I'll help," Melody said. "I'm staying anyway. I like it here."

Megan softened her tone. "To help keep you safe, ISBLIC will work with other countries to set up sanctuaries, places where travelers can gather and be protected."

"Starting with a community in the San Juan Islands," Eric added.

"Herd us into pens like cattle," the boy said. "No, thanks. I prefer to stay in hiding."

Stevie gestured toward his parents. "We've been hunted for years. You and your families can come with us. I know when bad people arrive and can protect us."

"I've seen him do it," said the girl from Melbourne.

Another child asked Stevie, "Those guards that fell in the Beacon, was that you?"

Stevie dipped his chin in the barest of nods. Megan understood his reticence. She'd read the reports—most of the blue-robed men inside the chamber hadn't fully recovered. Headaches, slurred speech, partial paralysis, and for two of them, the damage proved fatal.

"Safer together," Melody said.

Aunt Franny moved beside Megan. "The Church will cover all the costs: relocation, housing, lost wages, round-the-clock security—everything. The organization has more than enough resources to make that happen. I'll see to it personally that you and your families want for nothing."

The assembled children traded glances. Some nodded slowly, while others gnawed at their lips or shook their heads, plainly skeptical. The boy's face contorted, as if he'd tasted something sour, but he'd lost the defiant stare.

"Well," Megan said to him.

"I'll talk to my parents," the boy said. "See what they think."

A flicker of hope stirred within Megan. Trust would take time to build, that much was clear. Only through concrete action could she hope to win them over. But she'd walk through fire if that's what it took—not only because it was the right thing to do, but also because she wanted their cooperation for what she hoped would come next.

"You should all discuss this with your families," she said, then took a steadying breath, prepared to lay her cards on the table. "There's one more thing I'd like to propose. A request, not a demand, so please hear me out. If you're willing, I'd like to send an envoy to each of your homeworlds. One to start, someone who's both able and eager to serve as a bridge between civilizations. You'd have final say on whom we send, of course. Admittedly, we botched first contact—"

A derisive snort from the boy interrupted, causing Tina to elbow him in the ribs.

"I'm under no illusions," Megan continued. "But my hope—and it may prove to be a naïve one—is that when the people here learn of the wider universe, it will serve to unite rather than divide. I apologize for the nonsense you had to put up with. Inexcusable, but I hope you've encountered some good people along the way."

She spread her hands in a conciliatory gesture. "This is wholly my idea, not Stevie's or Melody's. They never once suggested or pushed for it. Ultimately, the decision rests with you and your people. You're under no obligation to answer now, or ever. I just wanted to put the possibility on the table."

Megan held her breath, waiting for a reaction. She slid the boy a sidelong glance, bracing for an outburst. But he remained silent.

Silence stretched as the travelers turned to face one another, a wordless communion flowing between them. Megan recalled Melody mentioning that while travelers couldn't read thoughts, they could sense emotions. Perhaps that's what she witnessed now—a conversation conducted in pure empathic resonance.

After what felt like an eternity, Tina stepped forward, apparently having been chosen as spokesperson for the group. "You already have an envoy. Did you want another?"

"One to start is fine," Megan said. "If that works out, we can expand the program to …wait, what did you say?"

Tina cocked her head, her eyes seeming to look through Megan. "You don't know."

"What is it I don't know?"

"She's talking about Dolores," Melody said.

Megan blinked, unsure if she'd heard right. "What was that?"

"Dolores is already there. Remember, she went into the Beacon with me and my dad. I hoped she'd go, but couldn't be sure. Not until Tina told me."

"She arrived before our departure," Tina explained. "As an infant, naturally. But the caretakers knew she came through the Beacon. I expect the one you called Dolores will find her way back here eventually. For all the reasons you've mentioned."

Megan pressed a palm over her heart, trying to rein in the emotions threatening to overwhelm her. She had never understood why Dolores had killed herself. But ending her life hoping to travel to another world made perfect sense. Dolores, brilliant, brave Dolores, had achieved her dream of traveling between the stars.

"Thank you," she managed to say. "I couldn't imagine a better representative. Truly. She represents the best of us."

Tina nodded in agreement.

The door creaked open, interrupting the conversation. An acolyte poked her head into the room and addressed Franny. "Pardon the interruption, First Disciple, but Brother Hosea asked me to relay a message. He says the congregation grows restless."

Franny flicked her wrist in a shooing motion. The acolyte, abashed, withdrew on near-silent feet.

Melody detached herself from the throng of children and came to stand at Megan's side, wordlessly taking her hand. Stevie moved in beside her, slipping his arm around her waist. Eric and Tara stood sentinel just behind him. Franny laid a steadying hand on Megan's shoulder. A rush of gratitude washed over her for these remarkable people. Her people. Her family.

Drawing herself up, shoulders back and head high, Megan met each young traveler's gaze, willing them to sense the depth of her conviction. "Thank you all for coming, for hearing us out, and for keeping open minds. You've been through more than anyone should ever have to endure, especially at your tender ages. For that, I'm truly sorry. But I promise you this: come hell or high water, we're going to get you home."

CHAPTER THIRTY-SIX

A biting chill clung to the air as I stood with my family and Megan in the vestibule abutting the narthex of the Temple of the Prophet. Beyond the imposing doors, the murmur of countless conversations mingled with the shuffling of feet and the solemn toll of ceremonial bells. Periodic roars surged through the unseen crowd like an approaching thunderstorm, making my stomach clench with unease. I reached for my dad's hand, grateful when he gave it a reassuring squeeze.

Mom tucked a stray lock of hair behind my ear. "Have you thought about what you're going to say?"

My gaze fell to the marble floor as I struggled to organize my jumbled thoughts. The people outside those doors wanted solutions to problems that couldn't be found in the words of a prophet or a traveler. Certainly not by slaying imaginary beasts. They needed to look within, not without for guidance. Everything was connected—the plants, insects, animals, even the rocks beneath our feet. Life was the mirror the universe held up to itself to find meaning. The same went for people, each soul a fractured shard of that same reflection. Including me. But how to put that into words?

"I'll tell them I'm no different from anybody else," I said, thinking aloud. "We're all travelers, moving from one life to the next, whether we realize it or not. And I'm no prophet. I've made mistakes, bad ones, and I've learned not to let those define me. I'll suggest they do the same."

"Spoken straight from the heart," Mom said.

My voice hardened. "I'll also warn them the Beast was created to distract them from realizing they're being used. That's an old trick of the being known here as Jezreel. For that reason, I've decided to denounce him. He showed no remorse when we met, so I expect he'll try to take power again—if not in this life, then the next. People need to be warned."

"That's all you can do," Dad said, "but I'm not sure that's going to help."

"Me neither," I agreed, having nothing else to suggest.

Aunt Franny twisted the unfamiliar pendant at her throat. "Nothing about the Beacon?"

"That's my job," Megan said.

Melody and I nodded, agreeing wholeheartedly. The Beacon wasn't a holy artifact, it was a tool used to bridge worlds. As long as I was associated with this church, I didn't intend to mix the two.

"Hosea may be a problem," Dad said, his expression darkening. "He seems cooperative now, but you know what they say about power."

"I'll keep him on a short leash," Franny said. "He'll do what he's told."

Her comment gave me pause. Wasn't that exactly what Jezreel accused me of doing—pulling strings from the shadows? But what choice did I have? Hosea, grateful for having been freed from his son's hold, had readily agreed to my demands. Or rather, Aunt Franny's demands. Even getting Megan reappointed as the Director of ISBLIC had required his intervention. Hosea held strings of his own, mostly connected to politicians. I needed him, but trusting him was another matter entirely.

Melody placed her hands on her hips. "He shouldn't be in charge of anything. Sure, he might have been possessed, but I bet he went along with it just fine…until he couldn't control his son."

"I agree," I said, thinking there would be no need for me to pull strings not attached to anything.

Aunt Franny's eyes gleamed with a sharp, calculating intensity. "We can gradually transition Hosea's responsibilities away until he becomes nothing more than a titular figure. But realize that means you'll have to be more involved, Stevie. Like it or not, this is your church now."

I extended my palms to ward off her words. "No, no, no, no. My only job is to make sure Jezreel doesn't interfere. People need to shape their own destiny."

Dad gripped my shoulders. "You're like everybody else now, remember? You have a stake in that future."

Melody intertwined her fingers with mine. "We're people now, and that's what people do, help each other."

Trapped by my own words, I could only sigh. But if shedding my past had one silver lining, it was this: I was undeniably human now. Perhaps the principle of non-interference no longer bound me as it once had.

Mom smoothed the folds of my robe. "I know you don't want to do this, but it's time."

Aunt Franny swung open the vestibule door, the sudden influx of sound making my heart skip a beat. I backed away until Megan rested her palm against the small of my back and gently nudged me toward the exit.

"You'll do just fine," she said.

"But what if I don't?" I whispered.

"Doing the right thing isn't always easy or popular. I know something about that. Tell your truth, regardless of whether people like it or not. That's on them, not you. Besides, whatever you say can't lead to a worse outcome than whatever that boy had planned."

"Thank you."

"You're welcome."

Drawing in a fortifying breath, I strode across the sun-warmed flagstones to the podium atop the staircase. Hosea awaited me there, clad in acolyte's robes and maintaining a respectful distance. As I neared, he bowed, a calculated show of deference to his former congregation.

I stepped onto the podium, my pulse thundering in my ears. Facing the crowd, I scanned the endless sea of faces—hundreds of thousands packed into the courtyard and beyond. One by one, they lowered their heads in waves until a revenant hush blanketed the multitude, heavy and absolute. The sheer weight of expectation stole the air from my lungs and the words from my mind.

Then their eyes lifted, shining with a raw, aching hope that cut into me like glass. With bated breath, they waited to hear from their new false prophet.

AUTHOR'S NOTE

While the Prophet's arrival may have been inevitable, I had never planned on writing his and Stevie's story. It was only the kind words and reviews from readers of the first book, *Melody*, that inspired me to write the second. Thank you.

Thanks also to my writing group, the Inkwells: Sarah Beauchemin (*author of Final Belongings*), Michelle Fogle (*City of Liars*), Ed Hanzel (*Avalon Found*), Drew Melbourne (*Percival Gynt and the Conspiracy of Days*), Steve Nickell (*The Treachery of Ravens*), Carol Pope, Ruth Roberts, and David Fairchild (*The Exodus*). After three years, I finally made it to the finish line! A special thank you to my wife, whose insights as my first reader made this story far stronger than it otherwise would have been. Additional thanks to my beta readers, Ed and Mike, and to my dad for his diligent copy-editing and proofreading. Your collective feedback and guidance lifted this novel beyond what I could have achieved alone.

A couple of notes the reader may find of interest: IGOR, like the AMIGO, is based on a project called the Laser Interferometer Space Antenna (LISA), led by the European Space Agency. As of this writing, it's scheduled to launch in 2035. Megan's backstory was inspired by the tragic events involving a cult called Heaven's Gate. While an extreme example of a demagogic leader leading others astray, the Prophet was planning far worse. That experience armed Megan with the drive and means to fight what she feared would become an unstoppable movement. Lastly, I didn't know the Prophet could rap—that surprised even me.

I hope you found this story worthy of your time. If you enjoyed the book, I invite you to leave a review and drop me a note at *david-hoffer.com*.